A NARROW ESCAPE
FAITH MARTIN

BLACK STAR CRIME™

First published in hardback by Robert Hale Limited in 2004

First paperback edition 2008
Black Star Crime
Eton House, 18-24 Paradise Road, Richmond, Surrey TW9 1SR

© Faith Martin 2004

ISBN: 978 1 848 45002 8

Set in Times Roman 10½ on 12¼ pt.
081-0908-70907

Printed and bound in Spain
by Litografia Rosés S.A., Barcelona

1

HILLARY GREENE rolled over, her eyes snapping open to a dim and curtailed light. It seemed to seep grudgingly into the tiny room, like a reluctant visitor trying to sell her something it just knew she didn't want.

She groaned. Only two seconds awake and already she was missing her old bedroom, with its flood of daylight pouring generously in through double-glazed, normal-sized windows.

The noise that had awakened her cheeped once again, and she quickly groped one arm out from under the thin bed linen, banging her knuckles against the wall only a few inches, or so it seemed, from the bed.

Yelping in pain, she managed to scuffle around on the floor for the mobile phone beside her bed and, bleary eyed, pressed the right switch.

'Yes. DI Greene,' she mumbled, knowing full damn well it couldn't be a social call so early in the morning. Dammit, what *was* the time? She peered downward, but her wristwatch, being on the floor also, was too small-faced for her to make out more than an impression.

Shit, what she wouldn't give for a decent bedside table. Not that she had room for one, of course.

'Hillary, morning. Hope I didn't wake you.'

Hillary's eyes came more fully open. She didn't exactly sit up straighter, but her brain synapses became impelled to make connections rather more quickly.

'Sir,' she said non-committally. In her mind's eye she could just see Superintendent Marcus Donleavy's heavy-lidded smile. His silver hair would be combed into place as neatly as a duck's backside, and no doubt his trousers had been creased to perfection by his wife's daily. Residing inside that impeccable exterior would be a glassful of freshly squeezed orange juice and two slices of toasted organic brown bread. Spread with that fancy margarine that was supposed to reduce cholesterol, to be sure.

Hell, what was the time? Surely she couldn't have slept in.

'Just thought I'd ring to save you a journey in to the Big House,' he said heartily, making Hillary wince. Why the hell he insisted on using police patois always confounded her. It didn't sit right with his nearly-Oxford-educated voice, or his much-joked-about ambitions for higher rank. Why not just call the Thames Valley HQ at Kidlington the HQ like the rest of his brass-wearing cronies?

She sat up awkwardly, stifling a yawn, trying to pretend that his words hadn't filled her with a seeping coldness.

'Oh?' she said, in what she hoped was a suitably unimpressed voice. Swallowing hard, she got one elbow under her and glared balefully at the cream-painted wall.

So this was it, then.

'Yes. Get yourself off to Dashwood Lock instead. That's right on your doorstep, isn't it?'

His words came as such a relief that, for a moment, she didn't really register their meaning.

So she hadn't been suspended. They hadn't found out anything.

This was just another case.

'There's a suspicious death been reported.' Marcus Donleavy's voice, with a certain growing crispness about it now which indicated that she'd better get on the ball soon, continued to flow into her ear. 'Since you're our expert in such matters, I thought I'd bat it your way. Report soonest, all right?'

'Yes, sir,' she said, with an equal crispness, and the monotonous blur of the dial tone answered back. Squinting her eyes again, she managed to find the off button on the phone, and lay back for a moment against the pillows, gloomily considering the idea of getting a pair of reading glasses.

When was the last time she'd had her eyes tested? Had she ever had her eyes tested? Must have done—when she was at school, if nothing else. So long ago, who's to remember?

She half sighed, half laughed at her own expense, and threw back the covers, swinging her legs around and nearly banging her knee against the wall. She reached up and drew back a pocket-handkerchief-sized curtain away from the round window, and yawned widely.

As she reached for her watch and slipped it on, she noticed its face read 8:15. She could see it perfectly now she had some light. The optician could go peddle his bike elsewhere then, for the time being.

Who said bits began to fall off when you reached the big 4-0?

She reached for her tights, wriggling into them, then pulled off the Def Leppard T-shirt, that one sure sign of her misspent youth, now doubling as a nightie, and reached for her bra. As she did so, she glanced down, wondering if it was her imagination or whether her breasts were sagging. Maybe it was just pre-coffee gloom.

Or, worse, excess fat.

Hastily, and rather inelegantly, she struggled into her Cross

Your Heart bra and stood up, walking exactly one step forward to her wardrobe and pulling the sliding door along.

That was another thing she missed—doors that opened outwards, like normal doors.

And, like most mornings, she cursed her husband. Or ex-husband. Or late husband. She never could get it straight in her mind which it was. But current, ex or late unlamented, one thing about Ronnie remained the same. He was, without doubt, the worst thing that had ever happened to her.

Selecting a pale blue blouse to go with a dark blue skirt, she dressed fast, moving exactly one more step to her right to stand in front of a small mirror.

Were those grey hairs appearing in the just-touching-the-shoulder–length bob of sensibly cut brown hair, or was it just the poor light again? Whatever, a few strokes of the brush, making sure of the parting and pushing back the two wings either side of her face, took care of it. A quick pat of powder, a dab of darkish lipstick, and she was ready.

Her stomach rumbled.

Well, almost ready.

She moved out through the permanently open door into the tiny passageway and into the open-plan lounge and kitchen area. No time for toast—which was probably just as well. Her constant battle with the flab was beginning to weary her, but not to the point of giving in.

She reached for the kettle, wondering warily if the gas bottles needed changing yet. But no, within moments it began to hum, as if in reproof for her ongoing pessimism. A spoonful of instant, a pill of artificial sweetener, and things began to look up. Not least because, in here, she had some decent windows.

Outside, things looked encouragingly blue and green. And yellow. A sunny day, perhaps? England in May, you never could be sure what you'd be getting once you were daft enough to stick your head outside your front door.

'Dashwood Lock,' she muttered, reaching for the old and battered *Ordnance Survey Guide to the Waterways—1: South* and rummaging through the pages.

Page 135, Oxford, down to Kidlington. Her finger paused on her own place of residence, the strangely named village of Thrupp, right on Kidlington's back doorstep. No Dashwood —must be north. Next page over, Lower Heyford, follow the line down, Cleeves Bridge, High Bush Bridge—yep, Dashwood Lock. Her finger tapped on it thoughtfully.

She noticed the natural nail polish on her index finger was chipped. Damn.

Dashwood Lock, it seemed, was right slap bang in the middle of precisely nowhere. Great. That meant no wits, no doorstepping to do, nothing to hope for in the way of possible leads unless the local farmer had some cows or sheep in the fields who were in a talkative mood.

'Damn,' she muttered, trying to gauge the mileage from her current position. Four maybe? Easy going up the towpath on the bike. Good for those thigh muscles. Think of the war against fat, and what a nice little victory that would be.

But turn up as the SIO at a crime scene on a bike? Not likely. She had enough image problems to live down as it was, thanks to bloody Ronnie, without turning up like some bornagain greenie.

No, the car it would have to be. Which meant finding the nearest village, which, by the looks of it, was Northbrook. Her lips twisted wryly as she contemplated the single dot on the map—no doubt a regular hive of activity, full of eager citizens all anxious to assist the police with their enquiries.

She gulped her coffee, keeping a wary eye on the clock. Barely five minutes since the phone call from Donleavy.

But why had she had a call from Donleavy in the first place? Her brain, with its first taste of caffeine, began to wake up. Mellow Mallow, as DCI, was surely far more likely the one to be doling out the jobs?

Unless he'd been told to lie low until the enquiry into Ronnie was over. In which case, Donleavy would probably be playing the kid-glove angle with her for some time to come.

That sick feeling was stealing back into her insides again, and she swallowed the last of the coffee hastily, hating the taste of the artificial sweetener and longing for sugar and comfort.

But she knew she'd be getting neither today.

Reaching for her bag and jacket, she side-stepped into the narrow corridor, making the detour into her bedroom for her mobile. She glanced at the unmade bed, then shrugged, ducking her head comically low as she walked up the iron stairs. Several extremely painful bangs on her head during her early days here had taught her to keep on doing the Max Wall impersonation whenever she left.

Unbolting the dual metal doors at the top, she emerged into a sunny May morning. A family of long-tailed tits were twittering their usual high-pitched calls in the willow opposite, and a woman walking her dog smiled at her in passing.

Yeah, yeah, Hillary thought, to both the birds and the woman, but she felt instantly better for being outside, with room to breathe and manoeuvre.

She stepped off the platform and onto solid ground, shutting and locking the doors behind her, then hoisting her bag over her shoulder.

She turned and walked the length of the *Mollern*—all 50 feet of her—and glanced idly at her paintwork in passing.

Like most canal boats moored in their posh private mooring at Thrupp, the boat was black bottomed and well maintained. But whereas her neighbours' boats were painted the cheerful bright blues, greens, reds and yellows that were so popular with native canal art, her uncle's boat was a combination of pearly grey, white and black with a touch of pale gold.

She remembered, vaguely, him telling her once that *Mollern* was the country word for *heron*. Like Brock was a badger, and Reynard a fox, she supposed. The colours of the boat were supposed to represent the plumage of the elegant river bird.

Yeah, whatever, she'd thought at the time—little realising that one day the boat would feature prominently in her own life.

But when she'd first moved in, as a supposedly temporary thing last November, it had just looked as grey and dismal as the weather. A fine echo to her own grim mood.

A robin began to sing heartily from a clump of sedge nearby. She caught a brief glimpse of his bright orange breast as he— or she—hopped about, and she felt her lips turn upwards as she walked to her car.

Her Volkswagen Polo looked good for its age. It was nearly twelve, but the pale green bodywork was immaculate. When you couldn't afford to buy a new car, it was uplifting to realise how quickly the human spirit could grasp the concept of wax. Even her own previously wax-free spirit.

Hillary opened the door and slid in, turning the key with an optimism that didn't let her down. The engine ran as smooth as a nut. She was sure that mechanic at the garage fancied her.

She reached for the seatbelt, then frowned. No, the mechanic couldn't fancy her. If he did, he'd service the car so badly she'd have to keep going back. Damn. Sometimes she hated thinking like a copper.

Driving down the narrow lane and onto the main Oxford-Banbury road, heading north, she finally let her mind drift to Dashwood Lock.

A suspicious death. Contrary to popular public belief, almost any death, in police parlance, was considered 'suspicious' until proved otherwise. Usually by the pathologist.

In her earlier career, like all lowly police constables, she'd seen death in all its usual shapes and guises. Domestics, RTAs, gang knifings, industrial accidents…you name it, she'd seen it.

But in this case, she didn't really have to stretch her imagination very far. A suspicious death at a lock probably meant a drowning. Some summer holidaymaker, unused to canal boats, perhaps boozed up, had fallen off the back of the boat and died.

Probably.

Hillary, with one eye on the map, turned off at Hopcrofts Halt. She was sure there was a quicker way to Northbrook but who the hell wanted to be fiddling with road maps on one cup of artificially sweetened coffee? Following the map towards Bletchington, she nearly missed the dirty, wooden signposted turn-off to Northbrook. As she steered carefully down the steep, single-track road, she looked around her.

Wheat-fields.

And that was it.

She'd lived in Oxfordshire all her life, and in Kidlington itself for the best part of 20 years, so she knew that the majority of villages were deserted in the day, as their commuting residents left every morning bright and early like released homing pigeons, and then returned, late and knackered, for their evening meal in front of the telly.

And a small village like Northbrook—no, make that a hamlet, for she couldn't see a church spire or tower in front of her—was no exception. Unless there was a pensioner or two about.

She followed the narrow road down past the few cottages and houses until it abruptly ended. And, there, parked off the road, was a bright red Mini.

She sighed. She was in the right place, then. What's more, DS Janine Tyler had been assigned the case with her.

Hillary's lips twisted wryly. She bet that had pleased her.

Janine Tyler walked wearily up and down and wished she could sit on the tempting black and white painted arm of the lock. She'd had something of a night the night before, and she'd been here nearly half an hour already, waiting for a Senior Investigating Officer to show up. She'd called in the doc, who now stood on the side of the lock looking down into the water below, and SOCO were on the way. And no doubt they wouldn't thank her for leaving her smudged bum-print on the arm of the lock.

She was glancing longingly at the grass, wondering if it was dry enough to sit on, when she heard feet approaching, and turned to look along the towpath. Detective Inspector Hillary Greene was walking towards her with her usual fast gait, controlled face and unnervingly competent manner.

Janine felt a flickering moment of disappointment.

Of course, there was no way it could have been Mel—or DCI Philip Mallow to give him his proper title—assigned to a mere suspicious death. Pity—she'd like to work with him. She was reasonably sure he was interested in her. And why not? He was divorced now. Twice, wasn't it? The other day, in the car park, he'd waited while she'd reversed out. OK, it was hardly a meeting worthy of *Brief Encounter*, but most senior male officers would just have roared away in their flash cars, and sod her and her brand new Mini.

But the DCI had smiled at her as she'd passed. In that way. The way that men who were interested did.

Yes, it would have been nice to have the excuse to get a bit closer to the very mellow DCI Mallow.

It was not that she had anything against Hillary personally.

In fact, the scuttlebut back at the Big House was generally in favour of Hillary, and always had been, even before this investigation into her late husband had started. It went without saying that any copper (or even fellow officer and wife-of-said copper) being investigated by an outside force automatically came in for near sainthood status and unstinting support from his own station. Except from those who liked to keep a distance, naturally.

But Janine wasn't one of those who thought that guilt through association was particularly dangerous. It was just that she didn't like having a woman boss. It was as simple as that. And it had nothing to do with jealousy, either. Hillary Greene, after all, was still only a DI even though she had to be gone 40. So she was hardly a go-getter, right? OK, getting to DI was good for a woman, even nowadays, but Janine was a sergeant already at 28, and intended to be a DI before she was 32, and a DCI long before she was 40.

She got on OK with Hillary. (In fact, apart from Frank Ross, the wanker, she couldn't think of a single cop back at the Big House who actively disliked her. Something of an achievement in itself, that, now Janine came to think of it.) It was just that once you got two women working on a case together, out came all the nudge-nudge, wink-wink jokes, and the Cagney-and-Lacey, all-you-girls-together mentality really pissed Janine off.

And it showed, if she had but known it, on her face.

As Hillary drew level, she noticed the younger woman straighten up, as if expecting some kind of reprimand. Just what was the sergeant's problem? Hillary wondered wearily. As far as she could remember, she hadn't done anything to step on her dainty toes.

It didn't help that she instantly felt awkward and ugly the moment she reached Janine. Janine, at five foot six, was a good three to four inches shorter than Hillary. And blonde. Damn her. And thin. Double damn her.

But she had the makings of a good copper, and like any SIO, Hillary knew it was part of her job to teach as well as lead. Even if the trainee would obviously rather be taking orders from anyone else.

Well, perhaps not from Frank Ross.

'What have we got?' she asked, trying not to sound like a growling dog that had just had its bone taken away.

'Boss,' Janine said, by way of greeting. She hated the awkward term *ma'am*, and no way was she about to sound like an extra from *The Sweeney* and call anybody, male or female, *guv*. 'A Mrs Millaker was out walking her dog this morning. Came across the body at roughly seven-thirty. She has a job that starts at nine—in a wine shop in Summertown. Called in on her mobile and waited for us to show.'

Hillary nodded. The usual, then. It was amazing just how often dog walkers came upon the remains of human beings. You'd have thought, she mused, with it happening so often both on the telly and in newspaper reports (which supposedly related so-called real-life events), the general public would wise up and just stop walking their mutts.

She glanced at the woman, who was standing a little way down the towpath, looking distressed, embarrassed, curious and excited at the same time, and fought the urge to tell her to buy herself a cat. Or a budgie.

She could leave it to Janine to get a full statement from her later.

Instead she walked to the edge of the lock and glanced at the doc.

Doc Steven Partridge would never see 50 again, although you'd never know it by the clothes he wore and the hair dye he used.

He played squash. And seemed to enjoy it. To Hillary, who loathed all sport and physical exercise, this said it all. Nevertheless, she kind of liked the man. He had the usual pathologists' gory humour, but he was respectful to the dead, and didn't treat coppers too harshly either.

'Doc,' she said quietly.

He turned his thoughtful, rather watery blue eyes her way for a moment, then smiled briefly, as if needing the few moments to recognise her. She didn't take it personally. No doubt he'd been miles away.

'Hillary. So you got this one, did you?' he said, somewhat unnecessarily.

She nodded, already looking down. She wished she wasn't. Looking at bodies wasn't her favourite occupation.

To make matters worse, the lock was out. And this one seemed deep. How far down was the body? Fifteen feet? More? She'd never liked heights. She felt a little light-headed and quickly looked up.

Swaying barley gleamed in the neighbouring field. Behind her, she noticed, was the typical English hedge—a mixture of hawthorn, blackthorn, wild damson, alder and other assorted bushes. Behind that a grazing field with seemingly nothing in it and beyond that a railway track. She could even hear a train approaching.

She turned more fully to watch it go by—a three-carriage, blue, green and white express. She doubted that, even if a train had been going by at the fatal moment, any of its passengers would have been able to see anything through the green thicket.

'He looks a bit battered about to me.' Steven Partridge's voice pulled her back from her thoughts and she turned and looked down once more at the body.

It was hard to make it out. Floating face down as it was, she could see dark hair and what had once been a white shirt bulged out in places due to trapped air. The legs looked very dark. Denim? Jeans? A youngster, then? A teenager, perhaps, on holiday with his mum and dad, who'd drunk too much last night? No. They'd have been looking for him by now.

But why was she assuming the body had gone into the water last night? It could have been in the lock only a matter of hours. Or even minutes. Could he have been one of a party of students? Oxford wasn't far away, and canal holidays were popular with them nowadays. Somewhere, a few miles up the towpath, there could be a whole host of teenagers, waking up with headaches, and wondering where old so-and-so had got to.

'See the angle of the left leg? And the dark stains on the bottom of the shirt, where it's tucked into the waist?' The doc's voice once again interrupted her musings. 'Looks to me like he took a right bashing.'

Beside her, she felt the svelte, blonde presence of her sergeant and ignored her stomach's insistence that, once back at the Big House, and no longer contemplating a corpse, she should tuck into the canteen's sausage and egg special.

'Propeller damage?' she said curiously, but it wasn't really a question. Police surgeons, pathologists and medical personnel in general were notorious for not sticking their necks out. Opinions came after the post-mortem. Not often before.

Steven Partridge sighed.

'I wasn't sure whether or not to open the lock, boss, and get some uniforms to wade in and move him. Or whether to flood the lock and bring him up. It'll be easier to get him out that way,' Janine said, already knowing what Hillary's response would be, but feeling, as she so often did in the DI's presence, the need to talk. To say something. Probably because, before all this guff had come out about Ronnie Greene, Hillary's track record had been good, and Janine wanted to know how she managed it. Hillary constantly got good results, so the scut-tlebut had it. In fact, old Marcus was known to think she had a 'real detective's mind'. Whatever the hell that meant, Janine thought.

'No, don't flood the lock,' Hillary said at once. 'In fact, I suppose we'd better call out the divers. Who knows what's fallen out of the victim's pockets down there by now.'

'Boss,' Janine said quietly, and politely moved a few steps away to use the phone and summon the police diving unit. Exercising this little bit of power made her feel up again.

Hillary, though, was long since immune to the sensation of giving orders, and was staring down as morosely now as the Doc. No doubt there'd be plenty of mud to sift through down there, she thought. She didn't envy the divers their job.

Thinking of professionals doing their job, how come the doc wasn't down there now, in his white overalls and wellies, courageously examining the body?

'You not going down there, then?' Hillary said, hiding her smile carefully, as the Yves Saint-Laurent–clad Dr Partridge looked at her, his expertly plucked eyebrows rising a scant millimetre or two.

'Are you kidding?' he said. 'Look what happened to the last silly sod who went down there.'

And with that unanswerable bit of logic, they both looked down once more at the gently bobbing body below.

2

SUPERINTENDENT MARCUS DONLEAVY leaned back in the comfortable leather swivel armchair he'd purloined from the police liaison officer many moons ago and looked up to turn a brief smile on DCI Philip Mallow, who'd just walked in.

'You wanted to see me, sir?'

'Sit down, Mel,' he said, his use of the officer's nickname a tacit acknowledgement of their friendly personal relationship. 'Just thought I'd bring you up to speed on the latest developments concerning the Ronnie Greene affair.'

Marcus was dressed in his usual navy blue suit and trademark black tie, but his face had a drawn look that wasn't at all usual.

Mel, who was in the act of easing his six-foot-two frame into the less comfortable chair in front of his superior's large and rather messy desk, glanced up, a grimace on his own clean-shaven face.

'Trouble?'

Marcus waved the flat of his palm in the air in a rocking motion. 'Yes and no. Seems they've definitely got their teeth into something, but nothing, so far, that ties in to us. Or Hillary.'

As Marcus mentioned the DI's name, he watched Mel speculatively. Station gossip had it that Mel was rather fond of

Hillary Greene, but Marcus could detect nothing of the sort in the thoughtful blue eyes now. And in truth, he'd never have thought of linking them together.

'Well, that's good. Mind you, I never thought Ronnie Greene would have been the kind to share his action with anyone else.' But even as he spoke, the image of Frank Ross's moon-faced, evil-eyed spectre rose up in front of him.

Wisely, he kept his mouth shut.

Besides, he knew that Marcus was almost certainly thinking the same thing. If Ronnie's corrupt little ways had infiltrated the Kidlington HQ, there was really only one place to look. Ronnie Greene and Frank Ross had been as close as two ticks on a sick parrot.

'They've requested an interview with Hillary this week,' Marcus said, the 'they' being the officers from the Discipline and Complaints Department, who'd been assigned by the Police Complaints Authority to investigate Ronnie Greene over two months ago.

They came from a North Yorkshire force, so everyone at the station was currently engaged in thinking up scathing jokes and insults about Yorkshire puddings, Leeds United, cricket and everything else Yorkshire. One university graduate had even come up with a War of the Roses pun that nobody got, but it was supposed to be very derogatory indeed towards Yorkies and so everybody laughed at it.

Mel sighed. 'Well, no point trying to put 'em off, I suppose. Sooner they're out of her hair, the better. It beats me what they expect to find. She left him more than, what, a good six months ago, didn't she?'

Donleavy sighed. 'Unfortunately, it's looking as if our Ronnie's had his hand in the till for a good few years now. So it's well within their purview to take a good long look at the wife, don't you think?'

The fairness of his words, however, were belied by the hard glint in his eye and Mel wasn't fooled. Like everyone else in the station, from the humblest PC to the highest brass, Donleavy didn't like cops investigating cops. Full stop.

'Yeah, right,' Mel snorted. 'I hope somebody's put them right on Ronnie Greene's wandering hands and eyes, though. Made it clear that theirs wasn't exactly a match made in heaven. If Ronnie has been raking in the dosh, Hillary's the last woman he'd have spent it on. Or trusted to hide it for him, for that matter. In fact, knowing her, she'd have been more likely to donate the whole lot to the Sally Army, just to see the look on his face when he found out.'

Donleavy grinned. Mel was certainly quick to defend Hillary, but was there anything more to it? No, Marcus couldn't see them as a pair. Mel, for all his laid-back reputation, was an ambitious sod, and although he'd always thought Hillary was too, there was a difference. A vast difference.

Mel wanted to be chief constable one day. He was political. He knew how to cultivate friends in the right places and play the game. Hillary…Marcus sighed. He'd always thought Hillary simply hated bad guys. And girls. Just liked doing the job. Enjoyed seeing crooks take the fall. To Mel, that was almost a means to an end, but with Hillary, he'd always felt, there was something far more personal about it. It was as if she enjoyed being a copper in a way very few of them did. He'd never known her to complain about public bias, for instance. Some cops got fed up with the 'pig' jokes, the carefulness of friends with their drinking habits whenever a cop was invited to a party, the endless innuendoes about racism, elitism, or whatever 'ism' was currently in vogue. But Hillary never seemed to care. If a member of the public barracked her at a crime scene, for instance, it made her smile, if anything. And that wasn't something that, for all his 'mellow' reputation, Marcus could ever see the Chief Inspector doing.

Mel was too wise about himself not to have at least some idea that they were oil and water. And since masochism wasn't one of his faults, who *did* Mel have his eye on? One thing Marcus was sure of, Mel's two previous divorces hadn't been enough of a case of 'once bitten, twice shy' to keep him away from the ladies.

'So, you want me to tell Hillary to keep herself available?' Mel offered now, a little surprised to see Marcus shake his head.

'No, I'll do it. Besides, I wanted to tell you, I've assigned her to a case.'

For a moment DCI Mallow looked surprised, as well he might. To all intents and purposes, Hillary had been practically desk-bound since her husband's death and the allegations of corruption that had quickly followed. What was the idea of giving her an assignment now?

But a second later, he had the answer. Of course, if Hillary was working an ongoing case, she'd have less legitimate time to give to the D&C people. Or the Yorkie Bars, as they were currently known at the station, for no good reason that Mel could figure out.

It was Donleavy's way of giving them the good old two-finger salute.

Not that she wouldn't have to co-operate eventually, of course. But still, he was with Marcus. Why make it easy on the buggers?

'So, what's the case?' he asked.

'Suspicious death.'

Mel frowned. A suspicious death could turn into a murder enquiry, and that might lead to ramifications in certain quarters. True, Hillary *herself* wasn't under investigation. Yet. But he wondered how long it would be before her bank statements would be subpoenaed and her neighbours questioned. Had Mrs Greene been going out a lot lately? New fur coat? New car? Where did she go on holiday last year? The year before?

Of course, they'd find nothing, because there was nothing to find, but to have someone under that kind of pressure heading up a murder case…

'Relax,' Marcus said, showing that uncanny (and sometimes downright unnerving) ability to read a subordinate officer's mind, and making Mel shift uncomfortably in his seat. 'It's a body in a lock. It's bound to be some boozed-up boatie who took a tumble. It has death by misadventure written all over it.'

Mel nodded. Or suicide, maybe. Just serious enough to give her some good excuses to be out in the field whenever the Yorkie Bars came a-calling.

'OK. I'll keep an eye on things.'

Donleavy nodded, then added thoughtfully, 'When I rang her this morning she didn't seem all that up. Still, no one expects her to be chipper, with her life in the crapper. Hey, didn't know I was poetical, did you?'

Mel smiled obligingly. 'I don't think she likes living on the boat.'

'No?' Marcus said, looking genuinely surprised. 'I thought it would have been most people's idea of a dream come true. Life on the open road. Well, open canal then. All that wildlife, kingfishers and stuff. A small space to keep clean, no housework to speak of.'

Mel shrugged. 'I suppose it all depends on the circumstances, doesn't it? I mean, it wasn't as if she'd always wanted to live on the canal, is it? It's just that when she left Ronnie, and the bastard kicked up rough about not selling the house till the divorce was final, or letting her live in it either, she had nowhere else to go until her solicitor could flex some of his own muscle. And you know what house prices in Oxfordshire are like these days, sir, she'd have been mad to shackle herself to another mortgage before she'd offloaded Ronnie for good. You know what a tricky bastard he was. And she had to stay local, and you know as well as I do, living so close to Oxford, what rents are like round here for anything even halfway decent.'

Marcus nodded. Luckily, he and his wife had bought their modest (but now very desirable) detached house in 'The Moors' nearly 25 years ago, before things had got so crazy.

'Right. Think the government's latest plan to help us and the nurses and firemen buy locally will be any use?' he asked, and for a while their talk turned to more broad and general topics.

It wasn't until Mel was making moves to go that their conversation got back to the internal enquiry that was causing so much aggro.

'If Ronnie has been pulling in the dosh for so long, he must have collected quite a wad,' Marcus said, automatically lowering his voice even though the door was firmly shut and only Julie, Marcus's secretary, sat outside. 'I know he was a brash working-class oik in many ways,' Marcus continued, thinking back on the late unlamented DCI Ronnie Greene without enthusiasm, 'but he could be surprisingly sophisticated in certain ways.'

But not with women, Mel thought, remembering the string of affairs, always with blondes, usually culled from the restaurants, pubs and hairdressers of nearby Oxford.

'So, with a bit of luck, they'll never be able to pin him down,' he mused. No wads of cash packed around the central heating lagging on the boiler. No gold coins in a safety deposit box. No stocks and shares and a portfolio with a city stockbroker that would have kept a professional footballer's wife happy.

'Let's hope not,' Marcus said, with feeling. 'At any rate, the bugger's safely dead. So that was one huge favour he did us.'

Mel laughed and nodded, then rose, stretching as he did so.

'Funny, who'd have thought there'd be so much money in tiger pricks,' he said.

Marcus Donleavy grunted.

The sun was definitely shining as if it meant it, Hillary thought, glancing once more at her watch. It was now gone half past ten, and there wasn't a cloud in the sky. Behind her some dog roses, the first of the season, were beginning to uncurl their pale pink petals to the world, and a squadron of ducks and one brave moorhen, no doubt attracted by human activity, were clustered around her feet, looking for a bread handout.

If it hadn't been for the presence of a black, rubber-suited diver below her, and the insistent presence of the bobbing corpse, it would be a perfect kind of day. The sort of day Evelyn Waugh would have set on the Isis, with Oxford's dreaming spires shimmering around his characters, rather than the more prosaic Oxford canal in the middle of nowhere.

'Ready, guv,' the diver called up to her, and she nodded, wondering why there wasn't a second one. Didn't divers always, for safety, dive in pairs? Probably cutbacks were the reason, she thought, with a non-accountable person's smug indifference to the cost of things. Or perhaps, with the water being barely four foot deep, the other diver had managed to skive off.

'Right, let's get the gate fully open,' she said, calling to the uniforms who'd since gathered. 'Give the man some room.'

As she spoke, she wondered if she was talking about the diver or the body.

Detective Police Constable Tommy Lynch moved forward, pushing the lock's arm without waiting for help. Not that he needed it. At six foot three, he was powerfully built, though Hillary had heard his particular sport was running rather than boxing or weightlifting. She nodded a silent thanks as she went past, and a little knot of professionally interested people gathered at the lock's edge to watch the proceedings.

Doc Partridge walked down to the end in anticipation of being presented with the body, and began to lay out a plastic sheet on the grass. From his voluminous bag, he pulled out a white coverall, that literally covered all, slipping over his shoes and coming to a hood at the top of his head.

Yellow police tape had already been set up around the lock, although who it was expected to keep at bay Hillary wasn't sure. Unless you counted a pair of curious crows, and the ducks.

Still, the season was getting on. There was bound to be a boat come along sooner or later.

And that reminded her.

'Janine,' she said, turning to look over her shoulder at her sergeant, who stepped a bit closer, 'you'd better call up the Rivers Authority—Thames Water, who-the-hell-ever—and warn them that this lock is going to be off-limits for a while. We'll be having boats backing up sooner or later, I know, but they might have some kind of CB or radio system whereby they can warn holidaymakers to avoid this area for a few days, if at all possible.'

Janine nodded, her eyes not on her boss but on the progress of the diver.

Not that he was doing much diving, poor sod. In fact, the muddy, greenish-tinged water only seemed to come up to his shoulders. He moved jerkily, as if wading through thick mud. As he probably was.

'I can feel something metal down here,' the diver called up. 'What's the betting it's a Tesco's shopping trolley?'

The diver looked impossibly young, Hillary thought, remembering that old chestnut about policemen looking younger the older you got. But this one really did look as if he should be in school. Riotous auburn curls, now tucked under the black rubber hood, did nothing to lessen the impression of a boy playing hooky from school. Now his pale, freckled face frowned in concentration as he got nearer the body.

Hillary tensed. She hoped he wasn't as much of a novice as he looked. It would be nasty enough down there as it was, without him puking his guts up into the water as well. But she needn't have worried. The frown was all professional.

'There's a lot of ground sludge here, guv,' he called up. 'We might have to dredge. I imagine visibility is practically zero down here. Especially with all this churning up I'm having to do.'

Hillary sighed. 'Let's have him out of there first. You never know, the water might clear.'

Out of the corner of her eye, she saw DPC Tommy Lynch grin widely. Yeah, right, she thought, with an answering smile. And she might sprout wings and fly.

The diver, whose name she hadn't caught, reached the body and carefully looked all around before trying to move it, just to make sure it wasn't caught up anywhere. Hillary nodded in unconscious approval. Finally, sure that the body was free-floating, the diver carefully and very gently wrapped a gloved hand around one wrist, to prevent post-mortem bruising, and then, with one hand slipped underneath the belly, began to slowly, almost courteously, usher the floating body out of the lock, towards the waiting ministrations of the pathologist.

Tommy watched the manoeuvre with interested but uneasy eyes. He never liked dealing with death. Strange in a man who'd chosen the police force for a career. He watched Hillary Greene as she kept a slow pace with the progress of the corpse. The sun was giving her hair a glossy sheen, like the kernel of a nut. She looked tired though, and there were dark smudges under her big brown eyes.

Tommy, like everyone else, knew she was being investigated

by the D&C Department, just because she'd been married to that clown Ronnie Greene. Everyone back at the Big House was up in arms about it. He wondered what she was doing as Senior Investigating Officer on a case like this. As if she didn't have enough on her plate as it was.

He caught Janine Tyler walking past him, mobile to her ear, and fought back a yawn. He'd been pulling double shifts last week, and he still hadn't caught up with his rest.

'Lynch, give the doc a hand, will you?' Hillary said, and Tommy quickly moved off the arm of the lock, where he'd been sitting, and crouched down beside the pathologist. The grass was warm beneath his knees, and gave off that crushed-grass smell as he knelt down. Like Hillary a few minutes before, he suddenly realised what a glorious day it was.

The diver slipped, went down on one knee, and automatically closed his mouth to prevent the foul canal water getting in. He righted himself, cursed under his breath, and got his footing back. The corpse, still floating face downwards, waited politely.

Within a minute, the diver had it at the canal bank. 'I'll push, you pull, mate,' he said unnecessarily to Tommy, who nodded without offence.

'Don't pull too hard, or grasp too tight. Try and get him under the armpits,' the pathologist said, also unnecessarily.

Again, Tommy merely nodded amiably, but he caught Hillary Greene rolling her eyes, and felt suddenly buoyant. At least she knew he didn't need to be taught how to suck eggs.

Yes, indeedy, it was a glorious day.

Janine Tyler turned off her phone and walked towards the scene, as eager as anyone else to have her first proper look at the body.

She'd done her time on the beat, of course, and had witnessed no end of burglaries, robberies, arson, assaults of various types, rape, and even, once, a kidnapping. (Though that had turned out to be a disgruntled dad, and he'd taken the kid to Lowestoft.) But despite what television series and crime novelists would have the public believe, dead bodies with any sort of mystery to them didn't come along all that often. So when one did, an ambitious sergeant made the most of it.

The pathologist, having examined the corpse's back, turned it over on the plastic sheeting, and Janine stared down at the face with what she hoped was the proper professional detachment.

She needn't have bothered.

'Ugly sod, isn't he?' said the pathologist.

The corpse was, indeed, even for a corpse, a very unprepossessing sight. His skin was extremely pock-marked and pitted, which even Janine could tell had nothing to do with the effects of water. Also, a scar ran over his right eyebrow, interrupting the dark shagginess of it with a pale white line. His hair was dark, as were the sightless, now slightly filmed-over, eyes. He had an angular face that leaned more towards the ferret than the feline. His teeth were yellow and uneven, reinforcing the rodent imagery.

An ugly sod, as Dr Steven Partridge had so precisely put it.

SOCO had arrived half an hour or so ago, and already the police photographer was snapping off shots. The ground immediately around the lock, especially where it was grass, had been cordoned off first thing, with the doc, Hillary and all the rest having been careful to keep off it as much as possible. Still, Janine had known straight away that it would be useless. The ground was too hard to take footprints, and besides, the best crime scene of all as far as SOCO were concerned would be the boat itself.

Finding it would have to be DI Greene's number one priority.

★ ★ ★

Hillary was thinking much the same thing. She knew that the speed limit on the canal was a whopping four miles an hour (not that she'd even so much as moved the *Mollern* from her mooring) so she doubted it could have got far.

In fact, she'd spent the entire time half-expecting to get a call on her mobile, patched through from the Big House, saying someone had already missed one of their boating party.

That, or getting a call from MisPer.

Now, though, as she looked down at the scarred and ugly face, she wondered if anybody would bother reporting this person as missing. She immediately felt guilty—just because he wasn't exactly a George Clooney look-alike didn't mean somebody didn't love him.

Even so.

She just felt, in her bones, that this wasn't going to be quite as simple as she'd first thought.

'Any ID, Doc?' she asked, although she knew it was impossible to rush him.

The doc grunted and didn't so much as lift his eyes from his inspection of the corpse's crotch.

Hillary sighed, walked to the arm of the lock, which had long since been dusted for prints by SOCO, and brushed some black powder off to form a cleaner platform to sit on.

'Young male, about mid to late twenties, I'd say,' the doc said, seemingly to nobody in particular, although Janine was the one taking notes. 'As of now, I'd say—but don't quote me—that he went into the water sometime between seven and midnight last night.'

Hillary rubbed the side of her nose with one finger. 'Earlier rather than later, I think,' she said and, noticing several people turn to look at her, explained, 'Narrowboats don't travel well at night. The majority of them aren't fixed with any kind of headlights, for example, and the canal authorities actively frown on people travelling after dusk.'

'Oh, right,' Steven Partridge said absently. There was something about his tone that caught Hillary's sensitive ear.

She left the lock and moved back to the canal's side, careful not to get in the way of any of the SOCO team. She'd supervised so many crime scenes now that this was second nature to her.

She crouched beside the doctor. 'What?' she said simply.

Steven Partridge glanced at her, then away. 'There seems to be a lot of damage in the lower abdominal region,' he said, deliberately non-committal. 'Of course, it's hard to say with the jeans still being on. And dark.'

'Propeller damage?' she asked.

'Maybe.'

He moved his gloved hands carefully over the pelvic region, finally dipping his hands into the pockets. It was not easy. The jeans were a tight fit.

'No wallet,' he said. The body was wearing a once-white T-shirt and a black leather jacket. He tried the pockets of the jacket, and shook his head.

Hillary sighed. 'Damn.' No easy ID, then. No witnesses, unless one counted the woman walking her dog. Great.

She got to her feet, feeling her knees twinge ominously. Ignoring her discomfort, she walked a few steps away. 'Right, Janine, you'd better get back to the village and do some doorstepping. Not that you'll find too many people home this time of day, so you'll have to come back tonight. The usual.'

Janine nodded and walked away, Hillary watching her go. She wondered what the pretty blonde got out of her job, then thought about why she herself had joined the force. Then she wondered why the *hell* Ronnie *ever* had. Unless it had been with the express purpose to hook up with an illegal animal-parts smuggler and make a fortune. She wouldn't have put it past him.

'Ma'am?' The voice, a gentle prompting, came from Tommy Lynch.

'You'd better take a walk along the towpath. Let's see…Say the boat came through as early as seven…four miles per hour, say it did eight before it moored. And this morning, say who- ever—' she nodded towards the corpse '—for some reason hadn't been missed, and the boat's done another few hours' travelling. Say the boat could be twenty miles away max. The lock was opened down stream, so head north first. Walk down the towpath for a couple of miles and talk to everyone on any moored boat you can find. You're looking for anything un- usual, a loud party on one of the boats, a boat going by after dark, any talk of a holidaymaker who's gone home early or in a huff. The usual.'

Tommy nodded and grinned. 'Ma'am,' he said happily.

Hillary talked to the dog walker, Mrs Millaker, again, this time describing the corpse. Photographs, in this case, might be a bit too grisly to inflict on the general public, she'd quickly decided. But the dog walker didn't recognise the description as that of anyone who lived locally.

Hillary, somehow, wasn't surprised. Nothing was ever *that* easy. At least, not for her it wasn't.

3

FRANK ROSS shook his head at the proffered smoke. 'No, thanks,' he said, watching Sergeant Curtis Smith put away the pack of Player's with a twinge of regret. As in all public buildings, there was a strict no-smoking policy at the Big House, and he'd have liked to indulge the chance to break the rules.

But not with the Yorkie Bars. Not even Frank was up for that.

'So, DS Ross,' the younger one began, leaning forward and ostensibly perusing the notes in front of him, 'we've been told that if anyone was close to Ronnie Greene, it was you. Is that right?'

Inspector Paul Danvers lifted his pale blue eyes from the file, and raised one blond eyebrow.

Prat, Frank thought. And typical of what the force was coming to. Smith was older, and probably knew more about coppering than this blond fairy ever would, but who was the mere sergeant, and who the high flyer? No doubt Danvers was putting in his time at D&C as a career boost before being shifted into something much sweeter. Buttering up the brass, showing he could do a nasty job if necessary. That he could be counted on to be unpopular and still come through.

Still, he'd learn.

Frank smiled. 'Sure, I knew Ronnie Greene well enough.

We went through training college together. Walked the same beat for a while. Then, when we got out of uniform, and he got his DI, me and him handled a lot of cases together. He had a good arrest record. But I s'pose you already know that. Right, sir?' he said, with another smile, and a passing nod at the file on the table.

He knew they didn't give a sod about Ronnie's arrest and conviction rate.

'Yes,' DI Danvers said, his voice as smooth as butter. Goes with the colour of his hair, that, Frank thought, with an inward snort. Bet he was the sort who went to the gym twice a week, too. Different now from when Frank was his age. Then just being a copper kept you fit. You got boxing lessons from the street gangs, and sprinting practice from the nimble young burglars who'd leg it as soon as whistle. But he doubted if old butter-face Danvers ever did anything more energetic than pull his chair out from behind his desk.

Idly he reached up and scratched his ear.

'So you must have been surprised when these allegations about Ronnie's dealing with these illegal animal traders came up.'

Frank shrugged his podgy shoulders and held up his hands in a mock-defensive gesture. He looked like a shocked Winnie the Pooh—a few stone overweight with thinning grey hair, a round pink face and deceptively innocent blue eyes. 'Could have knocked me over with a feather,' Frank said earnestly.

'So Ronnie never mentioned to you that he had a Jaguar XJS in a lock-up in Headington? You never went with him on all those junkets of his to Paris for the weekend, or all those little side trips to Amsterdam?'

Frank grinned. Amsterdam. What a place that was. And the red-light district…

'Sorry, I like to go to Benidorm for my holidays. And then only once a year, like,' he said amiably.

'Right,' Paul Danvers said dryly.

'So you never questioned his Patek Philippe watch, or all that gold jewellery he used to wear?' Curtis Smith put in sneakily.

'Give me a break,' Frank snorted. 'Ronnie didn't wear no gold jewellery when he was working.' Then his pink face flushed even more red. 'And it wasn't as if I was ever in his house, was it, when he wasn't working? I never saw him in his gladrags, did I?'

For a second, Paul couldn't understand the anger. But it was definitely there, flashing at the back of those clear little piggy eyes of his. Then he remembered overhearing something in the line of the police canteen yesterday lunchtime, and mentally nodded.

Frank Ross didn't like gays.

In fact, in his youth, Frank Ross had been disciplined for gay-bashing. So he was very sensitive when it came to discussing men's jewellery. And men's friendships. Too sensitive?

He wouldn't be the first closet gay copper to vent his feelings in open gay-bashing.

Interesting, but not relevant. It was all too clear that Ronnie Greene had been a rampant heterosexual for this line of enquiry to be worth pursuing. It wasn't likely Ronnie Greene would have given money to Frank Ross, for instance, unless as straight partners. He grinned inwardly. In the business sense, that was.

'So he never mentioned friends over in the Orient? No laughing references to Charlie Chan?' he pressed.

Frank casually reached up and scratched his chin. 'Nope. Besides, I wouldn't have even thought anything of it if he had, would I? I didn't even know there was much money to be had in animal trading till all this came out. Drugs, I'd have thought of, first thing. If anybody had mentioned bent coppers, I mean,' he added hastily. 'Well, you do, don't you?'

'Oh, come off it.' Curtis Smith snorted in disbelief, getting just a touch belligerent now, according to plan. 'Don't tell me that nowadays even the lowliest flatfoot doesn't know about stuff like that. What with wildlife documentaries on the telly beefing on about the ivory trade, and all the money to be had supplying China with traditional Chinese medicine. Bear bile is worth far more than its weight in gold. Or weight in diamonds, if it comes to that. If you really had no idea about the millions to be had in smuggling tiger penises, rhino horn or suchlike, you'd not be very much use to any bugger, would you?'

Frank flushed, an ugly look coming to his piggy eyes. 'Look, mate, I deal with crackheads in Blackbird Leys, yeah? Pickpockets in the shopping arcades. Your regular burglars, your gang bangers, your domestics. I don't know nothing about bear bile. So sue me.'

Paul Danvers smiled. 'Oh, you never know, Frank,' he said. 'We might just end up doing that.'

Frank Ross leaned back and grinned. 'Do I look scared?'

Hillary wanted to shrug off her jacket, it was getting so warm, but she ignored the impulse. She could feel the sweat start to prick on her forehead, though, and headed for the shade.

The SOCOs were winding up, and the doc and the victim had long since departed for their appointment at the mortuary and pathology department at the JR. Though who knew how long it would be before their corpse got his turn on the table. Hillary wondered if she should leave a constable on duty at the lock, but it seemed somehow absurd. By now even the ducks and the moorhen had taken themselves off, although the diver was still unhappily checking out the contents at the bottom of the lock. If a boat came through and disturbed any potential evidence after he'd finished it wouldn't look good. But then what evidence was there if the diver found nothing?

Oh, hell, life was too short (and the force too short-staffed) to worry about an almost-certain death by misadventure, she decided. 'When the diver's finished you can leave,' she said to the last remaining uniform, who looked at her and nodded with no especial pleasure.

'Yes, ma'am.'

Not that she could blame him. It would have been a cushy billet, stretched out in the sun on a day like this, with nothing more arduous to do than question any boaties that came along. Beat office work, break-ins or RTAs any day of the week.

She headed for her car and opened the door, sighing as a wave of heat came blasting back out at her. She left the door open for a while, then reached in for her waterways guide-book. Finding the lock, she let her finger run up the water-way to Banbury, then back down, pausing at the village of Lower Heyford, where there was a boatyard. No doubt it did a roaring trade hiring out boats for the summer, but that as-pect of it didn't concern her. Where there was a boatyard there were facilities. Water. Loo-emptying opportunities. Repair shop. Somewhere, in fact, where a boat with propeller dam-age could call.

She slipped behind the wheel. Only one way to find out. She turned on the engine, looking speculatively at Janine Tyler's new Mini. It was smart. Red. It suited her.

She wondered who Janine had found to chat to—she cer-tainly wasn't walking the streets of the vast metropolis that was Northbrook, that was for sure, because Hillary would have seen her.

She buckled up and carefully turned around, driving past the few houses and heading back to the B-road. She knew that a lot of constables and sergeants back at the Big House wouldn't approve of her being out and about interviewing witnesses. It was the growing conviction among a lot of them that anyone over and above the rank of sergeant belonged behind a desk, giving orders, doing paperwork and answering the phone.

But who the hell wanted to be doing that if they could be doing something else? Hillary grinned to herself, feeling, for the first time in what felt like years, a boost to her spirits. With a bit of luck, she could string this case out for a good while yet. At least until those plonkers back at HQ got fed up with sniffing around Ronnie's very unsavoury leavings.

Curtis Smith didn't seem to smell any unsavoury leavings as he watched Frank Ross pick his nose. But he smelt something else instead. Fear.

This man was dirty. He just knew it.

Unlike a lot of cops who ended up investigating their own, Curtis wasn't in this for a promotion or an easy working day. Regular nine-to-five appealed to some, but he wasn't married so to him it held no particular advantages anyway. Nor was he masochistic or one of those hot-heads who actually liked being universally loathed. No. Curtis Smith just didn't like bent cops. As far as he was concerned, one bad apple ruined the whole damned barrel, and if nobody else wanted to root them out, he sure as hell had no objections to doing it.

He was nearly 50, and had been doing this job for nearly ten years now. He was good at it. And his bosses, glad to have a capable man in the position, and one moreover who showed no obvious signs of restlessness, were more than happy to let him get on with it. Occasionally, as like now, they assigned him a high-flyer, in to do his time and learn some of the tricks.

Curtis didn't mind being a combination babysitter and teacher. In fact, he quite liked DI Danvers. The guy had brains, which was always nice, and ambition, which was less nice but at lease untainted.

On one memorable occasion, Curtis had had to bust one

of the members of his own team for corruption, when he'd found him trying to take over as main beneficiary for a call-girl ring, being operated by a bunch of coppers up Dundee way. But he had no such worries about Paul. The man was a straight arrow, and getting good at this too. He'd already come to the same conclusions about Frank Ross, he was sure, as well as picking up on the faint tint of whoofter. Not that that was relevant—not in this case.

No. What Curtis really wanted to know about was the wife.

'So, tell us about Hillary Greene,' Paul said, as if reading his mind. In truth, he'd done nothing of the kind. They'd already mapped out their strategy long before setting up this interview.

Frank shifted on his seat. His face tightened just a fraction.

Uh-oh, Curtis thought. Here we go.

'What about her?' Frank said.

'Do you get on?' Paul asked mildly.

'She's my best friend's wife,' Frank said.

'Was.'

'Eh? Oh, yeah, right. Was.'

'Now she's his widow,' Curtis put in, making it seem as if he thought Frank didn't have the nous to figure out what they meant.

Frank snorted. 'Only technically.'

Curtis looked, very obviously, at Paul, who looked, very puzzled, at Frank.

Frank felt like laughing. Who the hell had they sent out here? Laurel and bloody Hardy? Or did they just think they were dealing with a comedian themselves? It'd be a cold day in hell before Frank Ross couldn't handle a couple of bastards like these.

Still, Frank didn't mind dishing the dirt when it suited him. If it could get that bitch-on-wheels, Hillary Greene, scuppered, why the hell not?

'They were getting divorced, weren't they? Ronnie didn't give two figs for her. It won't stop her getting her widow's benefit, though, will it?' he said nastily.

Curtis nodded. The gossip—what little of it was allowed to filter down to them, that was—had it right then. Frank Ross wasn't exactly Hillary Greene's number-one fan.

'So we understand. In fact, there was a lot of rancour in their marriage, wasn't there?' Paul said.

Frank gave him a dirty look. 'Oh yeah. Very rancorous.' Who did he think he was, with his big long words? It was always the same with the brass—and those who wanted to become brass. They could never speak in plain bloody English.

Give him Curtis Smith any day. He was a bastard, but at least he was the right kind of bastard. In other circumstances, Frank thought he might have got on with Curtis Smith.

'That's why Ronnie wasn't letting her live at the house. And was in no hurry to sell it himself,' Paul carried on smoothly. 'Also he was contesting the divorce. Making her wait, wasn't he? Generally being a right pain in the neck?'

'Well, he wasn't hoping she'd come back, that's for sure,' Frank snarled quickly. 'He just didn't want the bit...didn't want her to have things all her own way. Women do, don't they? In divorces. Expect to keep the house, the kids, the cars, the lot. Well, Hillary sure learned different with Ronnie.'

He smiled with pleasure, some particular memory coming to mind.

'So it isn't likely that he'd have let her get her hands on any dosh he had hidden away, then?' Curtis said, watching the other man's face fall at this unassailable piece of logic, before he hid it with a masterly shrug.

'Wouldn't have thought so, mate,' Frank said. He might hate Hillary Greene's guts, but he wasn't about to get caught playing ball with the Yorkie Bars. It didn't particularly worry him that he wasn't the most popular man at the nick, but he knew how the world worked and knew he couldn't be openly thought of as a stoolie. Being disliked was one thing; being out in the cold was something altogether different.

'Still, before things went sour,' Paul put in smoothly, 'it wouldn't have been the same, would it? When it was all lovey-dovey. After all, Ronnie was at it for years, wasn't he?'

Frank opened his mouth, as if about to say yes. Then he grinned and rubbed his chin. 'Don't ask me, mate,' he said. 'I would have sworn up and down that Ronnie Greene was as straight as they come.'

Paul leaned slowly back in his chair. He smiled amiably. 'Of course you would, Sergeant Ross,' he said gently. But he was bitterly disappointed. They'd almost given the sod enough rope for him to hang himself there.

They played with him for a bit longer, but eventually had to let him go. Frank Ross slammed the door behind him.

'I'd have bet you a tenner he was a slammer,' Curtis said mildly. Interviewees, they'd invariably found, either slammed out or very gently shut the door behind them.

'I wouldn't have taken you up on it,' Paul said. 'So what do you think?'

'I think he fancied you,' Curtis said, and grinned as the DI scowled at him and shuddered.

'Shit, *don't*,' Paul said. 'I mean, is he dirty?'

'Course he is.'

'You think him and Greene were in it together?'

'Yeah. But as very uneven partners. Our Frankie boy lives above a dry cleaners here in town, doesn't he? Whereas our Ronnie managed to get himself a nice little detached in a quiet little cul-de-sac. And you can bet he's got the bulk invested and hidden somewhere.'

'And you can't see him trusting Frankie with a bigger share

of the proceeds?' Paul said, but it was more or less a rhetori-
cal question.

'Nope. He's the kind to like his share in cash that he can
spend. Wouldn't surprise me if he didn't blow all his cash on
booze and gambling, and rent boys in good ol' Amsterdam,'
Curtis mused.

'He doesn't like the wife, does he?' Paul said, with masterly
understatement. 'Jealousy?'

'Could be. Or it could be that she was getting a bigger cut
than him. Or that, now Ronnie's gone, she inherits more
than just a widow's pension.'

Paul sighed.

'The wife next, then?'

Curtis nodded. He was looking forward to checking Hillary
Greene out.

Janine Tyler accepted a digestive and sat forward on the chair.
She sighed and sipped tea, and listened to the 72-year-old lady
telling her all about how things on the canal had changed in
the last few years.

'You get a lot of foreigners, now, that you never used to get.
You can hear 'em as they go through the lock. Strange words
they use. Then of course, there's the teenagers. They don't
know how to use a lock, half of them. And the language…'

DC Tommy Lynch was also drinking, but in his case it was a nice
cold illicit beer and the chap doing the talking was also fishing.

Tommy sighed happily. You never knew with members of
the public. Usually, you could rely on the middle-aged and
older generation to offer you a cuppa, or at least talk to you
with some kind of respect. And you could normally rely on
the young to treat you like something on the bottom of their
shoe that they'd rather wipe off.

But there were always exceptions to every rule. Take the owner of *Babbling Brook* for instance. He looked to be in his mid-thirties, and was dressed in khaki shorts, revealing comically pale and hairy legs, and a black T-shirt. He'd been sitting on the top of the boat, dangling a fishing rod over the side when Tommy had come calling, expecting a curt 'see no evil, hear no evil, speak no evil' response.

Instead, here he was, sipping beer and watching a scarlet float bobbing about.

'No, like I said, I only moored up yesterday afternoon, so I don't know the site,' his host muttered, sucking on his bottle of beer. 'You usually get regulars, though, moored up at village sites. You know, those who aren't into travelling as such. You should find out which boats have been here longest. They'll know the most,' he advised helpfully, then suddenly leaned forward, eyes alert.

Tommy, who was no fisherman, couldn't see anything different about the float. There it still was, bobbing about.

'So you don't remember any speeding boats? Anybody arguing as they went by?' he pressed.

'Nope. We're a peaceable lot, for the most... Gotcha!' He yanked on the pole and Tommy looked forward, expecting a ten pound trout.

Instead, he caught sight of a half-ounce silvery thing that wriggled about on the end of the hook most unhappily.

'Gudgeon,' his host said, with evident satisfaction.

Tommy nodded, less than impressed, but far too pleased with his cold beer to say so.

Hillary almost missed the turn-off to the boatyard, situated as it was at the bottom of a steep hill and all but a blind turning.

She parked in the shade of a sumac tree and watched three golden-haired dogs and one big, long-faced black glossy dog frolicking about in the next field as she sauntered into the shop. It specialised in ice creams, basic staples such as milk and bread, and tourist-related items like postcards, ornaments, and boat memorabilia.

She found the manager working on a boat called 'King Alfred'. All the barges were smart, their colours being predominantly royal blue, gold and maroon, with a white piping.

After identifying herself, she informed him of the fatality at the Dashwood Lock, and then asked if he'd noticed anything suspicious the previous evening or early that morning.

The manager stepped lightly onto terra firma and shook his head. 'No, I don't think so. Nothing specific. But it's bad, isn't it. I've been working here nearly all my life, and this is the first death I've ever heard about. Course, people fall in the cut all the time, but it's not deep, so unless it's a nipper, there's never any real danger. And there's usually so many people about on a boat that somebody always notices and fishes them out. It happened in a lock? Well, that might explain it then. But still…'

Anxious to avoid giving any details, Hillary quickly prompted him. 'Did any boats tie up here overnight and then move on this morning? Did you notice any dents or scratches to the paintwork?'

'Not specifically, but then I wouldn't. I work on the boats here most of the time. And the water tap is under the bridge there.'

He pointed to the elegantly curved stone canal bridge, overshadowed by a big slate-blue iron railway bridge above it. Railways often ran parallel to canals, so her uncle had said, for the very obvious reason that the canal builders of a century or so before had already picked out the straightest, flattest route, so all the Victorian railways engineers needed to do was follow their lead.

'So I wouldn't see anyone taking on board water or such. And I don't work at night. No need,' the manager explained.

Hillary nodded, but she was already looking at the long line of privately owned boats. No doubt Tommy Lynch would be getting around to questioning them some time later today, when he got this far. Still, it wouldn't hurt to do a quick check.

She thanked the manager and retraced her steps, following a narrow tarmacked path to the top of the canal bridge, and then down the very steep sloped side at the other end.

She struck lucky almost at once. A woman sitting on a deckchair beside a freshly painted red and green barge looked up from her book as she approached, expressed the usual dismay and shock at a fellow boatie's death on hearing about it, and then nodded at Hillary's first question about whether she'd noticed anything unusual the previous night.

'Sure did. A boat come through—oh, it must have been nearly nine. It was practically full dark. Probably couldn't read the signs,' she said laconically, nodding her head to a British Waterways sign that asked passing traffic to please travel slowly past moored craft.

'Going more than the speed limit, huh?' Hillary asked, with genuine sympathy. She'd lost count of the times in the past few months she'd felt her boat being rocked by some Hooray Henry passing by on a speedy little river cruiser. Usually when she was dishing out soup or trying to pour out a cup of coffee, funnily enough.

It was yet another thing she couldn't seem to get used to. Her home rocking under her feet.

'Hell, yes,' the woman said, with a grimace. 'I don't know how they could see where they were going. There's a narrowing up ahead—I was half expecting to hear them hit it, but they didn't.'

Hillary nodded, trying not to let excitement get the better

of her. She'd originally thought the victim had just fallen off
the back unnoticed, and the rest of the people on board the
boat had just carried on, none the wiser, but this sounded as
if somebody was actually in a hurry to get away.

If you could use the word hurry when referring to a canal
boat, that is.

Which implied at least knowledge, didn't it? If not, by implication, guilt.

'Don't suppose you saw the name of the boat? Or who was
steering?' she asked hopefully, but her witness shook her head.

'Too dark. Mind, I did get the impression it was an older
man who was at the tiller. I think because his hair looked pale.
Although it might have been a young fair-haired man, as op-
posed to a grey or white-haired man.'

Hillary nodded and sighed. 'I expect a constable will be
along some time this afternoon. Would you mind making sure
you don't leave before giving him a statement?'

'Sure. We're staying for another week or two before heading up to Stratford anyway.'

Hillary smiled and walked on, only to pause a few minutes
later as someone walking a spaniel approached.

Of course, their body might not have come from a boat at
all. It could have been a walker.

She retraced her steps to the manager of the boatyard. He
could and did describe several regular walkers, from a tall, thin,
grey-haired man who walked a handsome dalmatian, to a
woman with a pretty sheltie and several owners of assorted lab-
radors and collies.

But none matched the description of the corpse.

Tommy peered into the boat's open door. 'Hello! Anyone
home?' He felt like calling jauntily, 'Ahoy on board!' but manfully restrained himself. The beer had put him in a good mood,

but humble PCs never forget their station in life. Or the station they belonged to, to whom members of the public could, and often did, complain about the behaviour of flatfoots.

A moment later he was glad he had restrained himself, as a nervous-looking, middle-aged and middle-class woman stuck her head up from the depths of the well-appointed narrowboat and regarded him with anxious eyes.

Big black Tommy Lynch didn't like it when people, especially women, looked at him like this.

He felt belittled.

He smiled widely and quickly reached for his ID. 'Detective Constable Lynch, ma'am,' he said, watching the fear fade out of her eyes, which was good, to be replaced by curiosity, which could be even better. 'I'm investigating a fatality that occurred somewhere last evening at the next lock up.' He paused, waiting for her to make the usual noises, which she did, then continued. 'I've been asking all the other boat owners in the vicinity if they noticed anything strange last night. The gentleman on the *Babbling Brook* suggested I ask those who've been moored here the longest.'

It was a roundabout way of putting her at her ease, but seemed to be working.

'Have you been here long, madam?'

'Oh, a few weeks, yes. But you should really speak to the man on *The Flier*. He's an artist. He notices everything.'

Tommy took her through the usual routine, but she was the sort who saw little and noticed even less.

And cared least of all.

He thanked her and, with some relief and a little bit of trepidation (he'd never met any artists before), made his way along to *The Flier*, a small but conspicuous boat, since every inch of it was painted with elephants.

Nothing else. Just elephants.

He saw at once that the windows were all shut and the door padlocked, and made a note to himself in his notebook to call back later. No doubt the artist had taken advantage of the good weather and vamoosed with his paints and easel to paint the English countryside.

Though Tommy doubted he'd find many elephants in it.

4

JANINE walked up the wide concrete stairs towards the offices, aware that the two uniformed PCs below were watching her. Both looked like babies to her, and she gave her bum an extra wriggle as she reached the top, just to give them a treat. She was wearing her standard office gear—dark blue skirt, white blouse and black knitted cardigan, a Christmas gift from her mother and therefore a 'must wear' garment.

So she wore it to work.

It did, in fact, offset her pale blonde hair to perfection, and it clung to her wrists and shoulders, adding to her misleading air of fragility. Sergeant Tyler was quite simply one of those much-envied women who looked good in anything.

There'd been the usual spate of burglaries, a ram–raid, one attempted assault and assorted drunk and disorderlies since the evening shift had taken over last night, and the paperwork was still being dealt with come the arrival of the day shift.

It was the graveyard shift Janine particularly despised. Nothing seemed to happen. Well, not when it got into the early hours anyway.

'Sir,' she said, noticing him noticing her, and giving just the right amount of smile. Too much and she'd look like a suck-up, or worse, up for it. Not enough and she might give him the feeling she was a grouchy cow.

What she wanted was just enough to make him notice and wonder.

Janine, of course, knew all about Detective Chief Inspector Philip (Mel) Mallow. The two divorces, the one son at a private boarding school. The education at Durham, and the fact that you could usually get a rise out of him by asking him if he hadn't been quite good enough to get a place at Oxford or Cambridge. He dressed well, looked fabulous, and had an enviable reputation for getting on with everyone. Hence the 'Mellow Mallow' tag.

But Janine wasn't sure that it wasn't all just a nice little persona for the real man to hide behind. And she wasn't sure, not yet, that winkling out the real DCI Mallow would be worth all the effort.

'Janine, how did it go yesterday?' he asked.

It could be just a simple conversational gambit, a response to her smile, a way of getting her to chat. On the other hand, he might really want to know how Hillary Greene had handled herself yesterday, and what the hell did she say to that?

She didn't want to be anybody's spy in the camp.

'Routine, sir,' she said, with what she hoped was the right amount of respect, tinged with 'back-off' overtures.

Mel smiled. 'Good,' he said vaguely, and wandered off to his office, leaving her staring after him.

Shit, he had a tight behind. He had a way of wearing clothes that she'd only ever seen on male models. Just once, she'd like to see him looking nonplussed.

'Boss,' Janine said a moment later, as Hillary Greene came into the big, open-plan office.

Hillary nodded, going to her own desk and slinging her bag

over the back of the chair. She was dressed in a rust-coloured two-piece outfit and cream blouse that did good things for her nut-brown bobbed haircut and dark eyes.

'As we thought, nothing from the house-to-house,' said Janine, filling her DI in on her work the previous day. 'I went back after dark, but nobody recognised the description, and nobody had been on the canal towpath during the crucial hours.'

Hillary sighed, but hadn't expected anything else. 'Still no joy on the ID?'

Janine shook her head. ''Fraid not.'

Hillary looked beyond her to nod a greeting to Tommy Lynch.

'We've got his fingerprints running through the usual, of course,' Janine continued, still talking to Hillary and barely breaking stride, 'but there's a backlog. Might not hear back for a while, they said.'

Hillary grunted. When wasn't there a backlog? How long would it be before the bloody Home Office finally went to bat for the force and got it adequately funded and staffed?

The words *hell* and *freezing over* swept in and out of her mind.

'Tommy, get on that computer,' Hillary said, waving vaguely at a terminal. 'Run his mugshot. A bloke with a face like his has either been a victim in his time, or far more likely a villain. That scar on his face looked like it was caused by a knife to me.'

Tommy nodded and pulled up a chair at a terminal. It was known that he was something of a whiz on computers, which was why the likes of Hillary and the older generation of cops tended to give him the jobs requiring even a modicum of technological nous. Not that Hillary couldn't use one, of course. Nowadays it was standard for everyone. Even that perennial grouser, Frank Ross had been rumoured to punch the odd button or two.

Tommy tapped around expertly before pulling his wheeled chair back and looking around. 'I've got the database and programmes running, guv, but it'll take a while. Some system's down in Cardiff.'

Hillary, engrossed in SOCO's preliminary findings, sighed heavily. 'Right. Anything come up from the boat-to-boat enquiries?'

'Nothing specific. Oh, I got to that lady in Lower Heyford, by the way. She said she'd seen you.'

Hillary glanced up quickly, wondering if there was censure in his voice, but his head was bent over his notebook. She shrugged and told herself not to be so damned sensitive. Tommy Lynch wasn't the kind to take the hump. Now if Janine had found her pussy-footing around what she considered her turf, no doubt she'd already have made her displeasure known.

'By then I'd had several vague nibbles along the same lines,' Tommy was saying. 'A white-haired chap driving, the boat going too fast, and when it was too dark for comfort. But no name of a boat. Though I've still got to call back at one or two barges.'

'Narrowboats,' Hillary automatically corrected him.

'Right,' Tommy said, and promised himself he'd remember.

'Well, first things first. Until we've got a name for our corpse, we're stuck.'

'Guv,' Tommy said, with a sigh. He rolled his eyes at Janine, who rolled hers back. They both knew what this meant.

Slog work.

A heron took off from the bank as an orange, green and white narrowboat chugged gently around the bend in the canal.

The old man at the tiller watched it appreciatively. You didn't see many herons nowadays.

He'd lived in the city, where you didn't see any wildlife at all, unless you counted what staggered out of the pub come closing time, and he'd lived in the country, where the odd squirrel, fox and bird-box attracted fellow critters. On the whole, he preferred the city. But he didn't mind the country.

He sniffed, then hawked and spat into the canal. Needing to turn right, he pushed the tiller left, and eyed the humped, red-brick canal bridge he was approaching.

Movement from inside the boat caught his attention.

A moment later, a second man emerged, his black curly-topped head being followed by a dirty T-shirt and faded jeans. When he looked up, his dark eyes were savage.

'We anywhere near a town yet?' he demanded, the tenseness of his body and the constantly shifting eyes looking out of place on the back of a slow-moving boat.

The older man shrugged. 'Banbury's not far.'

'Don't exactly sound like Liverpool to me. Will it at least have a pub?'

The old man smiled. 'More than one. It's a fair-sized market town. Remember the nursery rhyme? Ride a cock horse to Banbury Cross, to see a fine lady upon a white horse?'

'Eh? You been drinkin' or something?'

The old man sighed. 'There's no booze on board, you know that. Luke's orders.'

The younger man spent the next ten minutes graphically describing what Luke could go and do to himself. Most of it being a physical impossibility. The old man let him rage on, knowing as well as the other man did that if Luke Fletcher was actually here in person he'd be treated with the same fawning respect that he was used to from everyone else. Except coppers, of course. And even then...

The old man steered under the narrow bridge with ease, looking up at dank brickwork as they passed through. The sudden chill made him shiver. It was getting so that this was all becoming more bother than it was worth. Everyone knew he was just waiting to retire.

If he ever got the chance.

The younger man watched him and smirked, as if reading his thoughts, then scowled. A second later a knife was in his hand.

The older man's knuckles whitened on the tiller as he instinctively gripped it tighter, but his face, wrinkled, with a hooked nose and slightly receding chin, didn't falter.

The younger man pretended not to notice this display of toughness, and began to clean his nails nonchalantly. Still, you had to hand it to the old bastard. He had guts. He'd known a lot of people shit themselves, literally, when he'd done that trick.

Course, he had a proper knife halter strapped to the underside of his wrist, which helped. As a teenager, he'd practised and practised with it until he could make the four-inch steel-bladed stiletto appear in his hand as if by magic. Then he'd learned how to throw knives, how to use them properly. Close up and personal. That was why he liked knives. They were far more intimate than guns.

He began to whistle listlessly under his breath. He wanted a drink. And a shag. Maybe even a hit. No, perhaps not a hit. Not this trip. Not after what had happened last night.

Now was a good time to keep a straight head. Besides, everyone knew the old bastard was Luke's eyes and ears. Best not to antagonise the old buzzard.

He went below and lay out on one of the narrow bunks. Sodding boats. He hated them. They were so narrow and cramped and slow.

Hell, he didn't know it was possible for any motorised form of transport to be as slow as this. It was driving him crazy.

★ ★ ★

Hillary looked up as Mel appeared in front of her desk. 'How's things going?'

'Slowly,' Hillary said, leaning back. 'We've still not got an ID.'

'Suspicious, you think?' Mel asked, perching one half of his backside on her desk, and swinging one leg.

'Maybe,' Hillary said. 'Then again, if you're on a boat, on holiday, you dress casually. Your wallet, fags, whatever, might well be left on the nearest flat surface. You wouldn't necessarily feel the need to keep all your bits on you, would you? The boat's your home. Why wear ID? Although you're "out" you're not actually "going out", are you?'

Mel squinted a bit at this last rather enigmatic statement. 'Yeah. So perhaps not suspicious.'

'On the other hand —' Hillary began, and abruptly stopped. Her face, which could be intriguing, if not beautiful, suddenly looked almost downright ugly.

Mel looked behind him. 'Oh shit. The Yorkie Bars,' he muttered under his breath, and rose to his feet.

'We're looking for Detective Inspector Hillary Greene,' Curtis Smith said, totally unnecessarily, for everyone knew that they were well aware of who Hillary was. And *where* she was.

The entire room went quiet.

Hillary, aware of the sudden rush of animosity from her colleagues, followed by their silent but equally obvious support for her, felt herself flush.

She wasn't sure whether it was embarrassment, gratitude or anger.

She got up. 'I'm DI Greene. Have you been assigned an interview room?' she asked crisply. Better get it over with. And show them that she could be as professional as any brass. Also, it didn't hurt to let them know she was in charge, didn't give a shit, and wasn't about to take any crap.

She noticed the taller, younger, blond, good-looking one

watch her approach with something rather more than professional interest in his eyes.

Oh great. Just what she needed.

'It's Sergeant Smith and DI Danvers, isn't it?' she said, making no move to shake hands.

'Yes,' Curtis said, and nothing more.

For a second, nobody seemed to move. Then Paul Danvers spoke. 'We have a room on the bottom floor.' And then, to Mel, 'We hope this won't take long.'

Mel smiled wolfishly. 'I hope so too. DI Greene is working on a suspicious death. Some of us have proper work to do.'

Tommy Lynch watched Hillary's back as she disappeared. She was hurting. He could tell.

He sighed and went back to the mugshots he was perusing. No sign of Scar Face yet.

His mind wandered back to the previous night and he sighed heavily. He was going to have to move out, no way out of it. He'd been putting it off and putting it off, but things were reaching a crisis point. Living with his mother was beginning to really smart.

It wasn't the jokes he had to endure, or the stigma of being a 'mummy's boy'. Hell, everybody knew what the housing situation was like around Oxford. Even poxy bedsits were like gold dust, with students, like a horde of ravenous vultures, swooping on everything in sight. Plenty of people his age on the force shacked up with their parents. So the ribbing was rueful and good-natured, for the most part.

No, it was her constant harping on about Jean that was getting him down. When was he going to propose? What was wrong with her? Wasn't she good enough for him? And if so, why not? She had a better job than he did! If he had to listen once more to his mother's litany of praise for his girlfriend, he was going to go bonkers. And now Mercy Lynch had a new whip with which to flog her only son. She wanted to be a grandmother. And the black, Baptist, good-natured and respectful Jean Clarkson, who worked as a college secretary, was ideal daughter-in-law material. But the fact was, as much as he and Jean got on (and had been going steady for nearly two years with undoubted fidelity on both sides), he simply felt no desire to get married to her.

But tell that to his mother!

Hillary looked at the proffered packet of cigarettes incredulously. 'This is a no-smoking area,' she said. Besides, she didn't smoke. Never had. Even at school, she'd resisted the peer pressure.

Curtis put away the packet without comment.

Hillary Greene wasn't what he'd been expecting. He'd met several women, over the years, who'd been wives of serial adulterers. They'd all seemed, somehow, to be cut from the same cloth. They might look, physically, as divergent as any group of human beings, but emotionally, they could have been identical.

It was a mixture of rage, culpability and depression.

Hillary Greene looked angry, all right, but not at a now-dead spouse. She looked about as downtrodden as a Rottweiller, and if she was depressed, he sure as hell wasn't ever going to be allowed to know about it. He wouldn't have expected someone of Ronnie Greene's ilk to be attracted to her in the first place. They usually went for the helpless, hopeless type. Apart from that, she wasn't even a blonde, and hadn't all of Ronnie's squeezes that they'd tracked down so far been fair? And there was nothing 'fluffy' about DI Greene, that was for sure.

'I understand that this is awkward for you, DI Greene,' Paul was speaking, using his standard, soft, courteous gambit. 'Howev—'

'It's not at all awkward for me,' Hillary cut in, not in the mood for bullshit. 'Ronnie died, some nasties came out of the wood-work, and you've been given the task of clearing up the mess.' She shrugged. 'Fine. So somebody's got to do it. Go ahead and do it. Ask, investigate, then sod off. I've got other stuff to do.'

Paul blinked. Usually, when a woman spoke to him like this he could feel a number of things, depending on the woman doing the speaking. Usually it was wives or girlfriends of vil-lains, who were putting on an act of false bravado. These usu-ally aroused his pity. Or they were villains themselves, gutter-bred, hard-as-nails bitches, only being their own sweet selves. This produced a feeling of mild distaste. Sometimes the women were attractive, as Hillary Greene was, professional women, usually caught out in white-collar crimes. These pro-voked sadness or disgust, or a mixture of both.

But he couldn't quite make up his mind what to feel about Hillary Greene. She seemed to be in a class all her own. He couldn't even feel his usual brand of superiority when dealing with 'bent' cops, because he wasn't even sure that she was bent to begin with.

Curtis shifted uncomfortably on his chair, and Hillary transferred her mocking gaze to his direction. 'Yes?' she said impatiently.

'Did you know your husband had cultivated a relation-ship with this gang of animal-parts smugglers, DI Greene?' Curtis asked.

'No.'

'Did it surprise you when you learned of it?'

'No.'

'Do you have any idea where your husband stored his prof-its from the racket?'

Hillary snorted. 'If I did, do you think I'd still be here?' she asked. And instantly felt shocked. Because, even as she spoke, she wondered. Would she still be here? If she had the where-withal to be somewhere else, on a beach for instance, sipping piña coladas, would she really still be here, at Kidlington nick, trying to ID a nasty-faced corpse and then have to inform some poor weeping woman that her husband, son, brother or whoever, was dead? Would she still be trying to find out how he came to be dead in a lock, if she could be living it up in the Caribbean? Living in a nice, big, white, spacious, hotel room instead of a cramped series of rooms that bobbed about on occasionally foul-smelling water?

If she'd asked herself that question yesterday, she'd have expected the answer to come back loud and clear. Yes, she bloody well would. It was her job. Her life. It might not be perfect, but it was hers. She'd chosen it.

But now she wasn't so sure.

Frank Ross was a bastard, out to get her. Mel had all the backbone of a limp squid. Janine hated her. She hated the boat. Was it really so surprising that she should want out?

'If you were smart, you would,' Sergeant Curtis said, making her blink and, for a second, wonder if he was a mind-reader. Then she realised he was merely answering her question. 'Only an idiot, if she'd come into a sudden fortune, would advertise the fact,' Curtis Smith went on.

Hillary smiled wryly and got a grip. 'Quite right,' she said frankly. 'If I did know where Ronnie's money was, I would sit tight. Wait. Retire in a couple of years' time, when I got my guaranteed pension.' She nodded.

And didn't add the obvious rejoinder.

But.

But I'm innocent. But I don't have a sodding clue what Ronnie did with his dirty money.

Let the bastards work it out for themselves. What did she care if they ran their arses ragged trying to prove a false premise? It was their job. And it was an even shittier one than hers.

For some reason, this made her feel better.

'You were aware of your husband's infidelities, I take it.' It was Paul again, trying to calm things down.

Hillary turned her disconcertingly open, unafraid, and nearly-amused dark brown eyes to him. 'Of course I was. Why else do you think we were getting divorced?' she asked.

She refused to think back to the previous year. The humiliation. The shame. The sheer sense of outraged indignation. She wasn't sure what had hurt her the most—the fact that Ronnie had been cheating on her for years or the fact that she'd only just found out about it.

What kind of a detective did it make her?

The only consolation she had, and this she only gradually realised later, was that everyone, but everyone, had always assumed she'd known about it and turned a blind eye. Until things had got so bad, she'd eventually retaliated.

'Your husband wasn't happy with the idea of divorce, was he?' Curtis said.

'He wasn't happy with the idea of me getting half of everything,' Hillary corrected grimly. 'Forget the fact that I worked full-time, just like he did. Put the wages into the mortgage, just like he did. Paid half the bills, did...'

She stopped herself. Shit. She sounded like every whingeing divorcee friend of her mother's that she'd ever met.

'Is this relevant to a corruption investigation?' she asked coldly.

'It might be. If Ronnie Greene had been the kind of man to include his missus in on a get-rich-slowly scheme,' Paul Danvers said.

'Well, he wasn't,' Hillary said flatly. 'Ronnie didn't trust women. I'm not sure he even liked them much. Just needed them. If you want to find out who he might have brought in, ask...'

But she didn't say it. She was no fink.

But then again, it didn't need saying.

'Oh, we've already talked to DS Ross,' Curtis said mildly.

Hillary smiled. 'Charming, isn't he?' she said sweetly. And looked at her watch. 'Next question please. As DCI Mallow said, I am Senior Investigating Officer on a suspicious death case. Time's awasting.'

Curtis Smith leaned back and folded his arms over his chest. 'We have plenty of time, DI Greene,' he said, not even bothering to emphasise the 'we'.

Cocky sod, Hillary thought.

She looked at the other one, surprising him. He flushed. He actually flushed.

Oh, shit, Hillary thought.

Someone get me the hell out of here.

5

TOMMY printed off the info and read it with a whistle. The mugshot certainly looked like their corpse all right. He e-mailed his thanks to his opposite number in one of Birmingham's cop shops, and looked around to Hillary's desk.

He was going to enjoy this. His first chance to show Hillary what he could do. But he had to get it right. No swagger, no excitement. Professional, that was it. Like the lady herself.

'Guv, might have something here,' he said, walking towards her, paper in hand. He noticed both Janine Tyler and Frank Ross look up from their desks, faces interested, and felt a flush of pride. All those years in uniform were paying off. For the first time, he felt like one of the elite. A detective.

Hillary, too, lifted her head, and he noticed the darkening shadows under her eyes. The eyes themselves, though, were the usual snapping brown. Obviously her brush with the Yorkie Bars hadn't got her down too much, and he felt like grinning in applause.

He didn't, of course.

'Cop shop up in Birmingham. Does this look like our chap to you?' he asked casually.

Janine was already sidling across to get a look, but Frank Ross, sneering slightly, sat tight at his desk.

'Yes,' Hillary said firmly, after a few seconds' perusal. 'It does.' She leaned back in her chair, the action stretching her blouse tighter across her breasts.

Tommy was careful not to look.

'David Pitman, known as Dave, aka The Pits,' Hillary read the file out loud. 'Because, it says here, that's what he's generally thought to be. Oh, very droll. One conviction for rape, but two other cases never made it to court. Served five years, and another four later on for GBH. Charming chap,' she muttered, sitting forward, frowning. 'Lives locally now, but...'

'The Pits,' Frank interrupted from his desk, his loud voice cutting across the room, making all three look his way. Hillary thoughtfully, Tommy with apprehension, Janine with carefully disguised disrespect.

'Well, well, who'd have thought it,' Frank went on, aware that he had the floor now. He twiddled a pen playfully.

'Care to share, Frank?' Hillary asked, because she knew the sod wouldn't give out unless she asked.

'He's only one of Luke Fletcher's boys, ain't he?' Frank said, and laughed softly. 'As you'd know, if you'd been around as long as I have.'

Hillary smiled. 'Nobody's been around as long as you have, Frank,' she said, managing to make the statement sound like an insult. 'Tommy, give fingerprints a boot up the backside. Now we have a possible name, it won't take two secs to confirm,' she added.

'Right, guv,' Tommy said, moving away to the telephone.

'Janine, look out the relevant files on Luke Fletcher, and everything you can get on our friend Dave.' She handed the print-out to Janine, who glanced at the arrest sheet and mug-shot with a grimace.

'I reckon *The Pits* is right,' she muttered, and moved quickly to her own terminal.

Suddenly, the room was charged. They'd gone from a suspicious but almost certainly accidental death to the big time in a matter of a few seconds. Luke Fletcher was everybody's flavour of the month at the Big House. A big-time drug dealer, extortioner and pimp, rumour even had it that he ran some gambling joints from a fleet of lorries, always on the road and decked out like something from Las Vegas.

But Hillary rather thought that that last little morsel owed more to urban legend than feasibility. Still, no doubt about it, Luke Fletcher was a thorn in the side of the Thames Valley force that everyone would dearly love to extract. To see Mr Fletcher residing at Her Majesty's pleasure was the source of many a copper's wet dream, from the assistant chief constable down to the humblest uniform driving a patrol car.

And Hillary felt no different.

Frank began to speak, and since he was such a noisy git, with a voice like a foghorn when he wanted, no one had much choice except to listen.

'Fletcher's a nasty bastard. I remember back in eighty-eight, he had that poor Greek geezer beaten up so badly, he still walks with crutches.'

'Didn't he try to take over some girls from Fletcher's stable?' Hillary put in, just to show Frank, and the others, that he was not the only one who knew about the real low-lives that inhabited the city of dreaming spires. Including the local prostitution rackets.

Frank shot her a furious stare. 'S'right,' he said grudgingly. 'Course, his main trade is still in drugs—ask anybody from a toffee-nosed student of Brasenose to a ram-raider in the Leys. Fletcher's the man if you want anything to snort, sniff, shoot or chew. And one of his own has just turned up dead. I wonder now.'

Hillary was way ahead of him, not that Frank would ever

believe it. But she'd already asked herself the number one question. Namely, had Luke ordered it for some reason, or was he still in happy ignorance?

It was far more likely, she thought, that Fletcher would have ordered a severe beating if one of his lackeys had, in some way, overstepped the mark. Although some of the higher-ups assumed Fletcher might have actually ordered up to three actual hits, they'd never got anywhere near laying a charge of first-degree murder against him. It was bad for business getting the cops too riled up, so it would make sense for The Pits to be a beating-gone-wrong death rather than a deliberate murder or hit.

Unless.

Unless, of course, Dave Pitman had been doing something so bad that a very obvious lesson needed to be taught.

Frank reached for the phone and Hillary wondered what unfortunate stoolie was about to get his ear twisted. Unless he was calling in a favour from somebody else on the force. Although those had to be few and far between. Nobody liked owing Frank Ross favours—especially now his bigger and better buddy, Ronnie Greene, was no longer around to protect him.

'Guv, we should hear back in ten minutes or so.' It was Tommy who broke into her reverie. 'From fingerprints,' he added, as she gave him a rather vacant stare.

'Oh.' Hillary nodded. Then, 'What do you know about narrowboats, Tommy?' she asked casually, and saw him give her a surprised glance. It took her a moment or two to work out, and then she smiled.

It lit up her face. Or at least Tommy thought it did.

'No, it's not a trick question,' she said. 'I know I probably know more about the bloody things than most. I meant, what comes to your mind when you think of them?'

Tommy sat down slowly, wondering what it was she wanted. But since he didn't know, he thought about the question then shrugged. 'I dunno, boss. Just…holidays, I guess. Taking it slow and easy. The countryside, ducks, foreigners, an alternative break to the seaside, or going abroad. Sort of for the middle-class. Messing about on the water. That sort of thing.'

Hillary nodded. It was a disjointed list, but it about summed it up. You thought of narrowboats and you thought of an extended nuclear family—mum, dad, kiddies, the dog, an aunt or uncle—taking to the canal, running into the bank, having fun pretending to be Captain Pugwash, and talking pretentiously about how nice it was not to have the car, the phone, the telly, but getting back to nature and taking the stress out of life.

Of course, it was all bollocks. Nearly everyone took their mobile phone with them, every hire boat came with a television aerial, and Hillary, since living on the canal, had seen very nearly as many instances of boat rage as she had road rage.

'They aren't the first thing you think of when you imagine for instance, drug-running, are they, DC Lynch?' she asked.

Tommy stared at her for a moment, and then she watched his eyes narrow. 'No, guv, it ain't,' he said softly.

'But why not?' Hillary said.

'Well, it's not fast, is it?' Tommy said. 'Four mile an hour limit, on the water, isn't it? It would take weeks to get from one end of the country to the other—probably months. And yet…'

'Slow but sure,' Hillary said, nodding. 'And just think how much stuff you could store in a narrowboat. Take the flooring out, install some cargo boxes, and you've got no end of square feet of space.'

'Not to mention storing it openly under bunkbeds, in lockers, in wardrobes…'

'And who'd think of raiding a narrowboat?' Hillary mused, keeping her voice down and a watchful eye on Frank who was sitting hunchbacked, protectively guarding his own secrets over the telephone.

Janine, at her terminal, was happily sending the printer off on its merry way.

'But still, it's slow,' Tommy said. 'I don't, somehow, equate drug dealers with patience, guv.'

'Why not? Luke Fletcher, at least, is a canny bastard, or we'd have banged him up long since,' Hillary pointed out. 'The man must have something up here—' she tapped her forehead '—to keep on the outside of a cell for so long. Why shouldn't patience be one of his virtues? And remember, the canal network links up most of Britain—the London to Birmingham run alone takes in Oxford, Stratford, and all sorts of goodies in between.'

People tended to think only lower-class, poverty-stricken minorities made up the bulk of drug addicts. Cops knew better.

'Right,' Tommy acknowledged. 'And I suppose, if you had enough boats, and they set off at, say, one week intervals, within a few months you'd have a regular network with guaranteed supply all set up.'

Hillary nodded. 'Like I said, you think of a narrowboat, you think of holidaymakers. You don't think drugs. When was the last time you heard of a raid on the canal?'

Tommy, who'd been in the police force less than five years, couldn't remember any. Hillary, who'd been in the force nearly twenty years, couldn't either. She tried to rein in her exuberance. After all, one dead associate of Luke Fletcher's in the Dashwood Lock did not make a major drugs-related bust inevitable. He might simply have been dumped in the lock after a beating. The speeding canal narrowboat, seen by some witnesses on the evening of the death, might be nothing more than some juiced-up teenagers bored with barge living and having a high old time.

And yet…

She tensed as Frank Ross hung up the phone. At the same time, Janine came back with a sheaf of papers.

'Boss,' Janine said, beating Frank to the punch. 'This is interesting. Apparently Vice busted a couple of lorries last year, containing over twenty kilos each of grass, nearly a gross of ecstasy and related disco poppers, and a smaller quantity of cocaine, which they thought belonged to a haulage firm of Luke Fletcher's, but they couldn't trace the paperwork back to him.'

Hillary met Tommy's eye and gave an almost imperceptible shake of the head. She knew what he was thinking, because she was thinking it too. If Luke Fletcher had got his fingers that badly burned last year, then it made the possibility that he'd use alternative transport routes all the more likely. Obviously, now that Vice had the bit between their teeth, lorries were out.

She didn't want the relatively new and green DC spilling the beans in Frank's hot little ears. She reached for her sergeant's papers, noticing, with relief, that Tommy Lynch's amiable features hadn't changed.

'Seems Fletcher has a pub up Osney way,' Frank broke in. 'Called The Fluke.' He folded his hands across his podgy chest and leaned a thigh against Hillary's desk. She looked at it with distaste. 'Luke's Fluke. Very original. Anyway, it seems our lad Dave was a regular there, till he dropped out of sight a couple of weeks back.'

'I can't see The Pits giving up his free beer for anything less than a royal command,' Janine said. 'I wonder what Fletcher had him down for?'

'Let's just hold up a minute,' Hillary said warningly. 'Let's not get carried away. We don't know for a fact that he was doing a job for Luke Fletcher. We don't even know, for a fact, that his death was anything less than an accident.'

Janine all but snorted, but held off. Frank Ross wondered how to make capital out of this latest development. And Tommy Lynch was still thinking about how much crack, heroin, cocaine and other assorted goodies you could store on a 50ft barge.

Hillary was thinking something else entirely.

Hillary was wondering how the hell she could keep this from Mel Mallow. Working a suspicious death, one that was almost certainly a case of accidental death, was vastly different from working the case of a possibly murdered minion of their local bad boy. And sure as eggs were eggs, soon as Mel heard about this, she knew damned well her days as SIO were over.

Unfortunately for her, Frank Ross was thinking the exact same thing.

'Right, Tommy, get on to Doc, see if he can push our corpse to the top of the waiting list. Don't give out details, but tell him he's suddenly become more popular around here. Janine, I need a proper in-depth low-down on The Pits. Friends, family, did he have a habit, a cat, a favourite eating place, you name it.'

Janine sighed, but nodded. She longed for the day when she could delegate all the scut work, just like Hillary was doing.

Frank had already taken himself from Hillary's desk, but not back to his own. Hillary looked around the office quickly, but there was no sign of him.

A sick feeling swept over her.

Philip Mallow looked up as a knock came on his door, followed two seconds later by DS Ross. He initialled the bottom page of the report he was reading and then looked up again.

'Frank,' he said. 'I heard you'd been in with the Yorkie Bars. Any problems?'

Frank looked astonished. 'No, guv. No problems.'

Philip looked his most mellow as he smiled. 'Good. Didn't think there would be. Something up?'

Frank made sure the door was shut behind him, and as he did so, a look of acute distaste flickered across Mel's face and was gone.

When Ross looked furtive, Mel Mallow felt uneasy.

'It's this body-in-the-lock case, sir. Something's come up.'

Mel felt his heart sink even further.

Janine glanced up in surprise as Mel walked towards her desk. It impinged, but only vaguely, on her consciousness that Frank Ross had preceded him, and that they'd both come from Mel's office.

'Janine,' Mel said, glancing down at the pile of paperwork on her desk. He, like many before him on their way to a super-intendency, had long since learned to read upside down, and had no difficulty picking out the dossiers on Dave Pitman, Luke Fletcher et al.

Shit. Ross, the tattling little jerk, had been right.

'Fancy going to the pictures sometime?' Mel asked, surprising himself far more than Janine, who nevertheless gave a little jerk in her chair.

'Huh? Yeah, sure,' she managed to blurt.

Mel nodded, quickly getting back on an even keel. 'What do you like—action, comedy, horror or romance?'

Janine knew a cue when she heard it. She was supposed to say 'romance', then smile alluringly.

Well, sod that.

'Oh, I don't mind action flicks,' she said. 'If they've got one of those current Hollywood hunks in them. But you pick, sir.'

Mel, appreciating spirit when he stumbled across it, smiled a rather leading-Hollywood-actor smile himself and nodded. 'OK. Tomorrow night, then. I think there's something with

George Clooney in it.' It seemed a safe bet. There usually was something playing nowadays with George Clooney in it, he'd noticed. 'Do you want to meet in George Street, or shall I pick you up?'

'I'll see you there, sir, shall I?' Janine said firmly, wondering why Frank Ross was sitting back at his desk, looking half impatient and half smug. Like the cat that had had the canary but wasn't getting the satisfaction of the aftertaste yet.

'Right. Seven-thirty, then?'

'Sir,' she said, bringing her attention back to her superior officer, and with it, the suddenly surprising thought that she actually had a date with the station heart-throb.

Mel walked away, but not towards his office. Instead he veered towards Hillary's desk.

'DI Greene, a word,' Mel said, making Tommy Lynch's dark head lift up quickly from his computer screen. He watched Hillary Greene protectively as she got up and followed Mel back to his cubby hole. As she passed Janine's desk, their eyes met.

Janine grimaced, then glanced meaningfully at Frank Ross.

Ross, of course, was watching Hillary's back with the most disgusting expression of glee Janine had ever seen.

'Grassing dickhead,' she muttered under her breath.

Ross, aware of a coldness down his back, looked around, and found that big ape Tommy Lynch staring at him.

'What?' he said aggressively, and fully expected Tommy Lynch, Detective *Constable*, Tommy Lynch, to look away quickly. That's what constables did when challenged by sergeants. Instead, Tommy continued to stare at him for another very long moment before very deliberately turning his back.

Ross flushed. Rage swelled, then ebbed, leaving him feeling vicious. But he'd get him. Just give him time. The big, stupid black bastard would soon learn who really ran this nick.

As, no doubt, Hillary Greene was already learning.

He shot a smug glance at the closed office door of Mel Mallow and smiled.

Out of the corner of his eye, he saw Janine Tyler give him the finger.

'And just when were you going to tell me?' Mel said, his voice a good couple of tones lower than usual. It was, as everybody knew, the only way Mellow Mallow had of showing his anger. His open displays of rage and bad language were so rare as to have fallen into the rank of legend.

'Sir, with respect, I've only just learned of the identity of the body myself. What? Ten minutes ago?'

It was a lie, of course. She'd known about it at least an hour. Big bloody deal. A whole hour.

True, during that hour she'd been conniving ways and means of keeping the knowledge from Mel and holding on to her case as long as possible, but he wasn't to know that.

'And when I did, I thought it only prudent to get the background checks in place before coming to you,' she added. She wondered if she should add something about his workload, and merely doing her own job, but something in his eye told her she'd better not.

'Very thoughtful of you, DI Greene, I'm sure,' Mel said, although his sarcasm seemed to be tinged with traces of humour. 'Don't try and kid a kidder, Hillary. You know as well as I do that you can't stay on as SIO now. You were just holding out. Come on, might as well admit it.'

Hillary didn't like liking Mel Mallow at that moment. Normally, she had no beef with liking the DCI. He worked so hard, after all, at being likeable. But right now, she felt as if she was doing herself no favours by liking him, when he was in the process of snaffling her case.

'Sir,' she said, which was as much of an apology as he was

ever going to get. Let alone an acknowledgement that he had things right.

Wisely, he merely nodded. 'Right. So, what have we got?'

With a sigh, Hillary told him what they had, knowing that with every fact, she was handing her case over to him on a silver platter. When she'd finished, including her thoughts about the possibility of using narrowboats as an ideal smuggling vessel, Mel sighed.

He had to hand it to Hillary. She was doing a first-rate job. And a DI needed a break, they all did. His own break as a DI had come when he'd been left in charge as SIO on an arson case. That had all but ensured him his rise to Chief Inspector.

If it wasn't for the Yorkie Bars and their particular sword of Damocles hanging over Hillary's head, he rather thought that he could have made a case for her to Marcus.

But no, perhaps not. Not when Fletcher was involved.

'You know Superintendent Donleavy would have put me on the case the moment he heard Luke Fletcher's name mentioned, don't you?' Mel said.

Gloomily, Hillary acknowledged the fairness of his comment. Her misery, however, was palpable, and Mel, who really did hate to see good officers done down, sighed with her.

'Look, Hillary, as far as I'm concerned you've done well. Bloody well. And that'll be in my report to Marcus. In fact,' he added, 'I'm going to need an "assist" in this case anyway. I've got a feeling it's going to be big. And since you're already up to speed, you're the obvious choice. Fancy it?'

It was an olive branch, she knew. And although she winced internally at the thought of his pity, she was far too much of a pragmatist to turn down an offer like that. Even an 'assist' job on a big case was a career booster. And once the Yorkie Bars had departed the scene and the spectre of her bloody husband had shuffled decently off into the woodwork, she didn't see why a DCI-ship shouldn't be in the offing.

'Yes sir,' she said. 'Thanks, sir.'

Mel nodded and followed her out to inform the team that from now on he was SIO.

It pleased Frank Ross, anyway.

And whilst Janine quite liked the thought of being on a case with Mel, getting to know him better and learning from him up close and personal, she didn't like the fact that Hillary had been sidelined.

Tommy Lynch said nothing, but felt plenty.

'Another shitty day comes to an even shittier close,' Hillary muttered to herself as she turned off into the tiny narrow lane that led to Thrupp. She parked the car as far away from The Boat pub as she could manage and locked it angrily. Slinging her bag over her shoulder, she traipsed up the towpath, only looking up when a cheerful voice hailed her.

'Hey, Hill, you look like you need a good long G and T.' It was Nancy Walker, the woman who owned and lived on *Willowsands*, the boat moored next down to hers. 'I'd offer you some company, but you've already got it, I see.'

Nancy was a cheerful, lustful widow who liked to prey on the Mrs-Robinson-fixated young male students that Oxford had in plenty. Her freckled face looked with approval towards Hillary's own boat, and the youth who was stretched out, bare-chested, on top of the roof, soaking up the last of the hot May sunshine.

She looked approvingly at Hillary, who smiled back—damned if she was going to introduce them.

'Another time, maybe,' she said, not wanting to turn down a generous gin and tonic and the chance to spend some time off the boat, even if it meant spending time on somebody else's.

'Hey, Gary,' she said, watching her visitor who, alerted by their talk, had already sat up and was busily putting back on his shirt.

He was just Nancy's type. He was 21, but looked younger, and was tall and slim with a face that only just managed to stop itself from looking pretty.

'Hill,' he muttered, wriggling down the roof and landing his sneakered feet on the deck with a lithe leap.

Hillary opened the padlock and pushed it open, going down the stairs. 'Watch your…'

There was a 'whump' followed by a yell and then a full-throated obscenity from behind her.

'…head,' she finished wryly. 'How many times have you been on this boat?' she asked, turning around, watching as he duck-walked inside, rubbing his head furiously.

'Too effing many,' he said, as usual reluctant to swear fully in front of her. She was, after all, a policewoman. Not to mention a superior officer. Luckily, though, he didn't work out of her station. That would have been just too much.

'Want something to drink? There's some Southern Comfort in the cupboard I think.' Or was there? She had an uneasy feeling she might have finished it off last week.

'No, thanks. I just wanted to ask, you know, how things went. With the Complaints and Discipline people.'

Hillary snorted and slung her bag onto a chair. In the front of the boat, the lounge had only two chairs, and she slumped in one, then had to take her bag off the other so they would both have somewhere to sit.

'Oh, the Yorkie Bars. They're all right. One of 'em fancies me,' she said, finding it almost funny.

The young man sat down, still buttoning up his shirt. It was a curiously intimate gesture that would have had Nancy Walker salivating.

'Oh. No word, then? About Dad?'

Hillary shook her head at her stepson. Gary Greene had been twelve when she'd married his father, too old, really, to get a wicked stepmother complex. And since his own mother was still alive and well and waspish-tongued on the subject of Ronnie Greene herself, he'd come to look on Hillary as a sort of honorary aunt.

Now he looked at her miserably.

Hillary sighed. 'Uh-oh. I don't like that look. That's your *I-can't-tell-Mum-but-I-can-tell-Hillary* look.' She knew it well. It usually meant a crisis of some sort.

Gary had lived with his mother before, much against her wishes, then joined the police force and moved out. So he'd never been a burden or a strain on Hillary's marriage to his father. It was, perhaps, the main reason they were still friends to this day.

Gary also, for some less obvious reason, considered Hillary to be something of an oracle.

'Out with it,' Hillary said crisply, in no mood for playing nurse.

'Do you think Dad was on the take?' he asked.

'Yes,' Hillary said, not cruelly, but also with no doubt.

He blinked. Then sighed. 'Yeah. So do I.' His shoulders slumped. Since the allegations about his father had come out, Hillary supposed his life must have been pretty miserable. And now she felt the usual residue of guilt about the fact that she'd been relieved that, so far, Gary hadn't felt the need to confide or unburden himself on her.

Now she wondered what the hell was coming. Because one look at his tight lips told her that something sure as hell was.

'See, thing is, Hill,' he said, lifting his sandy-coloured hair off his forehead, then looking at her with woebegone eyes, 'Dad joked once about this account he had in the Cayman Islands. Said he'd set it up so that you didn't need a signature, or even identification. Just the number. I thought, at the time, he was joking. Then, later, I thought he was probably giving me a hint. You know. Son and heir, and all that. In case anything happened to him.'

As it had.

Their eyes met.

Hillary wished she'd accepted Nancy's generous-sized gin and tonic. She wished she hadn't finished the last of the Southern Comfort. She wished, in fact, that she could get nice and cosily sozzled.

Right now.

'Oh shit,' she said softly.

6

'UH-OH, here comes Vice,' Janine muttered under her breath, but Tommy, nearest to her, must have heard her because he looked up and scowled. Nobody felt particularly friendly towards cops who poached on their turf.

It was a bright new morning, still sunny, although the weather pundits were predicting the usual rain later. Tommy yawned, wishing he'd hadn't stayed up to watch the late movie last night—but Jean liked sci-fi, and the classic 1950s movie had, apparently, been a must.

If his mother hadn't been asleep in the next room, who knows. They might have got around to a little…

'Right, listen up, everyone,' Mel's mellifluous tones cut across his vaguely lascivious musings, and he stiffened automatically in his seat, as if he'd been caught out.

'This is DI Mike Regis and Sergeant Colin Tanner, from Vice. I filled them in on our case last night, when *our* Super had *their* Super assign them to our case, where we think Vice might have precedence. I expect your full co-operation.'

Yeah, right, Frank Ross thought, with an inner snort.

Regis looked a tough sod, Janine Tyler mused, eyeing the DI warily. Short, but with that vicious look you often got with little dogs. Just ready to give your ankle, or anything else he could reach, a nasty nip. He was balding, and could have been any-where from 35 to 55 years old. He had the craggy, couldn't-give-a-monkey's look of the kind of cop who'd seen it all and done most of it. The thing was, they could either be the best bloody thing since sliced bread to work with, or sheer hell on wheels. Especially if you were female. She'd have to wait and see.

She couldn't say that Hillary Greene looked all that appre-hensive. Could be she knew something about Regis she didn't, or could be she just had her armour plating already in place.

The other one, the sergeant, was as tall and lanky as a string bean, and as ugly as one too. He smiled vaguely at the room (nobody in particular, just the room) as Mel introduced them, then his face fell back into its crushed bog-roll look.

'Morning, everyone.' It was Regis who spoke, with the gravelly voice of a dedicated smoker. 'I come bearing gifts,' he added, waving a huge briefcase in the air. 'All we have on David Pitman, Luke Fletcher and known associates.'

Hillary mused briefly on the warning to beware Greeks bearing gifts, but didn't think that now was the time to air her Radcliffe College education. Although Radcliffe College wasn't affiliated officially with Oxford University, it was still, technically, an Oxford college, and some people, especially male cops, could get very nervous when confronted with an OEC—an Oxford Educated Cop. Especially a female one.

Like Janine, she had Regis pegged as a potentially difficult obstacle.

'So far, our boy Fletcher seems to be unaware of the loss of the The Pits,' Regis was carrying on, guessing that the room's single unused desk had been seconded for him and his sergeant, and walking to lean against it, already looking right at home.

'We haven't had much time, but we've had a watching brief since last night, and nothing seems to be stirring at Fletcher's. So far, we have only two others of his outfit currently missing in action. One Alfred Makepeace and one Jake Gascoigne. Makepeace is an old geezer, sixty-one last birthday, and just waiting to retire. He's had form, but none for violence. He's a bit of a dog-of-all-trades. Joined the merchant navy as a lad, no doubt picking up a load of bad habits as well as useful tricks of the trade and contacts abroad. He has an HGV licence, and did most of his time for forgery and some highly inventive scams. He's been working for Fletcher for some twenty years now, doing the jobs other villains don't want, and reaching the parts other villains can't reach.'

'Huh?' It was Frank, who was beginning to think this chap from Vice was all right, who spoke up.

'He's Fletcher's eyes and ears.' Hillary couldn't resist slipping in a bit of one-upmanship, having guessed at the Vice officer's somewhat clannish language.

Mike Regis's eyes, like missiles, shot her way. Janine felt herself tensing, and beginning to sweat, even though Hillary herself simply stared back. And—wonders of wonders—was that a ghost of a smile crossing DI Regis's face? A moment later, Janine thought not.

'Right,' he said curtly. 'We've long since supposed that Makepeace's only real function nowadays is to keep a general eye on things and report back to Fletcher on anything naughty. Now, Gascoigne, on the other hand, is a very different kettle of fish.'

As he spoke, he passed a load of slim folders to his sergeant, who began handing them out.

'As you can see from his mugshot,' Regis carried on, hardly waiting for the hasty rustle of paper that told him everyone was hunting out the relevant report, 'he's a good-looking bastard, who fancies himself with the ladies. More than that, he fancies himself with a blade. With good reason.'

Hillary, looking down at a black-haired, brown-eyed face that most women probably would consider handsome,

flicked her eyes over his vital statistics. Two suspected mur-
ders using a knife—neither brought home to him. In and out
of Juvie as a kid, natch, druggie mother, and currently em-
ployed by Fletcher, so Vice had it, as a kind of minder for
Luke's drug runs.

Nowadays, it seemed, not even drug runners were immune
from crime. Just last year, a drugs baron from up Edinburgh
way had had his shipment hijacked by some cockney chanc-
ers. Fletcher, it seemed, wasn't keen to be made a similar
laughing stock.

'These two have been missing from their usual haunts for
just over two weeks,' Regis reiterated.

'That's the same time span as when The Pits went AWOL,'
Hillary said. 'Do these three have a history as a unit?'

'Yes.' Once again Regis fixed her with a stare, and once
again seemed to nearly smile. Janine, for one, found it most
disconcerting—like approaching a dog with a friendly wag-
ging tail but also showing its teeth. Which end did you trust?

'On at least three other occasions, this combination have
been known to act together. Twice on lorries, working the
continental route, once doing something very odd with a
fishing trawler. Makepeace, apparently, can drive, navigate or
steer anything on land or sea. For all we know, the old sod
might even be able to fly a plane. Though not officially—he
doesn't have a pilot's licence, anyway. Right now, though, we
have no idea where they are or what they're up to. Except for
The Pits, of course. We know where he is all right.'

'DI Greene has a theory about that,' Mel put in, mostly because he could see all this attention to Hillary was getting right
up Ross's nose.

'Oh?' Regis said, looking once more at Hillary. He'd already
picked her out as the bright one of the bunch. Mallow was
still an unknown quantity. He'd have to ask Colin later about

the others—his sergeant had this knack of being in a room for five minutes and then having everyone sussed. Nobody knew quite how he did it, but it sure as hell came in handy.

'Yes,' Mel said, and went on to talk about Hillary's guess about a canal-network distribution scheme.

'And since she lives on a narrowboat,' Mel concluded, 'we can take it that she knows what she's talking about.'

Hillary wished he hadn't said that. She might live on a boat, but that was all she did. She didn't use the damn thing. Not as a boat, anyway.

Seeing Regis fix his gimlet gaze on her again, she wracked her brains for something intelligent to say.

'There are areas of the country that aren't covered by canals, of course,' she said, sounding as if she expected everyone to be well aware of the fact. 'So the network might, at best, be fragmented. Still, there are plenty of places to hide contraband, and narrowboats are so low-key as to be almost invisible. The only thing that worries me…'

'Is The Pits turning up in a lock,' Regis said.

Hillary nodded, glad to be able to knock ideas around with someone so on the ball. 'Right.' She nodded crisply. 'If Fletcher is using narrowboats, why advertise the fact by leaving a body in the lock?'

'Accidents happen,' Regis said, and nobody quite knew whether to laugh or not, because nobody could quite figure out if he was joking. Not even Frank Ross was sure.

'So, we have to get cracking and find out,' Mel said, taking charge again, not missing the way his DI and the Vice officer seemed to be clicking. 'Tommy and Janine, get cracking on seeing whether Fletcher owns any narrowboats. Remember, his haulage firm was hidden under a barrage of paperwork, so be careful. And extra thorough.'

Regis folded his arms across his chest as he watched his temporary co-workers sort themselves out. Quietly, Colin Tanner moved up alongside him.

'Frank, you know the low-lives around Fletcher better than anyone else,' Mel continued, with a certain bite to his voice that had Tanner perking up with interest. 'That can be your field. Get on to your snitches, find out if there are any rumours about The Pits or either of these other two—Makepeace and Gascoigne. If there are any fallings out between thieves, I want to know about it.'

'Well?' Regis said quietly.

Tanner knew exactly what he wanted. 'Greene is narked at having the case taken from her, obviously. She seems to be the brightest of the bunch. Something else is going on there, but I'm not sure what.'

Regis did. Before coming in this morning, he'd made it his business to find out about the people he'd be working with. But he'd fill his sergeant in on the investigation into her late husband later.

'The big black guy has got the hots for her, but is being careful not to show it. And is being successful too. I don't think anybody's twigged to it yet. Ross hates her guts. The pretty blonde has plans for our DCI, and I wouldn't be surprised if they don't coincide with his for her.'

Regis sighed. Usual mix, then. So long as none of it interfered with his plans to finally get Fletcher, he didn't give a shit.

'Sir, aren't we rather taking it for granted that this death is drugs related?' Hillary said, not liking the way Mel was giving everybody prime bites of the pie except for her. 'After all, we've barely begun an even bog-standard investigation yet. And if this turns into a high-flying case, we don't want to give the media, or anyone else, reasons to point the finger. The Pits might have had any number of people willing and able to kill him, enemies who have nothing to do with Fletcher.'

Frank snorted. Yeah, and pigs might fly.

'Right,' Mel said, suddenly seeing a perfect solution to all his Hillary-related problems. 'Hill, you can cover that. You're right, we shouldn't assume it's drugs or Fletcher related. You can get on to that. Check out his family, his personal life, look for the usual motives—money, love, hate, revenge, that sort of thing. That's great,' he added, looking away, not wanting to see the look in her eyes.

He was fobbing her off, and they both knew it.

At his desk, Frank grinned widely.

Hillary gritted her teeth and said nothing.

Mel took the two Vice officers into his office, and Janine sidled over, ostensibly to offer tea and sympathy but then, meeting Hillary's grim stare, thought better of it.

'I was wondering, boss, if you could give me a place to start. With tracing boats, I mean,' she said instead. Not that she needed it. She'd been a humble sergeant long enough to know her job.

'Sure,' Hillary said, guessing her dilemma and deciding to let her off the hook—she was determined not to be petty.

What was it Mel had said? Oh yeah. Be thorough. What a pearl of wisdom that was.

'First you can check on the fees. For a start there's mooring fees, which are paid yearly. Then you can check on licences—you get them from British Waterways, also paid yearly. The bigger the barge, the larger the fee. If that fails, don't forget insurance. It's mandatory and has to be third party. I'd check with the Thrupp Boat Club to begin with—there's probably insurance companies who specialise in that sort of thing.' For herself, she was still living off her uncle's insurance. No doubt she'd have to pay the next premium, though. 'Then there's a Safety Certificate—this might not help so much, as it's only issued every four years, and if Fletcher's bought his boats sec-

ond hand, they'll still be in place. Oh, and check with any private boat clubs—mooring there is extra, and I should think
Fletcher would like the privacy they offer more than public
towpath mooring.'

Janine, slightly glassy eyed, nodded, her shorthand still
flowing across her notebook. 'Right, boss.'

Tommy, who was already busy at his terminal, looked up
at her with a tea-and-sympathy smile of his own, but like
Hillary before her, Janine was in no mood for it.

Instead, she was looking forward to tonight, and her date
with Mel. If it was still on. She sat at her desk, tapping her pen
absently on her pad. He hadn't said it was off. Still, things were
hotting up, getting busy.

But then, a date was a date.

She turned her mind to the usual problems, multiplied in
her case by the fact that her date was also her boss.

He hadn't mentioned dinner afterwards, but if they did go
somewhere, she couldn't dress as casually as she would if she
was just going to watch a film. On the other hand, if he
turned up in jeans and turtleneck, she'd feel a right wally
wearing a little black number. And what about the goodnight
kiss? Awkward or what?

She sighed heavily and reached for the Yellow Pages. Boat
Yards. As good a place to start as any.

Just another exciting day in the life of a Thames Valley detective sergeant. When, oh when, was she actually going to
see some action? She'd joined the police force so she could kick
ass. As it was, she might just as well have become a secretary,
like her mother had always wanted.

Hillary, feeling even more cheesed off than Janine, and without even the prospect of a mildly problematical date to relieve
the monotony, read through the latest reports.

Some of them were standard, and had been implemented without her go-ahead. The Pits's mother, for example, had been traced and interviewed at her home. The constable's report was scrupulous, even though it told her nothing. A little postscript, almost apologetic, stated that, in the constable's opinion, Mrs Pitman was afraid of her son, but it did little to enhance her mood.

Pitman, rapist and all-round thug, was somebody that she assumed even his mother *would* be afraid of. It meant that, even if the poor old soul had known where her son was, or what he'd been up to, she'd never talk. Even with him dead, no doubt he still cast a long shadow.

She sighed and pencilled her in for another interview. Then shook her head. No. She'd be damned if she'd go over the leavings of a constable. Not even to suit Mel Mallow.

No, if she was stuck with the booby prize, she'd bloody well make the best of it. Even Frank Ross had a better assignment than she did, with far more chance to get a shot at glory.

She picked up her bag and, deliberately not telling Mel where she was going, marched across the office.

Tommy was the only one to miss her.

The address she had for the first suspected rape victim of Dave Pitman was nearly ten years old, and she didn't hold out much hope.

The house, in Banbury, was nice enough, one of those Victorian villas converted into flats. Sure enough, the flat number had a different name beside it from the one of the victim. No knowing where she might be now. A lot of rape victims, and victims of personal violent assault, moved away from the area, as if they could outrun the nightmares. But as Hillary well knew, a change of scene didn't do a thing to alter what was in their heads.

She ran her eyes down the list of six names, pausing on the third. Miss E. Carmichael. It sounded like the name of a spinster aunt. Of course, knowing her luck, she'd turn out to be a thirty-something highly efficient PA for some advertising firm.

But no. The voice that came over the intercom was reassuringly old. And wary.

Hillary introduced herself. 'Detective Inspector Hillary Greene, ma'am. I was wondering if you knew Diana McGraw? She lived here back in 1993.'

The lobby door buzzed, and she pushed through, walking across cracked linoleum and up one flight of stairs. As she turned the bend into a gloomy corridor, the door at the far end was already ajar. She was glad, and sad, to find the chain was still firmly attached. Had Miss Carmichael been the victim of a forced entry? Or did she just read the papers?

Hillary already had her warrant card out, and carefully showed it through the crack in the door.

A moment later, the door opened. Miss Carmichael was old, but she wasn't little, standing an inch or two taller than Hillary herself. But she had white hair, weak blue eyes, and an air of vulnerability that Hillary wondered, uneasily, if she might not herself wear given another 20—oh, OK, 30—years' time.

'Come in, Inspector. Yes, I knew Diana.'

Ten minutes later, Hillary was sitting on a settee, sipping Darjeeling and admiring the canary. It wasn't hard. The tea was good and the bird could sing prettily enough. Since she was in no hurry to get back to the Big House and watch Frank smirking his triumph at her or dodge Mel's hang-dog, not-my-fault looks, she was prepared to take her time.

And it had been a while since she'd done some interviews. Getting out of touch with the public was an occupational hazard as you climbed the ladder, and one that could be a grave mistake.

'Poor Diana. She never was the same after…the incident. It didn't help that her mother was dead at the time. It might have made a difference, having a mother to talk to,' Miss Carmichael mused. Obviously she had known the McGraws well—unless she was just the household busybody. 'And then her dad died a couple of years ago. But by then, Diana was gone. To London, or so her father said.'

Hillary sighed. That was one potential suspect out of the way then. She'd known fathers who'd tried to kill or settle old scores with men who'd attacked, raped or robbed loved ones. Still, the timing was all wrong on this case. Usually, if a family member was going to take revenge, it was whilst the attacker was out on bail, if bail had been granted, or when they first got out of jail.

In this case, the alleged rape had happened too long ago.

'I daresay her brother keeps in touch,' Miss Carmichael said, momentarily raising Hillary's hopes before dashing them again, 'but I don't know what the post's like from Saudi Arabia. He's in oil,' the old lady went on. 'An engineer. His father was that proud of him.'

Hillary lingered for a few more minutes. In her car she made a few notes in the margin, then checked the details of the rape victim who'd at least succeeded in getting The Pits jailed. Not every woman was prepared to testify in open court.

But she'd been in care, she read, and had had priors for prostitution since then. She'd also disappeared into the city's underbelly long ago. Either moved on, married or ended up dead somewhere, probably from an overdose, Hillary supposed grimly.

Not the kind, anyway, to have an avenging angel hovering in the wings.

That just left Sylvia Warrender.

★ ★ ★

Deirdre Warrender flung open the door and took a stagger-
ing step forward. Hillary found herself holding up a hand to
stop her lurching over, before the woman caught herself and
stared at her.

'You're not Brenda,' she said, accusingly.

Hillary agreed that she wasn't, and held up her warrant card.
The usual look of disconcerted guilt crept across the woman's
face. Hillary could almost hear her sorting through her mind
for any misdemeanours she might have committed. She looked
like the sort who might shoplift the occasional bottle of gin
or packet of fags. She was certainly the worse for drink now.

'Oh,' Deirdre said blankly, blinking at the warrant card. She
had frizzy blonde hair, very much dyed, and a once-good figure running to fat. Too much make-up badly applied. And she
was wearing what was probably her best dress—a floral tent-
like construction.

'I thought you was Brenda,' she said, her words the carefully enunciated words of someone not quite drunk. 'We were
going to Mecca,' she said, making Hillary blink. With her
nearly-Oxford–educated brain, her first thought was that
Deirdre Warrender made an unlikely Muslim, let alone one
who even knew which way Mecca faced. 'Bingo,' Deirdre said
helpfully.

'It's really your daughter I wanted to see, Mrs Warrender.
Sylvia. Is she here?'

'No, she ain't, see,' Deirdre Warrender said aggressively, the
mother hen instantly aroused to clucking fury over a threat-
ened chick.

'At work, perhaps,' Hillary said mildly.

'No,' Deirdre said, reluctantly. 'Got made redundant last
month. She's on the social,' she added, sounding ashamed of it.

'Sorry to hear that,' Hillary said, wondering if she was ever
going to get invited in. 'It's about her…' She looked around,

lowering her voice, but she needn't have bothered. The street, lined with poor terraced houses on either side, was as deserted as a pub after closing time. '…trouble a few years back. The attack,' Hillary added, not sure she was getting through, and deliberately avoiding the use of the word 'rape'.

'Oh,' her mother said blankly, and swayed back into the hall. 'You'd better come in, then.' She led the way to a cold and tiny lounge. 'Didn't think you rozzers were still on that. Bugger got away with it, didn't he?'

She fell, rather than sat, on to an overstuffed sofa, and stared belligerently up at her, rather cross-eyed. Hillary wondered if she was seeing double.

'Your daughter accused David Pitman of the attack, didn't she, Mrs Warrender?'

The older woman's eyes, a clear blue set in puffy, red-veined cheeks, narrowed. She looked, suddenly, very sober indeed.

Hillary had her down for a loving mother but useless at the job. She'd have been furious at anybody who'd hurt her ewe lamb but basically impotent. She might have, on the spur of the moment, attacked Dave Pitman with her handbag, or bottle of gin, or whatever she happened to be holding, had she run across him in the courthouse or on the street. But she couldn't see this woman planning or executing a cold-blooded revenge killing.

She was also the type who stayed close to home. Home being, in this case, Cowley. She doubted if Deirdre Warrender had even been outside her portion of the city, let alone ventured into the countryside. In fact, she probably despised the country, and all it stood for. A city sparrow down to her marrow, if ever Hillary had seen one.

Pity the daughter wasn't in. Still, if she took after her mother…

'What's this all about, then?' Deirdre asked, but Hillary was not about to fill her in. If her daughter had had something to do with it, she didn't want her forewarned.

She'd have to come back later and interview the daughter separately.

'Just routine enquiries, Mrs Warrender. Was Sylvia your only child?'

'Yeah, she was. Only wanted the one. Had such a bad time with her, I thought, never again. Not like some round here. Have brat after brat. All of them up to no good. My Sylvie's a good girl. She did typing at school. Worked as a receptionist, she did. Well, before they gave her the push.'

The tone had become whining now, and Hillary nodded quickly. 'Yes, I'm sure she's done well for herself. How about her dad? I'll bet he's as proud of her as you are.'

Deirdre snorted. 'Huh. *Him!* Don't know if he's even still alive. Ran off, didn't he, as soon as he heard I was up the duff.' A cunning, curiously humorous look crossed her face. 'Joined the French Foreign Legion, or something, I 'spect.' She began to laugh raucously.

So bang goes another possible suspect, Hillary thought morosely, and, then, with a nasty jolt, caught Deirdre Warrender looking at her with knowing eyes. She suddenly felt her hackles rise. She really was getting out of practice if she couldn't read a witness better than this.

She asked a few more desultory questions but after a while was forced to call it quits. She got back into her car feeling out of sorts. Then she laughed. The likes of Deirdre Warrender and her poor bloody daughter just didn't like cops, it was that simple. And since they'd failed to jail the man who'd raped Sylvia Warrender, who could blame them?

Besides, it was obvious that whoever killed The Pits had something to do with Luke Fletcher and one or another of his crooked schemes.

She was just wasting her time with this personal angle stuff.

But thanks to Mel bloody Mallow, it was all she had to play with. Unless she wanted to linger around the Big House and get pounced on by the Yorkie Bars.

Which she didn't.

7

It wasn't George Clooney but Brad Pitt. Janine didn't seem to mind, though.

As Mel watched the action up on the big screen, he found himself wondering idly what the real actor would do if he'd really been hit in the gut like that. One thing he was sure of—he wouldn't bounce back like a bloody rubber ball and vault a nearly six-foot-high wall. He'd probably bend over and groan, then be spectacularly sick all over the street. Maybe even cry a bit. He'd seen men, punched in the stomach, do varieties of all three, be they big bad villains, or bigger badder policemen. He'd even done some himself, in his younger days, back on the beat. Pain brought tears to the eyes, and a fist to the stomach after a plateful of fish and chips was a recipe for disaster for anyone.

Except Brad Pitt, of course.

Beside him, he felt, rather than saw, Janine Tyler smile. He focused on the screen again, and saw the scene had changed to that of a romantic moment.

What had made him suggest a film anyway? Why not dinner? That was far more his line. He hadn't been to the cinema in years. Perhaps it was because, unconsciously at least, he'd realised that Janine would prefer the cinema to a dinner in a smoky little jazz club. And why would he have thought that? He followed the line of thought wryly, like a man with a toothache, compulsively and painfully probing the cavity with his tongue.

And the answer came back loud and clear. Because she was just the age to enjoy big Hollywood blockbusters. She was just the age to find in it escapism rather than world-weary scepticism.

She was, in fact, just the age to be nearly twelve years his junior.

He sighed heavily, wishing heartily that he was Brad Pitt. Then feeling old. Very old.

In The Boat, one of Thrupp's two pubs, the night was hotting up. Hillary resolutely refused to patronise the Jolly Boatman. A boatswoman she might have been forced to become, but jolly she sure as hell wasn't. Of course, hotting up in Thrupp meant somebody had a darts match going.

She walked through to the bar, about to order a very large vodka, but didn't get the chance to so much as open her mouth. For, at the other end of the nook, was a Yorkie Bar.

The good-looking one. The one who fancied her.

He saw her, of course, and a brief look of consternation, followed by wry guilt, chased across his even, eye-pleasing features.

No wedding ring, she'd noticed, but she'd bet there was a girlfriend in the offing somewhere. She could just see him in ten years' time—probably a DCI or even a super by then, married with the mandatory 2.4 kids, a new car and a crippling mortgage.

'DI Greene,' Paul Danvers said, coming over to her and indicating the bar with a nod of his fair head. 'Can I get you a drink?'

Hillary snorted. 'Don't you have to watch that sort of thing?' she heard herself jeering like a belligerent teenager. But who the hell cared? 'What if your DS caught you buying me a pint—won't he begin to look at you sideways too?'

Paul laughed. 'I'll risk it.' Though, now he came to think about it, he *could*, actually, imagine Curtis raising a knowing eyebrow.

He uncomfortably ordered a cider for himself, and Hillary, reluctantly, asked for and received her vodka. They took one of the tables at the back, away from the rowdiness of the darts game. Those women from the Tea Emporium could get rough. Especially when they took on the toughs from the Baker's Oven.

'So, found out anything interesting about me and my nefarious and highly suspicious activities?' Hillary asked, smiling wickedly. 'Or are you going to say you don't know what I'm talking about?'

Paul swallowed and grinned sheepishly. 'No, I wasn't going to say that,' he said, with discomfiting seriousness. 'You've had no recent fancy holidays abroad, no luxuries coming on to the boat, so far as anybody's noticed. You've not even bought a newer second-hand car.'

'I've got a Volkswagen,' Hillary said grimly. 'I won't need another new car until…oh, at least another ten years' time.'

Paul smiled but Hillary didn't. The fact was, she *really* could see herself driving her VW Golf when she *was* 50.

'So, how's the investigation going?' she asked, then immediately held up a hand. 'I know. Sorry I asked.' Briefly, it occurred to her to wonder why she was being such a prat. Still, the vodka helped her to push the thought away.

Paul's usually amiable blue eyes looked back at her steadily from across the table. 'So why did you ask?' he demanded quietly.

Hillary looked away, feeling somehow ashamed, like a kid who'd been caught pulling wings off a butterfly. Great. Just

what she needed. To be psychoanalysed by a Yorkie Bar over
a vodka at The Boat.

Surely there wasn't anybody in the city having a better time
than her right now?

Mel opened the gate to the small, weedy little garden, and
looked around nervously. Terraced, converted, Victorian. Say
that, and you've said it all. He knew what went on inside bed-
sitland. Beans on toast for main meals, and the laundry basket
always full. He remembered living in digs like these himself.

Years ago. Years and years ago.

'Better not come in,' Janine said firmly. 'We share—three
of us. The other two are both in.'

Of course they were, Mel thought grimly. Flatmates. He
was out with a girl who had flatmates. Worse, a member, albeit an extended member, of his own team. Was he going to
let his dick rule his brains for ever?

'Well, goodnight, sir,' Janine said, then shut her mouth
with an audible 'click'. Startled, Mel looked down at her. She
looked so miserable at the absurdity of what she'd just said that
he just couldn't help but burst out laughing.

Sir. On the doorstep, with *the kiss* looming in the background like an ominous thundercloud.

Janine, after a second or two, slowly stopped wishing the
ground would open up and swallow her whole and began to
gurgle herself.

'Sorry,' she burbled. 'I'm nervous.'

Mel sighed. 'Yeah. Perhaps this wasn't such a good idea.'

Then Janine stood up on tip-toe and kissed him.

And suddenly, it didn't seem like such a bad idea at all. But
it had been a while since he'd played this game. The second
divorce, not to mention the stark reality check that was double alimony, had, for a while at least, inured him to celibacy.

Now, with her small hands on the back of his shoulders, her young and firm body pressed into his, he felt the old familiar stirring.

Janine quickly moved back. She was breathing fast. 'I have to go in,' she said, but at least, this time, didn't add the hilarious 'sir'.

Mel nodded gloomily and watched her using her key to open up. The light from the hall illuminated her fair hair, and her face when she turned to shut the door behind her, looking vaguely apologetic.

Hillary traipsed back to the *Mollern* and carefully hung up her clothes in the tiny wardrobe. She used only a few mouthfuls of water to brush and rinse her teeth, since her water supply was dangerously low.

She'd have to fill the water tank tomorrow. She'd been putting it off for days now.

Her stomach rumbled hungrily. She'd restricted herself to a salad at the pub, when what she'd really wanted was the steak and kidney pie. With sauté potatoes.

She heaved a fed-up sigh and dived under the duvet.

Mel stared up at the ceiling, noticing, for the first time, a long crack in the artex. He rolled over, wishing Janine Tyler were next to him. He missed having a woman in his bed. And not just for the sex, either, but for what came afterwards. The smell of warmed-up perfume. The soft, tickling strands of hair on his cheek. The warmth of another body.

He turned back on to his side.

Two divorces his career could survive, but a third would make him a joke. And going out with a young dolly-bird sergeant would make him what? Envied? Admired? By his juniors, perhaps. But what would Marcus Donleavy and others like him make of it?

He shook his head and closed his eyes. At the office tomorrow, he'd have to be careful.

Tommy was on a high. He and Janine had been at this job almost all day yesterday and all this morning, and finally things were clicking.

He caught Janine's eye when Hillary and Mel, talking together over her desk, looked about to break it up. He got up, meeting Janine a few yards short of Hillary's desk. For some reason, she seemed to want him to do the talking for once. Normally, she'd already be launching into speech, careful to point out—not brag about, you understand, but definitely point out—her own cleverness in coming up with the goods. Now she simply stood and waited.

'Guv, we think we've got something,' Tommy finally said, realising she wasn't about to speak. 'About Fletcher's boats.'

'He actually owns some?' It was Mel who spoke, turning sharply, his eyes fixed on Tommy.

'Well, not Fletcher himself, no, sir,' Tommy said calmly. 'But then, we didn't really expect to find his name on any paperwork, sir. Here…' He bent forward, laying out the paper trail on Hillary's desk, going over the complicated process by which he and Janine had put it all together.

Hillary was impressed. Holding companies leading back to other holding companies, boards of directors made up of either fictitious or dead characters, or people from domestic cleaners to schoolteachers who simply signed on dotted lines for a no-doubt nice little annuity left her cold, but by the time Tommy had finished, she found herself agreeing with him that Archer's Boat Hire and Luke Fletcher were one and the same.

'It was the name that made me start back-tracking them in such detail,' Tommy said, still surprised that Janine wasn't taking her fair share of the glory. 'Fletcher—Archer. Get it?'

'Huh?' Mel said, puzzled.

'A fletcher, in the old days, was the craftsman who made arrows,' Hillary said helpfully. 'You know, like coopers made barrels and cartwrights made wheels. Usually villains like Fletcher have egos the size of Everest,' she mused. 'Even if they're trying to find a way of hiding behind corporate lega-lese, their vanity demands that they simply have to make some kind of a stamp on something they own or consider to be theirs.'

Tommy was nodding. 'Right. Anyway…'

'Hold on,' Mel said, 'let's get our pals from Vice in on this.'

Both Regis and Tanner responded promptly to their mo-biles, and within ten minutes Tommy, patiently, went over the paper trail yet again. 'Now, Archer's Boats has only five nar-rowboats that we've been able to track down so far. If they have more, it'll have to be under a second company name.'

Tommy selected a rather crumpled print-out and tapped a dark finger against it. 'Of these five, three are in dry dock.'

He paused significantly, but it didn't really need spelling out. Fletcher was obviously having the boats outfitted to take con-cealed cargo. 'One boat was taken out nine days ago from a boatyard in north London, supposedly to carry on north, to-wards Oxford way.' He looked up, waiting, but Janine still wasn't catching his eye. 'Sergeant Tyler's enquiries located it just south of Oxford right now. By tomorrow it will probably be moored up in the city itself—if it sticks to the speed limit.'

'Which it will,' Mike Regis said, before Hillary could make the same comment.

'Fletcher will have drummed it into his boys to keep a low, law-abiding profile,' she agreed dryly.

'Right. But it's the last boat that really interests us,' Tommy said. 'According to this, the last boat has disappeared. That is, we can't find mention of it anywhere. We think,' Tommy said,

with an uneasy glance at Janine, since this was pure specula-
tion now, 'that they've renamed the boat and neglected to
mention the new name on any forms. It'll have the same reg-
istration number, of course, but what we really need, if we're
going to locate it, is the name.'

'That's odd in itself,' Hillary said quietly. 'Real boaties don't
like changing the names of boats. It's a tradition, or supersti-
tion, or whatever. My uncle would never think of buying a
second-hand boat and changing its name.'

'Then we need to find it,' Regis barked. 'Shake up the buggers at British Waterways. Don't they have some sort of system for coping with this sort of thing? I can't see them letting
anybody get away without coughing up the dough for licences or what have you just because they've changed the
name on the boat.'

'They have boat wardens,' Hillary put in. 'Volunteers, citizens whose job it is to see that boaties behave themselves, deal
with any problems, that sort of thing. They might be the best
people to ask. If a boat calling itself *The Jolly Roger* suddenly
becomes *Rumpelstiltskin*, ten to one a warden would have noticed it,' Hillary said.

'Right,' Regis said, looking almost impressed.

'In the meantime,' Mel said, not to be outdone, 'Janine, get
cracking with our friendly judge. We'll be needing a search
warrant for the boat at Oxford, right? The…what's it
called…?' He craned his head to read the upside down listing.
'*Kraken*? We *are* going to raid it?' He glanced at Regis for confirmation.

'Oh I think so,' Mike Regis said, smiling wolfishly. 'Don't
you?'

Suddenly the atmosphere became electric. Tommy looked
as if he could hardly believe it. All this time he'd been going
cross-eyed, getting telephone finger, and generally checking

and rechecking minute bits of information, without really re-alising what it would mean.

Now, suddenly, it was real. Very real. The boat might ac-tually be full of drugs and drugs smugglers. And he, and the others, of course, were going to raid it. It was the kind of stuff that made the newspapers. Hell, if the haul was big enough, even the telly. It was what he'd laboured in uniform for—this chance to make the big time. And when it came, it came so suddenly, he almost missed it.

The room was buzzing. Even those officers not working the case seemed to have sensed the excitement. Most of them kept looking up from their desks and over at them.

Janine, too, felt her breath catch. A raid. With Vice. Would it be done at dawn? She'd never been on a real dawn raid be-fore. At last, something good.

Hillary felt merely apprehensive. Raids were all well and good, all glory and high-profile soundbites on the local radio, but what if they were tooled up on the *Kraken*? The Pits had ended up dead and mangled in a lock. One of their chief sus-pects was known to be a very handy slice-and-dice merchant with a knife. What if Fletcher's jolly band of boaties came armed with automatics? Or even plain and simple knuckle dusters, for that matter.

Hillary had once seen a WPC's jaw broken into smithereens with a knuckle duster. She'd been on the beat for twelve days when she'd seen it. The constable concerned had taken the in-surance money and run for it—probably to a nice safe job in a library somewhere. And who the hell could blame her? She'd had to eat through a wired-up jaw for months.

But Hillary's fear, as even she herself was well aware, was a calculated thing. She wasn't terrified, for instance. She knew, as a senior officer, and a woman at that, she'd be well at the back when it came to the rough stuff. Besides, in her time, she'd been knocked about a bit. She knew what pain was. What police officer didn't? Nobody got to be 40, after an adult lifetime spent on the force, and not know how to look after number one.

But Hillary was worried about Janine. Her sergeant was still young and relatively green. Moreover, she was the kind who, through sheer ignorance and gung-hoism, could get herself seriously hurt. She knew what it was like to be a woman copper. You always had to keep on proving to yourself, and your male colleagues, that you weren't yellow. That you could hold your own, and more. And she knew just where that attitude could get you.

But worried as she was about Janine, she was even more worried about Tommy. As a mere DC, and big and black to boot, he'd be one of the forerunners. It was expected of him, and he himself, no doubt, wouldn't even question it. But all it needed was for one of Fletcher's thugs to be a racist prat as well, and Tommy Lynch could well become instant enemy number one.

Still, it was no use fretting. It had to be done. And if they *did* find a good-sized drugs haul and it could be traced back to Fletcher...

Mel was beaming like a cat anticipating a canary cocktail followed by cream hors d'oeuvres.

Regis and his sergeant were conferring quietly. As if sensing Hillary's eyes on him, he glanced up and caught her gaze. For a second, Hillary had the absurd idea that they were the only two coppers in the room who really understood what was going on. He seemed to hesitate, as if surprised, and then, slowly, nodded.

For some reason, it made Hillary's day.

The go-ahead came just as Tommy was knocking off. The judge had been reluctant to agree to a search warrant, since, in his opinion, probable cause was extremely shaky. But either Marcus Donleavy or the super over at Vice was owed a favour and the paperwork got signed.

It was, as Janine had expected, going to be a dawn raid. Tanner and one of Vice's plain clothes were even now checking out the exact whereabouts of *Kraken*, and would report back with its location at 5 a.m. the next day.

All those officers concerned were to be back at the Big House by 3:30. It was hardly worth going home, and he knew he'd be too keyed up to sleep, but Tommy also knew Jean was expecting him.

She was going to cook him and Mercy a new recipe tonight. Something Jamaican.

Sometimes, Tommy wished that his mother could marry Jean. It would make everybody happy.

Janine didn't bother to go to bed either. Instead, she curled up in her favourite armchair next to a big floppy-shaded standard lamp, with her favourite author, James Burke. He was American, and wrote about tough American cops. As a girl, Janine had wanted to live in America. Come to think of it, she still did.

Still, tomorrow would make up for living in staid old Oxford. Forget Morse and all your dreaming spires. Tomorrow, she and her mates were going to bring off a major drugs bust. She just knew it.

She imagined phoning her mum, sounding cool and offhand, casually describing her part in the drama her mother had been watching on telly that lunch hour. Or tea time. It depended on whether Mel wanted to crow to the media right away or keep a lid on it.

Mel.

He'd been avoiding her today. She knew it. Not surprising, really, since she'd been doing the same thing. But still, why shouldn't they get together? It was the second millennium and sex was just sex.

She smiled over her novel and, had she been a cat, would have purred.

Hillary set her alarm and cursed herself for not making the bed that morning. Within moments she was asleep. Unlike the others, Hillary knew the importance of getting plenty of rest before a raid. Excitement took it out of you far more than toil.

She just knew Mike Regis, if he wasn't in contact with that curiously silent sergeant of his, would be asleep too. Mel, for all that he was a pal, simply wasn't as competent as Regis.

Tommy ate spicy chicken and complimented Jean fulsomely. She was looking good tonight, in a simple, sleeveless white dress with a square neckline, setting off her ebony skin to perfection. As she and his mother washed and wiped up, laughingly consigning him to the living room, he wondered what his mother would do if he brought Hillary home for a meal.

He couldn't help but smile. She'd have three thousand fits, all at once.

She was white. She was a cop. His superior officer, no less. She was old enough to be Mercy's own sister. She was so unsuitable, so unthinkable, she'd probably, for once in her life, be speechless.

Tommy's smile faded. Of course, he'd never bring Hillary home. He wouldn't want to hurt Jean. And besides, why would DI Greene want to have dinner with a mere detective constable and his mother anyway?

He sighed, leaned back and stared at the muted screen of the television. A game show was on. He hadn't told Mercy or

Jean about the raid tomorrow—only that his shifts had altered and that he had to be back on duty by three. He knew they'd worry.

He wasn't scared, not really. But he wasn't a fool. He knew there were plenty of cops out there who didn't like working with black or other ethnic minority police officers. And in a raid, things got confused. If the suspects were armed, things could get really nasty, really fast. Especially in such a small and cramped space as a narrowboat. There wouldn't be much room for manoeuvring if things went pear-shaped.

He'd been in a street riot once, during his early days in London, so he knew just how much you had to rely on a fellow officer to watch your back. He himself had prevented another black officer from getting a broken milk bottle buried in the nape of his neck.

But Tommy couldn't let thoughts like these worry him now. In all probability, the raid tomorrow would go like clockwork. Be nothing more than a damp squib. They might not even find anything more drugs-related on the *Kraken* than mentholated teabags.

Mel knew he needed this bust to be a good one. Even though Vice would be collecting most of the glory, all those who mattered would know it had been a joint affair. When Marcus moved up, as rumour had it that he was going to, and soon, it would do his own chances of taking over as superintendent no harm at all if he was known as the man who'd taken down Luke Fletcher.

OK. Helped to take down. Was at least in on it when the first nail was hammered into his coffin.

He frowned.

He hoped Janine kept her head down tomorrow.

8

FROM the top of Headington Hill, the city of Oxford would have looked spectacular. It was just getting light, and a soft peach colour was highlighting the greens of the tree tops, and the pampered lawns of the college quads. Some of the lawns, centuries old, rolled, trimmed, fed and all but venerated, were host to the early birds of legend. Blackbirds, mostly, avidly catching out worms which had been seduced to the surface by the mist and morning dew that dampened the ground.

The same low-lying mist that was the worm's undoing carpeted the city from about ten feet or so upwards, leaving the skyline clear. Through this dream-like, peach-toned miasma poked every one of the spires, pergolas, arches and domes that made the city famous, and would have had any photographer snapping away like a crazy person, thinking happily of commissions from postcard manufacturers, calendar makers and the tourist board.

For working cops, however, the mist was a bit of a sod. Frank didn't mind it so much—in his opinion, if you couldn't get a clear view of the bastards, then it meant the bastards couldn't get a clear view of you, either.

Frank rather liked it when they couldn't see you coming.

Nothing on the canal was moving. Not even a cat. The bottom end of Walton Street, all the way up to Canal Street, was as yet deserted of students, Japanese tourists or even milkmen or postmen. It was unusual, even at this hour, not to hear the sound of a car, but here, on the canal, the city might have been a million miles away.

There wasn't even the sound of lapping water, for the canal wasn't tidal, and the water just sat there in its narrow confines, like a dull greenish brown ribbon. The muffling mist had even the church bells sounding as if they came from the other side of the world as they rang out the half hour.

Hillary checked her watch. It wasn't yet 4:25. That was the thing about Oxford—it had hundreds of damned church clocks, college clocks, bell towers and chiming gongs, and not one of them seemed to keep the right time.

She glanced across at Mel.

The raiding party had met up in Walton Street, and had been co-ordinated by Regis, who undoubtedly had more experience of this kind of thing. It had reminded her of her days in training college. There were cops in protective gear everywhere, but none of them, as far as Hillary was aware, were actually armed. She wondered, uneasily, if it was a mistake not calling in the armed response unit.

Even though Tommy Lynch and all the rest looked impressive in protective padding, with riot shields hard helmets and nice big hefty truncheons, she knew how false such a look of armoured imperviousness could be. Bullets shattered shields, broke helmets apart, and did very nasty things to flesh and bone, no matter what padding it had.

Still, she could understand why the powers-that-be had vetoed guns. For all that they were on the canal, they were in the heart of the city, with snoozing terraced cottages on one side and other boats moored around the *Kraken*.

She'd listened in approval as Regis had outlined his softly-softly approach. There was no point going in there yelling like a raiding party of Mongols.

'Picks' Pickering, a sergeant older than Methuselah, had been co-opted to see if he could get into the boat without the aid of a battering ram.

When Hillary had arrived at the Big House over an hour ago, she'd been the first one he'd approached, asking about boat doors, locks, safety features, alarms and such that he'd be likely to come across on a narrowboat.

She'd told him all she knew. Her own boat had bolts, top and bottom. Her uncle had never fitted a Yale lock, since the doors on boats weren't anything like the front or back doors of houses. At least, they weren't on the *Mollern*, but then she was an old boat. Twenty years old at least. She wasn't so sure about the new state-of-the-art range of boats. She'd seen a hotel narrowboat once, long, sleek, and from the glimpse through the windows she'd got, complete with every mod con you could hope for. Now *those* might have Yale locks *and* a burglar alarm.

However, she'd been relieved to see from the photos taken by Tanner and his mate yesterday that the *Kraken* wasn't brand new by any means. Which was good news for Picks.

Nobody knew what Picks's real name was. Hillary found this rather alarming as she watched the old-timer creeping along the towpath now, as if not knowing his name was a bad omen. The mist seemed to swirl around him, but he was in uniform and the dark blue suit enabled them to watch his progress with relative ease. Regis and Mel had binoculars, but Hillary wasn't sure that they'd be helping much, not in these conditions.

She wished Picks wasn't quite so old. Surely he should have retired by now? Or was he just one of those men who looked ancient when they were really only 50? He was a tall, skinny, scarecrow-like figure, the kind that looked to be permanently in danger of being bowled over by the least bit of wind.

She supposed she wasn't the only one to be feeling beset by pangs of guilt. Here they all were, in places of strategic cover, the men young and fit and pumped up on testosterone and memories of *The Bill* on telly, whilst it was poor old Picks who was actually in the front line.

She glanced across to her right. She was crouched behind a parked car, a Mazda in a rather off-putting shade of purple. Beside her was an armoured PC she didn't know, but beyond him, she caught the unmistakable glimpse of pale blonde hair. By leaning to her left, she could make out her sergeant's face clearly. Janine's eyes were glued to the crouched, advancing figure of Picks. Behind him, as per plan, crept the first of two big police constables. It was their job to come to Picks's aid if the sleeping crew on the boat were woken by his faint scratching as he tried to gain access.

As Regis had said, raiding a narrowboat was going to be a bit of a bugger. For a start, it was narrow, and Hillary had warned them it would be narrower still inside. The alleyway between front and rear, where the bathroom was located, for instance, would allow single access only. Cops on raids, as a rule, preferred to stand shoulder to shoulder to shoulder, covering each other front, back and sides if possible. But there was no way you could do that on a narrowboat.

This meant they had to be very sure of the plan. They had to go in single file, hard and fast. No Keystone-Cop stuff, like getting jammed in the entrance ways. They had to be quick and silent.

Hillary had seen the pictures of the boat yesterday, and had been able to give a good guess as to its internal layout. Most canal boats either had the lounge area at the front, like hers, incorporating the kitchen area, leading off to a narrow corridor that allowed access to the bedrooms and shower/toilet that were at the back, or vice versa. From the pictures of *Kraken* she was sure that the layout followed much the same as that of her own boat. But without blueprints, which weren't available, it was impossible to be sure.

Regis's plan was, therefore, simple. If Picks succeeded in gaining access at the rear door, he was to leave one PC stationed at the rear and give the signal to the others. He'd then immediately go to the prow of the boat with the other PC and see if he could gain access, quietly, though that door as well. Providing that was successful, the raiding party would split into two groups—one coming in from the rear, the other from the front. They were to meet outside the bedrooms.

That was the plan. Hillary could think of a hundred things that could go wrong with it, but then, she had no doubt, so could Regis, Mel or even the greenest cop fresh out of training college.

Janine cursed the mist as Picks disappeared briefly from view in a particularly thick patch, but then re-emerged. She sensed someone staring at her, and turned her head, first one way, then the other, finally encountering Hillary Greene's unnervingly unruffled gaze.

She nodded coolly, still feeling resentful about her DI zeroing in on her during the briefing in Walton Street, and all but lecturing her about safety. She felt like a kid at school, being told by a bigger kid to keep out of the way of the school bullies. Hillary looked away, and Janine found it impossible to know what she was thinking. She supposed the DI was getting past it now, and was just trying to look out for her. Her heart was probably in the right place.

Come to think of it, Janine had never heard anything on the rumour mill about Hillary Greene's bottle—or lack thereof. She knew for a fact that she didn't play any contact

sports, not even squash, which seemed to be the woman police officer's holy grail of fitness. That or martial arts. But she
didn't think DI Greene was the kung-fu type. Not that it mattered, of course. By the time the DI and Mel and even Regis
entered the boat, the suspects should all be nicely handcuffed
and yelling for their briefs.

Janine could still clearly remember her self-defence training from police college, and the big burly sergeant who'd
taught her how to throw men twice her weight, and how to
avoid getting stabbed if some berserk junkie came at you with
a carving knife. She wondered, briefly, if they'd even had
training sessions like that when Hillary Greene had attended
College. Come to think of it, hadn't she heard that her DI had
been a university copper? In her day, for all Janine knew, fast-
track intellectual female officers might not have had to even
go to training college. So where the hell did she get off telling her to keep back and keep her head down?

On the other side of Janine, crouched behind a big Dumpster
used by the boaties as a communal waste bin, Regis stiffened
as he saw Picks reach the boat. Hillary had warned him about
how a boat moved when someone got on it. She'd even had
him, and the raiding party down to Thrupp to demonstrate
on her own boat before setting off for the city.

It had been useful. He wished he'd thought of it himself.
Now he watched, approvingly, as Picks, mindful of his early-
morning lesson, stepped on to the back, right into the boat's
centre of gravity, and carefully, very carefully, knelt down.
Through his binoculars, Regis couldn't see the boat make any
appreciable movement.

He glanced at his watch. Good. It was getting lighter now.
Light enough, in fact, to give good visibility inside, even with
all the curtains drawn.

Mel, on the opposite side of the canal, behind the garden wall of one of the terraced cottages, glanced through the open gate, and then across at the others. He couldn't see Janine. He guessed Hillary had taken her aside back on Walton Street to warn her to keep a low profile, and he hoped she'd listened.

He cursed the fact that he had a bad view of the proceedings, and kept his ear glued to the radio. He glanced uneasily behind him, but the curtains in the cottage windows were all still safely drawn.

Usually, whenever a raid was to take place, the public were warned and possibly even evacuated, but in this case, given the fact that they didn't know until the last minute where the boat would moor, plus the fact that, in such close confines, it would have been almost impossible to silently evacuate the cottages without those on the boat cottoning on, it had been decided that what the public didn't know wouldn't hurt them. Mel only hoped some little old lady needing a pee didn't look out the window and call out, asking what he was doing standing in her rhubarb patch.

From the buzz on the radio it seemed Picks had got the back door opened, for he'd stepped carefully off the boat and was giving the signal.

Mel risked craning his head around the gate and looking around, down the towpath. The boat was moored up about twenty feet away. Through the mist, fast thinning now as the sun's power came to elbow it aside, he could see a big, padded constable step onto the back of the boat, ready to be first in. Coming past Mel now, crouched, were four others, waiting for the signal to join him. In a few minutes, if Picks got the front door open, another group of raiders would come past, ready to converge on the front.

Mel felt the sweat break out on the back of his neck. He was wearing a white faux-silk shirt and a navy blue Giorgio

Armani knock-off jumper. He felt slightly ridiculous. Not because of the clothes—hell, nobody would wear their finest on a job like this—but because being crouched in someone's garden at five o'clock in the morning, waiting to follow a group of gung-ho coppers on to a narrowboat, seemed faintly silly. He couldn't, at times like these, remember exactly why it was he'd joined the police force in the first place. His brother taught mathematics at a private boys school in Harrogate, for Pete's sake.

He wiped off the sweat which had surprised him by running down his forehead and onto the bridge of his nose. Shit. He must be more tense than he realised. He jumped as the second wave of uniforms passed. Picks must have succeeded in getting the second door open. Sure enough, he was coming back now. The old sergeant slid in beside Mel, whose safe spot was nearest, and crouched down. He was breathing hard. No wonder, poor sod. He'd drawn the short end of the stick, no mistake. Everybody knew that if the gang inside were Luke's boys, and were tooled up, they might have shot first and asked questions later. There had been more than one cop who'd been shot through a locked door and killed in the line of duty.

Mel reached out and patted the old man on his shoulder. 'Good going, Picks,' he said softly.

Picks nodded and smiled. He looked just a bit sick.

'Right,' Mel said tensely, hearing the squawk on the radio. 'This is it.'

He duck-walked a few paces to the open gate. Picks stayed leaning against the wall, looking at the cottage, wondering how much one would cost. He'd always fancied retiring to the city. Most of his pals did it the other way around, living and working in town, and then moving to the seaside or a country village on collecting the pension. But he'd always lived in villages, and quite fancied being an Oxonian in his old age.

His youngest granddaughter reckoned he looked quite Don-like. Perhaps he could buy a pair of pince-nez and hang out near the Bodleian reading a book and fooling the tourists into thinking he was some emeritus professor.

With a start he realised he was maundering—something he always did after a shock or a particularly stressful episode. He also realised he was alone.

DCI Mallow had gone.

From her position behind the car, Hillary watched the by-the-book, best-of-all-scenarios being played out, and took a few deep breaths, letting them out slowly. So far, so good. They had both doors unlocked, one constable at each end, and four others, also at each end, ready to go.

She glanced across at Regis, who was talking into the radio.

'Come on, come on,' Janine muttered under her breath, her own breathing coming in ragged, excited little jerks.

'Go,' Regis said quietly into the radio.

Something went wrong. In this case it was simple, and should have been foreseeable.

Somebody had used the lounge sofa as a bed.

They were designed to convert to single beds, of course, since holidaymakers liked to cram as many people on to a boat as possible, making the cost of a boating holiday cheap. From the size of *Kraken*, Hillary had—rightly, as it was to turn out—estimated that it could sleep at least eight, maybe even nine. It would have at most two bedrooms, probably doubles, but could, at a pinch, be converted into bunkbeds sleeping four in each.

But they hadn't expected anything like that number to be on board.

Given that they were almost sure that The Pits, Makepeace and Gascoigne made up one unit, they were expecting three or maybe four, tops, to be on board. One, like Makepeace, to be a sort of dogsbody, driver and probably cook. One or maybe two for muscle, like Gascoigne and The Pits. Gascoigne probably to guard the haul at all times, The Pits to help out at locks, drawbridges and suchlike.

But this team was a lot bigger.

The constable who went in through the front entrance was the first to figure this out. Rising from his left, and already moving frighteningly fast, was a near-naked figure. Aware of Regis's plan to keep everything quiet, the constable's first instinct—that of yelling blue murder—was quickly stifled. Even though he could hear the sound of footsteps at the rear of the boat, meaning the other raiding party was already moving in on the bedrooms, he still didn't call out. He did, however, swing around to meet the challenge.

Behind him, the other constables were already boarding—but so confined was the space that only one was coming through the door.

He lifted his shield just in time, as the dark-haired suspect, dressed only in a pale blue pair of boxer shorts, lifted something that looked like a radio alarm clock and tried to smash it down on his head.

Behind him, he heard one of his pals yell out a warning. After that, several yells, thuds, curses and assorted sounds came from the back of the boat. But for the PC in the lounge, who was called Brian Herbert, and was 21 years old next Monday, the heartening knowledge that the rest of the gang had been caught safely napping didn't help *him* much.

He pushed forward with the shield, to try and squash his opponent in one corner and contain him until he and the others could get cuffs on him. At the same time, he was trying to shift his rear end around so that his pals could get in behind him and give him the necessary back-up.

It was at this point that the suspect did something totally unexpected.

He slithered out of the open window like an eel.

Brian hadn't, until then, even realised that the barge window was open, let alone that it was big enough to allow somebody to get out.

He gave a startled yelp and darted forward to grab an ankle, but his shield was in the way, and he had a truncheon in one hand, and by the time he'd dropped the shield and transferred the truncheon to his weaker left hand, it was too late.

He heard a splash and cursed.

To make matters worse, the two cops still outside hadn't seen what had happened. Brian ran to the window and looked out, expecting to see a dark head and flailing limbs or someone swimming raggedly to the bank.

He saw nothing.

He swore graphically. Surely the cut wasn't all that deep? Why wasn't the bastard wading along the side of the boat? He backed up, bumping into the last of the four who'd come in the rear. They were already heading for the back of the boat, where there were sounds of furious scuffling.

Shit.

Brian ran to the front of the boat and again looked fore and aft. Where had the slippery little bastard gone?

He reached desperately for the radio strapped to his collar.

Mel and Regis were already running along the towpath as Brian Herbert spoke, making the use of the radio obsolete. If he wanted to tell his superiors what had happened, all he had to do was shout.

He began to do so.

Unfortunately, there was a lot of noise now coming from the *Kraken*, waking everyone in the cottages. Heads began to poke out the windows, irate sleep-interrupted members of the public calling out and asking what was going on.

Brian didn't panic. He knew a lot of binoculars and pairs of eyes had been watching the boat. They would all have seen one of the suspects trying to leg it.

Hillary Greene, for one, certainly had.

She noticed the big, black figure of Tommy Lynch going in the rear, just as something white and fast seemed to fall from the front of the boat. She saw the feet first—the unmistakable kicking motion of an expert swimmer. But why swim in only four feet or so of water. Why not stand and wade?

The answer to that was obvious. You swam to go underwater. And you went underwater to hide.

Shit.

Then, out of the corner of her eye, she saw the flash of a pale gold head and she knew that Janine was on the move.

Too soon. Dammit, too soon.

'Janine, no!' she yelled, but no notice was taken of her. Quickly, Hillary looked for Regis, but he was already on the towpath, along with Mel and his sergeant and everybody else and their Aunt Fanny by the looks of it, running towards the *Kraken*.

Hillary stood up, torn. Should she go after Janine? No, not necessary. She was surrounded by cops.

Instead, she scanned the canal. Whoever had gone over the side had to come up for air any second now. How far along could a strong swimmer go before surfacing? She had no damned idea. Twenty yards? Too much?

She glanced left, then right. The trouble was, the canal water was filthy—the khaki mud colour unrelieved by bubbles of any kind.

Had he gone behind the boat? No, surely not, it was already overrun with coppers.

On the front of the boat she saw a single constable who, like herself, was searching fruitlessly for air bubbles.

Brian Herbert was swearing frantically under his breath. He could see the scene now. His furious superior officer, barking out questions, asking why it was that every other villain on the boat had been nabbed, save for the one in the lounge. The one that PC Brian Herbert was supposed to nab.

He cringed as he imagined the sarcasm as he tried to explain. Oh, like an eel, was he? Slithered through the window before you could catch him, did he? Greased, was he, like one of those pigs at an old-fashioned fair? He was so agitated he was almost sobbing. Where the hell had the bastard gone?

Janine was running down the towpath, her eyes on the back of Mel's head. From the back of the boat, the first of the suspects emerged, handcuffed, wearing, comically, a pair of pyjama bottoms with some sort of kids' characters on them.

Boy was he going to be embarrassed later, when he had time to think about it. Then something hit her.

Hard.

One moment she was running, the next she simply wasn't. In fact, she was skidding painfully along the tow path, her hands, knees and cheeks flaming as if they'd been torched. In fact, they had merely been skinned as they scraped along the rough stone mix that the River Authority used instead of concrete or asphalt.

She didn't have time to yell. She didn't really know what was happening to her. All she knew was pain, and sudden, stark fear. Confused fear.

From her view behind the parked car, Hillary Greene saw exactly what happened. Seeing a break in the line of coppers running along the towpath, a pale-skinned figure had emerged at the edge of the towpath, standing upright, holding something long and thin—no doubt a pipe, or some other such piece of metal, that had been tossed in the canal who the hell knew when. The swimmer couldn't have seen it, not in the gunge that passed for canal water, so he could only have felt it with his fingertips as he'd swum along.

What Hillary couldn't understand was why he'd used it in the first place. Perhaps panic. Perhaps hatred of cops. More likely hatred of women. Whoever the suspect was, he must have known, in his heart of hearts, that there wasn't any getting away.

For a start, the stretch of canalside where Hillary was standing was lined with corrugated iron, too steep to climb up. Even if he'd managed it, there were cops all along this side of the street. And the side he was on now was even worse. The towpath was lined with cops, from Mel to Regis, to the now emerging and victorious PCs from the boat. Even if he'd managed to get out of the canal unseen, he was hardly likely to blend into the background and manage to slip away. Skinny, white, dripping foul-smelling canal water, he looked like nothing on earth.

But, as Hillary well knew, his adrenaline would be up. He'd be feeling pumped and pleased with himself for getting off the boat at all. He'd be feeling like superman. So why not floor the silly bitch copper running by? Perhaps he even thought her colleagues would all be so filled with chivalrous remorse, they'd go to her aid and forget about him.

Who the hell knew what was going on in his mind?

Hillary knew what was going on in hers. He was out of the canal now, on his knees, but with the weapon still in his hand. And Janine, stunned, was an easy target well within reach. One swing of that metal bar on her head and...

'Hey, you! You bastard, look at me!' Hillary bellowed, her furious voice cutting across the air, making everyone, including the perp, look her way.

It was Regis's sergeant, the silent, unimposing Colin Tanner, who saw him first. He yelled, a nameless word that seemed yanked out of him as he spun and sprinted towards the woman police officer lying on the ground, her golden hair spread around her, looking wildly out of place.

Then everyone was moving. One of their own was in trouble. They absorbed the fact more by osmosis than logic.

It was enough to utterly confuse and demoralise the perp, who began sprinting for all he was worth. Away from Janine.

Hillary too, was moving, although not really aware of it. She knew, vaguely, that there would be someone coming across the bridge ready to tackle the fleeing suspect—it simply wasn't procedure to have everybody in only one place. There was always back-up.

And so there was. Even now she could see two uniformed cops, not in armoured gear, true, but both men of a good size, running across the bridge to intercept the perp. She was just coming up behind them when the suspect did a crazy dodging manoeuvre that reminded her of nothing so much as a ferret.

Brian Herbert, watching from the back of the boat still, felt a silent sense of justification for losing him in the first place, as he displayed the same eel-like ability to wriggle and dodge. See, he could say. The sod must be as double-jointed as a bloody snake.

Tommy Lynch was the first to see the obvious danger—that Hillary was now directly in his way. And being on the boat, he was utterly unable to help her.

Hillary had very little time to feel dismayed. She'd watched, wide eyed, as the white-skinned, desperate-faced perp dodged first one lunge, and then ducked under the unloving embrace of the second cop, like a manic limbo dancer. She heard both of her colleagues curse, even had time to see them bang into each other, fumble and start to turn.

But by then, the perp was almost upon her. He looked young, and desperate. And mean. Very mean. Worse, he could taste freedom. She could almost hear his thoughts. He'd been on the boat, trapped like a rat, but he'd got off the boat, hadn't he? He'd given that tart of a cop a good whack, and dodged those other two like Michael Owen shrugging off a whole Arsenal-load of defenders. Now all he had was one middle-aged, suit-wearing, desk-jockey, *woman* cop and he'd have the whole city to get lost in. No doubt it stretched out behind Hillary like the promised land, Walton Street and the maze of side streets leading off it.

Of course, she knew there must be other colleagues behind her, some probably no more than a few yards away.

But that didn't help now.

He was coming at her with all the fastness of his youth, all the strength lent to him by the desperation of his situation, his fear leeching him of any finer feeling he might once have had. All he wanted was to steam-roller over her and be away.

Hillary briefly contemplated just stepping aside and letting him surge past her. She doubted that anyone would blame her if she did. The two cops behind him were nearly on him anyway. And she could hear angry shouts behind her, telling her indeed that back-up was on the way.

Some might even argue she'd be right to do just that. The brass didn't like it when women officers got hurt—especially not those of the rank of DI.

But she just couldn't stand there and let him pass, could she?

Of course she couldn't.

When he was just the right distance away from her, she lifted her foot in a classic, high-kick, the likes of which would have impressed even a veteran of the Folies Bergère, and kicked him squarely in the balls.

9

HE DIDN'T seem to like it much. His face went white then suddenly suffused with blood, his mouth projecting itself into an O of agony. He bent double, unintentionally head butting her in the stomach. She took a hasty step back, but he was down on one knee now, heaving and retching.

Behind him, the two uniformed officers were already reaching out for him, cuffs at the ready. Behind Hillary, a ragged cheer went up. Mel, puffing a little from his dash across the bridge, pulled up beside her, grinning fit to make even the Cheshire cat look at him askance.

'Shit, Hill, that was the best kick in the goolies I've seen in a long while,' he congratulated her admiringly.

'Yeah, nine-point-nine for artistic merit,' Mike Regis said, not at all out of breath as he joined them on the bridge and looked down at the gasping, red-faced perp. He reminded him of a guppy he used to keep as a kid.

'But a straight ten for technical expertise,' Mel added, straight-faced, and suddenly Hillary found herself embarrassingly and gratifyingly surrounded by laughing colleagues, all set to see who could tease her the most.

From the opposite side of the bank, Tommy watched with relief as his DI dealt smartly with the danger, then felt flooded

with jealousy at the fact that he didn't dare go over and join
in the teasing.

He walked instead to where Janine half sat, half sprawled
on the towpath, surrounded by burly constables not quite
sure what to do with her. One was radioing for an ambulance.

Tommy crouched down in front of her. 'You OK?' he
asked softly.

Janine swore at him, loudly and roundly. Then added, in a
wobbly voice, 'Of course I'm not sodding all right. Do I look
all right?'

She could feel nothing but pain. Pain, pain and more pain.
She wasn't used to it. Worse, she hadn't expected it. Not
really. The concept of being injured in the line of duty had always been an abstract one.

And she simply hadn't realised it would make her feel like this.

Its intrusive, omnipotent force made her want to puke on
the towpath. She was shaking, and somewhere, deep inside her
head, she knew she was in trouble. She wanted nothing so
much as to cry her eyes out to release some of the tension, then
ask to be taken home to her mother.

But of course, she could do none of these things.

Her skin, where it was scraped, burned and stung, making
her want to scratch. But she knew if she took her hand off the
towpath, she'd collapse back onto her nose again.

She didn't know where to put her face. Why did all these
men keep hanging around her, looking like shame-faced, worried sheep?

How had this *happened* to her?

'An ambulance is coming,' Tommy said, making her feel ten
times worse. 'Just take it easy.'

'I don't need an ambulance,' she said, and made to get up.
Pain, this time like a lash from a red-hot whip, flickered across

her back where the perp had swung the iron bar and caught her across her shoulder-blades.

The world swam.

She lay back down on the towpath, and concentrated on not being sick.

Still, somewhere deep inside her head, she knew she was in trouble.

They brought the sniffer dogs and their handlers in from the vans still parked in Walton Street within minutes, whilst the crew from the boat—all five of them—were being carted off, as per the arrangement, to the nick in St Aldates.

Tanner went with them to start the interviews and co-ordinate things from that end, but Regis, not surprisingly, wanted to hang around and see what they came up with. Thanks to the great Houdini, as they were already calling the one who'd made a bolt for it, they were sure there had to be something on board, and some of the tension at the thought of coming up empty-handed had begun to dissipate. And it totally disappeared when the dogs, big professional-looking Alsatians, began to go crazy the moment they were led on to the barge.

Hillary, back at her perch by the purple Mazda, watched as the ambulance pulled up, following the progress of the attendants as, with professional sympathy, they transferred her sergeant to the stretcher. She'd had quite a whack, but Hillary was pretty sure her shoulder hadn't been dislocated. She wanted to go over there, but she knew from past experience that she was probably the last person Janine wanted to see right now. She'd be feeling humiliated enough, without having Hillary as a living, breathing, I-told-you-so to rub it in.

She knew what it was like to take a beating. She'd once got on the wrong end of a domestic, where a wife-beating hubby, unusually, decided to give Hillary a taste too.

She'd have to keep an eye on Janine now, and make sure she didn't lose it to such an extent that she couldn't get it back again. Try and show her that what had happened today wasn't the disaster it felt like, and that people weren't laughing at her behind her back, but that it was just one of those learning experiences that everyone has to go through.

Of course, there would always be male chauvinist prats, like Frank Ross, who *would* rub it in. But that, with a bit of luck, would only have the effect of stiffening her sergeant's backbone. She refused to believe that the likes of Janine Tyler, blonde harridan from hell extraordinaire, would ever let Frank Ross or turds like him put a dent in her self-esteem. Or so she'd tell Janine, once she was back at her desk.

A sudden yell of triumph from the boat told her the good news. They'd found something.

In fact, they'd found something very big indeed. All morning, carefully, and with photographers, SOCO and by-the-book procedure with them every step of the way, they retrieved what would later turn out to be the sixth biggest drugs bust in Thames Valley history.

'Fletcher must be chewing off the wallpaper by now,' Regis said to Hillary as they sat in her car, eating hamburgers that one of the uniforms had been sent to Burger King for. She would have liked fries and a big chocolate milkshake to go with it, of course, but when you had a high like this morning to carry you over, even she, she supposed, could do without a chocolate fix for once.

'Poor chap,' she said, sotto voce.

Regis nodded, taking a huge bite out of his burger. 'Makes you want to cry for him, don't it?'

Everyone back at the Big House had heard about the bust, of course, and its mammoth haul of crack, coke, heroine, ecstasy, and assorted other goodies not even tested yet. The atmosphere as Hillary, Tommy, Regis and Mel walked into the office was electric. The cheers and hails had begun in the hall, with the desk sergeant giving them cheerful grief, and continued with ribbing from everyone they met on the stairs. In the office, they got a burst of applause that made Hillary feel all warm and gooey inside.

Until she realised they still hadn't found out how The Pits had met his end. It was now almost certain that he'd fallen off a second boat, with or without assistance. She knew Regis and Mel would be throwing everything into finding the second boat, although she thought that their chances of making a second spectacular haul were near zero. Fletcher would be on the mobile the instant he learned of the Oxford bust, and any drugs on the second canal boat would be offloaded faster than a stereo from a car parked in Blackbird Leys.

Paul Danvers and Curtis Smith weren't immune to the air of celebration either. Up in the canteen, the jubilation was as redolent as the scent of frying bacon. Not surprisingly, when the dynamic trio walked in, they got a heroes' welcome. Mel lapped it up, of course, but Regis, after a smile that looked cracked in stone, seemed to shrug it off.

'She looks a bit embarrassed, don't you think?' Paul said, looking at Hillary with what he hoped was a bland face. 'See, I told you she was a good copper.'

'She can do her job,' Curtis agreed, spearing an egg yolk with a satisfyingly thick chip. 'I never thought she couldn't.'

Paul reluctantly looked back at his partner. 'You heard from Scotland yet?'

His partner nodded. 'Yep. It's confirmed.'

Paul sighed heavily. Shit. Still, he supposed it had to be done. 'Let's leave off confronting her until after this dies down, though, yeah?' he said, looking around a shade apprehensively.

Hillary was heroine of the hour at the moment. Stepping up the investigation a notch wasn't going to go down too well.

Curtis had no problem with that, and nodded. He too looked around, and wouldn't have been human—or a cop—if he hadn't felt an echoing sense of pride. They'd obviously done good. And, like every other cop in the place, he liked the thought of a big-time drug dealer going to the wall.

'Sure,' he agreed amiably. 'We can wait a while.'

Paul caught his eye, and knew damned well what he was thinking. Hillary Greene might be a good cop, but if she was as bent as her husband, she'd be going down.

Paul pushed his plate of vegetable lasagne away and wished he still smoked.

Gary Greene pulled off his marked patrol car at the Bicester straight, and signalled left, sighing as the old, grey metallic railway bridge hove into sight. He signalled left again, into the new, pale, gleaming nick that was supposed to be Bicester's answer to the rise in crime statistics.

He hadn't been there before. He'd spent some time in the old Bicester nick, at the bottom of the road from the sports centre and Bicester Comprehensive, now called something more upmarket. And he knew his dad had worked out of that nick too, and still had a lot of friends in this one.

He just wished one of them hadn't called him last night and told him he might like to pop around when he had a moment. Like, soonish. He parked the car and walked in, feeling apprehensive, and asked for Sergeant Pete Glover.

Glover turned out to be one of those men who looked like a professional wrestler and couldn't stop talking about his kids. After the usual compulsory ten minutes of reminiscing about Ronnie, being told what a good bloke he was, a real copper, and how sorry the sergeant was about him being dead, Glover eventually took him to the locker room.

'See, thing is son,' Glover said, glancing around, although the room, which smelt habitually of dirty socks and aftershave, was completely empty, 'old Ron liked to keep a locker here. Not strictly legit, see, seeing as he wasn't serving here, but what the hell? Right?'

'Right,' Gary said miserably, with a bright smile.

'So when I heard there were some nosy parkers sniffing around up at the Big House, I thought I'd better check, you see, just to make sure…well, that there weren't nuffin' hanging around that you wouldn't want your old lady to see. See?'

Gary nodded, ignoring the sick feeling in the pit of his stomach.

'Turns out there was nothing much there. Well, a bit of porno, got off a raid years ago, but you can buy worse than that now in W H Smith. Get me?' Glover said, giving him a painful nudge in the ribs with his elbow, and laughing like a blocked drain. 'But I thought I should clear it out anyway. Just in case them sods from down your way get to hear about Ronnie's little arrangement here. I bagged it up,' he added, opening the locker concerned and dragging out a Tesco's shopping bag. 'I, er, got rid of the porno,' Glover said, not quite meeting his eyes. 'Didn't think you'd want to run the risk of getting caught with it. You still being a nipper of a constable, and all that.'

What he really meant was he'd sold it to some sleazy geezer he knew.

Gary nodded, feeling relieved. So that was it. Just some wary sergeant wanting to cover himself. Fair enough. He took the bag, admired Glover's youngest, an unprepossessing brunette of ten years old or so, and left, feeling like laughing.

Being big bad Ronnie Greene's son was both an asset and a liability. He knew damned well he'd have to keep his nose extra squeaky clean to get promoted, and knew the brass would always see his name and wonder. On the other hand, a lot of the troops in the trenches secretly admired Ronnie Greene, and he'd had a few spectacular collars in his time before things had turned sour.

So he walked a tightrope, and prayed for memories to fade.

He drove off, but pulled up in the nearest lay-by. In the bag was a pair of old trainers, a wallet with no money in it but credit cards that he was sure Hillary knew nothing about, some toiletries, caked around the rim with green, pine-smelling ooze and a paperback novel.

The novel was a Dick Francis thriller. He glanced inside, surprised to see an inscription from Hillary. He'd give it her back. Who knows, she might want a small keepsake.

Yeah. Right. She'd probably burn it. When he was alive, his father had given her nothing but grief. And now that he was dead, he still couldn't seem to get out of the habit.

Tommy was back on the towpath but nowhere near all the excitement of Oxford. Right now, the *Kraken* was cordoned off and being gone over by jubilant cops from the Oxford station.

When he'd got back to the Big House, feeling the usual washed-out lethargy that came after an adrenaline rush, Hillary, far from coming it with the compliments, had rather sourly reminded him they still had a suspicious death to investigate, even if Regis and Mel seemed to have forgotten all about The Pits.

Her grim reminder had prompted him back to his notebook, where he'd come across the message to himself to return to question the missing boaties from up Dashwood Lock way. In particular, the artist who liked elephants, and who, according to one witness, saw everything in clear detail.

The day was overcast now, the earlier sun having slunk off over the horizon, but in other respects he was in luck. The elephant-bedaubed boat had a door that stood open, and from inside was the sound of a radio.

With nothing to knock on, he stood outside and coughed. Nothing. 'Excuse me. Hello in the boat,' he said, feeling like an extra from a pirate movie. Well, at least he hadn't said 'Ahoy there!'

The radio was immediately silenced, and a second later a mass of blond hair, with a face somewhere in the middle of it, looked out. The long hair fell to bare shoulders, the long beard lay on a bare chest, and somewhere on the lip, a furry blond caterpillar made inroads into his cheeks.

A pair of dark brown eyes twinkled out of the hairy mess, and a moment later, the rest of him followed. He was covered in paint smears and something that looked like sawdust.

Tommy hadn't expected a walking cliché. Didn't the chap know the sixties were, like, gone, man. Or was this new eco-warrior stuff? Tommy also had no desire at all to know what he'd been doing down in the boat. Anything that required paint was something he tended to stay away from.

He introduced himself, showing his warrant card, and tried not to notice that the artist was running his eyes over him like he was a prime Aberdeen Angus at a cattle show.

Tommy said his piece about the body of a young man being found. 'So I was wondering if you noticed anything unusual that night,' he finished. He'd tried hard not to lay any undue emphasis on the word 'young man' but wasn't sure he'd suc-ceeded. The implication that if a young man had been found dead, this gay man might have something to do with it, seemed to hover in the air, despite the fact that Tommy had no reason to suspect him of anything at all. And didn't.

But if the artist had taken offence, he didn't show it. Instead he seemed to squint up his eyes and think. It looked a painful process.

Tommy cleared his throat after a long silence. 'For instance, did you notice a boat going faster than it should, or travelling after dark?' he prompted, a little desperately.

'Oh yeah. *Time Out*, it was. I thought it rather twee.' The artist, who hadn't given his name, spoke for the first time in a thick, Welsh accent. Tommy, for a second, had trouble deciphering the sing-song words, then grasped their significance.

'The boat was called *Time Out*? And it was definitely the night of the eighth?'

'It surely was. The lady who was moored up a few berths down complained about the bow wave the next morning. I noticed it too—I was trying to paint an elephant's eye at the time. You try doing that when your boat suddenly starts rocking.' And he laughed. 'Talk about someone rocking your dreamboat, look you.'

The combination of all that pale hair, his sing-song voice, and the way he kept looking at Tommy, as if imagining him stretched out in a big bad bed, was enough to make the policeman break out in a sweat.

But DCP Tommy Lynch wasn't the kind to be put off easily.

'Did you notice who was driving?' he asked, his voice at its most constabulary.

'Navigating? Yeah, sure, an old bloke. About sixty, I should say. Silver hair, and lean as a whippet, he was. Good facial bones. If I was into portraiture, see, I might have been interested.'

Tommy blinked, hoping his own facial bones were of the common or garden variety. *Real* common or garden.

'I see. Did you notice anyone else on the boat?'

'Oh no. They had the curtains drawn, look you. Floral ones.' And he shuddered. It set all his hair rippling. Tommy managed to keep his eyes averted.

'Did you hear any conversation from the boat?' he pursued doggedly.

'Not a dickie bird.'

Tommy tried a few more questions, but got nothing more. Still, it was a starting point. Of course, *Time Out* might be a boat with nothing more to its discredit than breaking the four miles an hour speed limit—although Makepeace, one of Fletcher's gang, was supposed to be a bloke in his sixties.

It was something to take back to Hillary, anyway.

Frank liked scaring his stool pigeons. He refused to call them narks, let alone informers, and the specimen in front of him now was particularly loathsome. He'd pulled him from one of his regular haunts at the dog races, and a little light slapping around plus the offer of a twenty to put on the 4:37 had produced results, of a kind.

But nothing earth-shattering.

'Look, I don't know nothing about drugs, honest, Mr Ross. Only what I already said,' the snivelling specimen assured him, wondering if he really should put all the twenty on 'Shanks's Pony', or split it and put a tenner on 'Mary's Lamb' as well. His mother's name had been Mary.

'Yeah, yeah,' Frank said in disgust, lighting up a foul-smelling cigar. 'Word has it that Alfie Makepeace asked for The Pits specially. For this holiday of his. Don't suppose you know the name of the boat he was going on holiday in, d'ya?'

He slapped the little runt around some more, but he wouldn't even admit to knowing Makepeace had rented a canal boat.

'I thought he was off to Tenerife or somewhere. You know.'

Frank did. A lot of Fletcher's lads went on holiday abroad, and came back via Amsterdam. Very lucrative.

'So why did he ask for Dave Pitman, special, like?' Frank pressed, but the snitch wasn't saying. Frank, after a while, was sure he didn't know, and reluctantly tossed the little git a twenty.

He drove back to the Big House in a pensive mood.

He'd been left out of the raid on the Oxford boat, ostensibly because they hadn't needed another sergeant there. They had the likes of Mel and Hillary bloody Greene, and Regis's sidekick, plus the muscle boys. Frank thought Hillary had probably put the boot in, keeping him out of the action just for spite.

So he was already in a foul mood by the time he got to the office. Word was already filtering out about the size of the bust, and the brass were all beaming. The air of congratulations still hung in the office, so when he got to his desk and found that Tommy Lynch, of all people, might have come up with the name of the boat they were now all hot to get their hands on, his cup of happiness truly overflowed.

Not.

With a name to go on, it wasn't long before two sharp-eyed constables from Banbury way spotted the boat *Time Out*, moored north of the market town. It was unusual to find a boat there in the first place. Most boaties either liked to moor up in the town, where they had close and easy access to the shops, or else get right out into the countryside, and into the peace and quiet. So to find a boat moored up far from the shops, but still not quite out in the sticks, struck them as unusual, even before they'd confirmed the name of the boat. They radioed back their find to their station, who got on to the Big House at Kidlington.

The switchboard put the call through to Mel, who wasn't answering, mainly because he was having his ego massaged by Marcus Donleavy up in the Superintendent's office.

No doubt they were both licking their chops over the press conference they were about to give. It would go down a treat on the six o'clock news.

Hillary, walking by, answered it instead, and took down the details gleefully. When she walked back to her desk, however, she was surprised to see Janine Tyler's fair head drooping over her computer terminal. She moved across to her.

'Have you been discharged, then?' she asked, watching as her sergeant's face swung nervously around.

'Sure. You know how it is—the usual six-hour wait in casualty, followed by ten minutes of prodding and poking about by a quack, then another two-hour wait for an X-ray only to be told nothing is broken, given some painkillers and told to go home. Who says the NHS isn't wonderful?'

'So why aren't you at home?' Hillary said, telling from the way that Janine's pupils were working (or rather, weren't working at all) that she'd taken the painkillers all right.

Janine went to shrug, remembered just in time that she really didn't want to move her shoulders at all, and smiled instead. 'Nothing there. Besides, I thought I'd just call in for a while. Shift's nearly over.'

'Yeah,' Hillary said thoughtfully. Obviously, her sergeant didn't want to be alone, which was understandable. Being attacked, no matter how hard-bitten a copper you were, always left you feeling shaky. Which was only human. As was the desire to get back on the horse again before you had time to become afraid of falling off again.

Still, she wished Janine hadn't chosen now to come back to work. She glanced at Mel's still empty office, and knew she was going to be stupid.

Knew it, but didn't intend to do a damn thing about it.

'We've got a lead on the second boat,' she said casually. 'I was about to nab Tommy—and probably Frank—and check it out.'

She didn't really want to take Frank, but there was no doubting that he was a very useful ally to have in a scrap. He was a vicious little jerk, and after this morning, if *Time Out* really did prove to be the boat they were looking for, things might get hot. She should, at the very least, tell Mel about it, but she knew what he'd say. Or rather, do. Take control. Call out a small team and do things by the book.

And it might all be for nothing. The boat might contain nothing more dangerous than a granddad who liked to go to the wire by speeding in his boat, two grandkids bored out of their mind with only an over-excitable dog for company, and a grandma who resented cooking on a tiny stove.

'Yeah?' Janine said, something in her voice catching Hillary's attention.

Tommy, sensing something afoot, sidled over, his face tight with left-over excitement, and obviously open for more.

Oh shit, Hillary thought. Why the hell not?

10

'RIGHT, we're going to check out a possible lead on the second boat, the one our victim *might*, and I stress the word *might*, have come from. You think you're up to it?' Hillary added, knowing Janine could never say 'no' to a question like that.

Her sergeant nodded, wondering uneasily how hot the lead was. Although she'd felt satisfactorily macho when leaving the hospital, and had enjoyed laughing off solicitous questions and making sure everyone knew just how tough she was, she'd planned on taking it easy today. 'Course, boss,' she said, reaching for her bag.

'Right. I suppose we'd better bring Frank,' Hillary said, glancing over at Ross's desk. He was hunched over some paperwork, pretending to read it.

Tommy Lynch audibly groaned.

Reluctantly, the trio ambled over to Ross, who looked up, smiling widely, for all the world looking like a beatific cherub.

'I hear you got whacked, love,' he said to Janine, eyeing her pretty face eagerly for signs of bruising. But apart from a scraped red patch on her cheek, she looked remarkably fit.

'It was nothing,' Janine said curtly, feeling her shoulders ache abominably, and hoping against hope that the slight weak feel-

ing she had in the bend at the back of her knees was only due
to the painkillers.

'You lot off to the pub, then?' Ross said, smirking unpleas-
antly. 'No doubt you and ol' Mellow have got some celebrating to do,' he added to Hillary, with such obvious meaning that
Janine stiffened, then bit her lip as the pain pulled tight across
her back.

What was it with Ross? Did he think everyone was at it
like rabbits, as he no doubt wished that he was?

Hillary gritted her teeth. 'That's right, Frank, want to
come?' she asked sweetly. 'I'll even buy you a pint.'

Frank, momentarily, looked surprised, then scowled fero-
ciously. 'Nah, don't think so. Not in on the raid, not in on the
party afterwards.' He turned his back dismissively, ostentatiously
flipping over a page on a fingerprint report from SOCO.

Hillary abruptly turned and headed for the door, knowing
she was being an idiot. She was going to a possibly dangerous
interview with one injured sergeant and a solitary DPC.

Not smart. Why did she persist in letting Ross push all her
buttons?

Frank waited until they'd gone, then chucked his pen down
in disgust. It was all right for some. The shift still had—he
checked his watch—half an hour or more to run, and here she
was, the heroine of the hour, swanning off with her little gang
of arsehole creeping acolytes to live it up at the pub.

It made him feel sick. But there was no way he was going
to let the bitch buy *him* a pint.

Hillary drove, fast and skilfully, towards Banbury, conscious of
the way Janine, sitting beside her, leaned forward so as to prevent her back resting against anything. In the rear, Tommy
sprawled massively, and thus reassuringly, across nearly all the
back seat, still looking hyper enough for anything.

As she approached the town, then drove down through the centre, negotiating the nightmare roundabout that had the famous Banbury Cross for its centre, her mind ranged back to the description of Gascoigne.

And his handiness with a knife.

She glanced at the radio in her car, wondering if she should call back to base and tell Mel where she was and what she was doing. But he'd still be in with Donleavy, and by now the press conference would be starting. She smiled to herself. She knew she could hardly interrupt her boss in the middle of a press conference, now, could she?

Once through to the northern part of town she slowed to consult a map, and only then realised that she wasn't quite sure how far north of the town *Time Out* was moored, or even if it was still there. Going on a guess, she turned down the next narrow, rutted path that she knew, from the *Ordnance Survey*, ended at the canal.

It was still overcast, but warmer, and the cloud was thinning. It was hard to believe this was still the same day, so much had been crammed into it.

Over in a growing wheat-field, a skylark was bursting its lungs in usual fashion, and May blossom dotted the hedgerows.

Tommy was first onto the towpath, and looking both ways, saw that there wasn't a single narrowboat in sight.

'Which way, guv?' he asked, not unreasonably.

Hillary nodded north. Well, she had a 50-50 chance of being right.

Frank only realised that the press conference had started when two DCIs came in, talking enviously about it. Which meant, of course, that Mel and Superintendent Donleavy, and probably a CC or two, must be down in the media room right now.

So where the hell had Hillary Greene and her band of merry men gone?

Curious, he got up and wandered over to Hillary's desk, and read the message she'd left on the pad that had come in from Banbury.

She'd gone off on a lead. Without him.

For a moment, he went dark red and ugly with rage.

Then he began to smile.

They didn't, as it turned out, have to walk far. Just to the next bridge, in fact. The narrowboat was blue and red, one of the more popular colour schemes, and had its back to them. There was no name on the stern, which meant they'd have to walk past it to where the name would be painted on one of the side panels or on the prow of the boat, thus alerting anyone inside that they had company.

Worse, there was no village nearby, so walkers this far along the towpath would be rare.

But there was nothing for it.

Hillary didn't have to warn Tommy or Janine to stop talking, and in silence they got closer to the barge.

Hillary felt her heart sink as she realised the only thing on the side panels were stylised painted flowers, in typical canal-ware tradition. They walked past the first window, a round porthole, and glanced inside. Net curtains obscured the view. Almost certainly a bedroom, Hillary thought, for she could see that bigger, oblong windows were placed at the front. That would be the lounge/kitchen area, and where anyone on board was likely to be.

As she approached, craning her neck forward to try and catch the first letters of wording on the prow, she thought she heard a noise from inside. It sounded like movement rather than a television or radio.

She felt the hairs on the nape of her neck rise, but her stride didn't falter.

The word *Time* was now clearly visible.

It had to be the boat.

Mel Mallow was feeling good. The press conference had gone well. As a rule, journalists liked going in for the kill, but even they, hardened bunch of barracudas as they were, had been impressed by the size of the haul, and were willing to paint the police in a good light for a change.

One or two cheeky sods had made pointed references to Luke Fletcher, and asked questions that they must have known nobody was going to answer, but on the whole Mel and Marcus tended to think that was a good thing. At the very least, it put the pressure on Fletcher, and let him know that everybody and their granny knew what a dirty little crook he was.

Donleavy had been expansive in his praise, and the Assistant Chief Constable had obviously marked Mel down in his mental notebook as a name to be remembered.

So he was feeling particularly happy when he walked back into the large open-plan office that looked nearly empty. For a moment it puzzled him, then he realised that it was only the change of shift in operation. Perhaps he'd ask Janine out on another date. After all, they were grown-ups and should be able to handle any little awkwardness that came along. It had made his heart leap to see her lying on the towpath that morning, and he'd been scared. Even when she moved, and the ambulancemen made it clear there was nothing too seriously wrong with her, he'd felt sick to his stomach.

But now his equilibrium had returned. He was looking forward to getting off himself. A bath, perhaps a phone call to one of the boys, followed by a nice big glass of Southern Comfort.

Then he found Frank Ross zeroing in on him like a determined pouter pigeon, and his good mood abruptly vanished.

Ross was looking pleased with himself—never a good sign.

Hillary glanced at the closed door which, no doubt, led to two or three steps that in turn deposited a visitor into the tiny space that passed for a narrowboat lounge.

There was nothing else for it, of course, and she stepped on board and knocked loudly.

Tommy hovered anxiously on the towpath, ready to leap on board should he be needed. Janine, feeling sick, glanced up and down the towpath nervously. If only they weren't so isolated. There was nothing but rows of willow trees on one side and a row of sedge bordering a wheat-field on the other. Not a sign of civilisation. Some jackdaws in the trees were having an argument about something, and the noise was getting on her nerves.

Her back hurt.

She felt sick.

What the hell was she doing here?

Her mind snapped back from its precarious descent into self-pity as a snicking sound alerted her to the fact that someone was opening the barge door.

Hillary looked down into the face of Alfie Makepeace, and thought, *Yes!*

'And you think she's gone there?' Mel said, his voice dangerously tight, as he stared down at the piece of paper Frank had just handed to him. It was Hillary's handwriting all right, the directions clear enough.

'Well, guv, she took Tommy Lynch with her. And Janine,' he added slyly, watching his DCI closely. His antenna was telling him that randy old Mel had his eye on the luscious Janine.

Mel's face didn't move by so much as a millimetre.

'I thought Sergeant Tyler was on sick leave.'

'She was in casualty for a while, but came back here,' Frank said, not wanting to say anything that might put Janine Tyler in a good light, but wanting, at the same time, to drop her in it as well. 'DI Greene seemed keen to have her along,' he added.

Mel looked up, his hand willing him to form itself into a fist and smash right into Frank's soft, piggy little face.

'Really?' he said casually. 'In that case, we'd better go and check it out, just in case they need back-up,' he said mildly.

He'd have to inform Regis.

Well, perhaps later, if it turned out to be the boat they were all after.

It never occurred to him that he was doing exactly the same thing that Hillary had done—namely, trying to hog the good stuff for himself. And even if it had, it would have done nothing to cool the anger simmering under the surface.

Nothing was going to stop him from giving Hillary a right bollocking.

'Yes?' Alfie Makepeace asked, chewing something. A digestive biscuit, it turned out, as a moment later he took yet another bite.

He looked the epitome of a boatie, laid-back, taking his time over a cuppa and a biscuit, raising one shaggy white eyebrow lazily.

Hillary felt like sitting down with a bag of popcorn and watching the show. Makepeace was certainly some actor.

She smiled and showed him her badge. 'Mr Makepeace?'

The old man's eyes glinted. 'That's me,' he said, a fraction of a second too late. 'What's up?'

'Can we come aboard?' Hillary asked.

For a moment, Makepeace hesitated, and she could almost sympathise with his dilemma. On the one hand, he wanted coppers aboard his boat about as much as a pedigree Persian wanted fleas in his silvery fur. Yet he was reluctant to refuse. To make things difficult would put backs up and rouse already sky-high suspicions. Besides, Makepeace probably wanted to know how much they knew. And he could only gauge that by sifting through the questions they asked him.

Eventually he shrugged and stood to one side. 'Course. Come on in. I've just made some tea. Want a cup?'

'I'd prefer coffee, if you have it,' Hillary said, glancing back significantly at her two juniors.

Tommy was on fast, his bulk surprisingly graceful, and she noticed Makepeace running an expert eye over the big black youth. Janine got on much more carefully, obviously uncomfortable in both body and spirit.

Hillary Greene watched Alfie Makepeace with thoughtful eyes. For a second, the two seasoned pros, vastly different and yet, in a single flash of a second, uncannily alike, seemed to acknowledge one another.

Then Alfie went into the kitchen and reached for the instant.

Hillary glanced quickly down the narrow passage, only one thought in her mind.

Where the hell was Gascoigne?

Mel wound down the window pointedly as Frank Ross lit up a fag. The two hapless uniforms he'd picked up on the way out sat in the back, quiet as church mice, wondering just what Mellow Mallow wanted with them. Neither minded that their shift had been due to end in another quarter of an hour or so— Mel was the man of the moment, and any way of getting in on even a little of the action was a welcome change from assisting at RTAs and doing paperwork.

Ross puffed happily and warmed himself on the thought of Hillary's face when Mel showed up, breathing thunder.

* * *

Jake Gascoigne climbed the stile, cursing as the milk cartons squashed against the wood, threatening to spill their precious cargo. Trust Alfie, the useless bastard, to run out of milk miles from the nearest shop, he thought.

He caught his foot in a tuft of grass, nearly went over, and cursed yet again. He was still swearing graphically as he climbed out on to the towpath just a few yards short of the boat.

'So, you don't remember Dashwood Lock?' Hillary said, sipping her coffee and wishing that he'd put in a more generous amount of sugar. Without her artificial sweetener, the coffee was bitter.

Tommy Lynch stood with his back to the passage, preventing anyone slipping past him, and Hillary only hoped that he had his ears turned up to their highest notch. Though between them they should notice if anyone tried to sneak up behind him.

She was sitting on a deck chair, that had been folded away against one wall, giving the second of two padded seats to her sergeant, who was beginning to look distinctly peaky.

'Well, not particularly, like,' Alfie said. 'I mean, if you say so, I know we must have gone through it, but there was nothing to make it stand out.' He shrugged. 'Once you've been through one lock, you've been through 'em all,' he added, making a meal of his biscuit, knowing it was annoying DI Greene.

He was beginning to relax, somewhat. Unless she had a whole squad of helpers concealed behind willow trees outside (and he didn't think she had), the cops were just fishing. They wouldn't have sent just two females and a humble PC if they suspected anything important.

And the younger girl didn't look fit enough to even scratch and bite, if it came to a scrap. He wondered, uneasily, what had happened to her. He didn't like to think of violence and women in the same thought process. To his mind, they didn't go. Women, to Alfie, meant either the generation of his mother, plump, homely, cheerfully practical and to be cherished, or bed bait, to be used but never abused.

The DI he could respect, in a way. The pretty, hurting blonde girl, however, made him feel deeply uneasy.

Not that Alife was worried about anything else. The stuff was long gone now, anyway, so even if the boss woman had got a warrant to conduct a search (and again his instinct told him that she hadn't) they'd come up emptyhanded.

And besides, so far all she'd asked about was Dashwood Lock.

'We?' Hillary said now, casually. Very casually. 'You're not alone?'

Makepeace sighed. 'Me and a pal.'

'Only two of you?' Hillary said, sounding surprised. 'Makes for a very expensive holiday, doesn't it? With the rental, I mean?' she added, glancing around. The boat was well but not expensively outfitted, but its rental wouldn't have been cheap—had Makepeace been paying any, that was.

Makepeace shrugged. 'It's worth it. Peace and quiet nowadays is like gold.'

This sod isn't even going to admit The Pits was on board, Hillary realised, feeling suddenly frustrated. Almost certainly, any drugs that had been on board would have been unloaded the moment Fletcher had heard about the raid that morning. They'd had hours to get rid of it, along with any evidence of David Pitman ever having been on board. If only she knew for sure whether his death had been an accident or murder, she might at least have a solid starting point from which to chip away at this old oyster.

But it was no good supposing murder. Even villains had accidents. They were just as much prone to the pitfalls and bad luck that plagued the rest of mankind as anyone else.

The PM *had* come back that morning, but she'd barely had

time to glance at it after the raid. She knew he'd been drinking, but whether or not it had been enough to make him lose his balance and fall overboard depended on his drinking habits. Some men, she knew, could drink ten pints of beer and still be compos mentis.

The PM had stated that David Pitman had been very severely mangled between his lower stomach and upper thighs, and propeller damage hadn't been ruled out. What it meant, she wasn't yet sure, but accident still had to be high on the agenda.

According to Frank's snout, this old man had specifically asked for Pitman, but why? One thing was for sure, she wasn't going to get any answers here.

She felt suddenly foolish and ill prepared. She'd let her pique at Mel and being side-barred on the case affect her judgement. Worse, she was feeling too tired to think on her feet. Which was a cardinal sin for a copper.

It was just as she was thinking this that she heard Janine give a little squeak.

Someone had just walked past the window.

Jake heard the voices just as he was halfway along the boat. And froze.

Unless Alfie had finally gone senile and taken up talking to himself, he had company.

But it couldn't be the lads come back.

Luke Fletcher himself had called him that morning on his mobile, telling him about the disaster at Oxford, and to be prepared to offload the cargo ASAP. A load of men had descended, with transit vans parked up in the woods, and hastily hauled the drugs from the boat.

He and Alfie had then spent the rest of the day up to their necks in bleach, scouring every surface on the boat just in case the rozzers came calling with sniffer dogs.

And Fletcher would have wanted to keep as much distance between himself and the boat as possible, so there was no way he would have had any of the lads return. What for? As far as Luke was concerned, neither he nor any of his own had ever even heard of *Time Out*.

Jake knew that, if ever questioned, he was to say that he and Alfie had hired the boat themselves to take a break. Sure, the coppers would laugh themselves sick over that, but they wouldn't be able to prove anything else.

He stepped warily onto the prow of the boat and peered in through the glass on the door.

A black face stared back at him.

Instinct took over and he leapt off the boat on to the towpath. He had taken two running steps before he forced himself to stop.

Tommy Lynch was just unbending his height from the back of the boat when Gascoigne turned and walked cautiously back towards him.

Mel turned off down the same rutted path that Hillary had taken a half hour before, and muttered something under his breath on spotting her parked car.

In the back the constables perked up. Frank Ross grinned and chucked his fag out of the car.

'Put it out,' Mel snapped at him savagely. 'The last thing we want is for you to start a bloody fire.'

Frank slammed out of the car, glancing back to make sure neither of the uniforms were sniggering at him behind his back. They weren't. They knew better.

Mel climbed out, wondering what the hell he had to do to get Hillary reined in. He wished now Marcus had never assigned her the case. Of course, if Donleavy had known what it would lead to, he never would have.

With a sigh, and a sign to the uniforms to follow, he set off up the towpath. The sun was beginning to shine. It was going to be a lovely evening. Pity nobody was in the mood to appreciate it.

Tommy wondered why Gascoigne had changed his mind about running for it. It was obvious that was what he'd been about to do. Now he watched, warily, as the curly-haired, dark-eyed geezer walked reluctantly back.

Behind him, Hillary stood a little way up the steps, not wanting to leave Janine alone with Makepeace but needing to watch Tommy's back as well.

'Mr Gascoigne, is it?' she called from the boat, knowing she had to get control of this situation and fast. 'I'm DI Greene, this is Detective Police Constable Lynch. Inside is Sergeant Tyler. We were just having a few words with your friend Mr Makepeace. Care to join us?'

Taking his cue, Tommy stepped aside to let Gascoigne past. He wondered where he kept his knife. Up his sleeve? In his boot? Back pocket?

Gascoigne stepped, wary as a cat, on to the boat, and went through to the lounge. He looked surprised to see Janine, probably because she was young and blonde and pretty.

She was on her feet, looking paler than ever, but succeeding, just, in hiding her fear. Hillary knew she could do nothing to help her—she had to find her own way through it.

'Please, have a seat, Mr Gascoigne. Alfie was just telling me about Dave Pitman,' she lied outrageously.

Well, it was worth a try.

'Dave who?' Makepeace said at once, shooting Jake a telling glance.

Jake, making a great show of it, sat down in the chair that Hillary had been using, legs arrogantly splayed, and reached for an apple from the fruit bowl.

'Do you remember the night of the eighth?' she asked, without much hope.

Gascoigne munched noisily.

As if triggering him, Makepeace reached out for the packet of digestive biscuits and took a handful. Together the two crooks munched in harmony, regarding Hillary quietly.

It was enough to make her want to spit.

Mel found the boat five minutes later. He heard voices, female and grumbling male, all of which stopped as he, Ross and the two constables passed. He read the name of the boat with a mixture of triumph and chagrin.

Trust Hillary to come up trumps. And trust her to try and nab it for herself.

He didn't bother to knock as he let himself in.

Makepeace picked up on the friction at once, even though Mel pretended that Hillary had always known he'd be along, and Hillary pretended that, yes indeed, she always had.

'Mind if my lads look around your boat?' Mel asked Makepeace, who didn't get the chance to speak.

'You got a warrant?' Gascoigne snarled instead.

Mel, mildly, admitted they didn't.

'Go ahead,' Makepeace said, glancing at Gascoigne with something approaching contempt. He, obviously, knew how to treat coppers.

They found nothing, of course.

Hillary, reluctantly responding to Mel's hints, followed him outside. Frank Ross hovered, ears flapping, but was bitterly disappointed. Mel merely told her that he'd be applying for a warrant, and seeing as she was on the scene, and was so obviously keen, she could supervise the search.

But she was being punished, and everyone knew it.

Including Makepeace, who seemed to regard the tension amongst the ranks with appreciative amusement.

It was getting dark by the time they got back. Janine, feeling like something the cat wouldn't even bother to drag in, all but collapsed at her desk. It had been a bad day—the stark fear and pain of the morning, followed by the dispiriting hospital visit, culminating in the slow Chinese water torture that had been the abortive interviews on the boat.

She knew, as well as Hillary and Mel, that they'd find nothing on the boat, and as for Makepeace and Gascoigne, they couldn't even be made to admit that they *knew* Pitman. The only thing they'd admitted to was going through Dashwood Lock on the evening of the eighth.

Big sodding deal.

Tommy was morosely typing up reports, checking his watch, knowing his mother would be worrying about him not being home to eat his evening meal. He kept throwing worried glances at Hillary, who was obviously in deep shit. He hadn't realised that she hadn't checked in with Mel before following up the lead. He didn't really blame her, but even so, he knew Mel had a right to be miffed.

To make matters worse, the Yorkie Bars were about. Hillary spotted them the moment they walked in.

Unfortunately, Mel didn't. Frank had gone home, so he had no reason now to hang fire.

'Just what the bloody hell did you think you were playing at?' he exploded the moment he was within yelling distance, causing the heads of the other workers in the office to dip over their desks.

'Sir,' Hillary began, trying to warn him of the approach of Smith and Danvers.

But Mel was in full flow. 'Damn it, you know Gascoigne's

reputation with a knife! And did you have to take Janine? She's been wounded, for Pete's sake!'

At this Janine had to interfere. 'Sir, I volunteered,' she put in. She sounded pathetically tired, but Hillary judged that being in on the scene at *Time Out* had done her, pscyhologically at least, a world of good. Soon she'd start congratulating herself on holding up, on doing her job. Later, when the physical pain faded, that boost to her self-confidence would be vital.

'And why didn't you at least take along some back-up? Even a uniform or two wouldn't have hurt,' Mel thundered on.

'Sir,' she put in firmly, not liking the interested look on Smith's face, and especially not the sympathy on Paul Danvers's, 'at the time we didn't even know if *Time Out* was the boat we were looking for, let alone that Makepeace or Gascoigne would be on board. You were at the press conference, so I didn't want to interrupt you.' Mel opened his mouth to speak, but Hillary rushed on before he could. 'Time was obviously of the essence,' she pointed out reasonably. 'If it *was* the boat, I wanted to make sure we got to it as soon as possible. Yes?' she added, confusing Mel, for the last word was uttered with unspeakable contempt, and seemed to be directed over his shoulder.

He spun around, saw the Yorkie Bars, and scowled.

'We'll be needing to re-interview DI Greene tomorrow.' It was Curtis, the junior officer, who spoke.

Mel swore. He shot Hillary a half furious, half supportive look and shrugged helplessly.

Hillary smiled sweetly at Paul Danvers. 'Of course,' she said reasonably. 'Any time you like.'

In their dreams.

11

THE next morning, Regis read the report on the search of *Time Out* with a certain gloom. As nice as it was to have the success of the Oxford boat raid still wafting around like expensive perfume, it would have been even nicer to have the cherry on top of the icing too.

Next he read DI Greene's report on her interviews with the suspects, easily reading between the lines. He knew her DCI had given her a bawling out for going off to investigate the lead without telling him, but he understood her reasons.

Of course, she'd probably known, as Regis had the moment he'd been told of it, that her chances of finding a second drugs haul on *Time Out* had been practically zero. But then again, if a miracle *had* happened and she *had* been successful, she'd be woman of the hour, with a promotion almost certainly guaranteed.

If he'd been in her place, he'd have done exactly the same.

'Mellow is still on the warpath,' Colin Tanner said, having walked up to his desk unnoticed. Now he slipped into the chair opposite his boss and nodded at the report he was reading. They were back at the Big House in Kidlington after spending most of yesterday at St Aldates nick. But with charges now filed, and with plenty of Indians around with no need of cow-boys, Regis wanted to check in with his temporary mates back at Kidlington. Only to walk into this quagmire.

'I reckon it's more to do with Greene taking along the blonde as much as anything else,' the sergeant added, making Regis look at him blankly for a minute, then smile knowingly.

'Ah. You can understand why she did it, though. Greene,' he clarified.

Colin gave his boss a long thoughtful look that made Mike Regis shift in his seat.

'Oh, yeah, she did good,' Colin agreed. 'But she'll be feeling the backlash for some time yet. I hear the Yorkie Bars are going to re-interview her today as well.'

Regis snorted, then followed his sergeant's gaze as Janine Tyler pushed through the door and made her way to her desk.

'I'll bet she's feeling stiff as a board,' Colin mused. Although he hadn't seen the blow to her back, he'd taken enough wallops in his time to imagine it. And injuries always felt worse a day or so after they'd been inflicted.

They watched, amused, as Mel emerged from his office and walked over to the blonde girl.

'Janine, you didn't have to come in. In fact, wouldn't it be better to take some sick days? Have a break while you can?'

Sick days were like gold. In fact, so gold-like were they that most coppers were loathe to use them when they were feeling ill, preferring to inflict the flu on their friends and workmates and suffer in a nice warm office, using them instead when Arsenal were playing.

'I'm fine,' Janine said dismissively, hoping nobody was watching and wishing Mel would sod off. The last thing she wanted was a reputation for being teacher's pet. Or Mellow Mallow's latest squeeze.

'OK. I was wondering, did you fancy eating out tonight? Save you cooking?'

Janine couldn't believe what she was hearing. Was he hitting on her? Now, of all times?

'Thanks, sir, but I think I'll have an early night tonight. You know, take it easy.' She was careful not to look up from the file she was busy not reading.

Mel smiled, an automatic defence mechanism that was wasted on the top of her head. 'Sure. Another time, perhaps.'

But they both knew he wouldn't be the one doing the asking.

Janine sighed heavily, and not totally in relief.

'DI Greene's not due to come in until two,' Colin mused innocently. With the floor-show over, his eyes followed the loser back to his office. Silly sod should have known better than to push his luck.

'So?' Regis snarled dangerously.

His sergeant grinned, unabashed. 'Nothing.'

Gary approached the boat nervously. Luckily, the praying mantis who lived on the boat next to Hillary's wasn't home. He supposed, philosophically, that it was only a matter of time before he answered the call of her knowing eyes. Didn't they say every lad should have a middle-aged woman lover once in a while, just to show him what was what?

Thing was, he couldn't seem to summon up much enthusiasm for it.

'Anyone in?' he called, feeling foolish as he always did, wishing Hillary would have a doorbell fitted.

'Come on down.' The muffled voice sounded sleepy. Had he caught her trying to catch up on forty winks? Like the rest of the constabulary world, he knew about the raid in Oxford yesterday, and the grapevine had it that his stepmum had been well in on it.

'Sorry, were you kipping?' he asked, following her down the cramped passage into the lounge.

'No,' Hillary lied, rubbing her eyes. 'What's up?'

'Nothing.'

'Come to get the gory details about Luke Fletcher's nasty little wake-up call?' she said, heading for the kettle. The water trickled out of the tap like a reluctant bladder. Damn, she'd *have* to fill the water tank. She glanced at Gary, wondering if she could wheedle the offer of doing it out of him.

'I dare say he wasn't a happy bunny,' Gary said, grinning widely.

'Especially if he'd already sold that stash on, in which case we'll be investigating his murder soon,' Hillary said, with a certain amount of very un-copperlike relish.

Gary looked vaguely uncomfortable and Hillary realised that he was still too young to actively want anyone dead. Hillary could have told him that, given a few more years on the force, he would be thinking like her, when he'd seen a few more dead teenagers who'd wasted their lives and other people's money on crack, or heroin, or whatever they could get their hands on. Or when he'd seen a few more obscenely wealthy drugs barons like Fletcher walk free from court, due to high-priced lawyers, bribed juries or threats to witnesses.

But she didn't tell him that.

'Biscuit?' she said, thinking of Alfie Makepeace and his digestives.

'No, thanks,' Gary said, plonking himself down in one of the two armchairs.

'Good, because I haven't got any,' Hillary said. If she bought them, she'd eat them, so she didn't buy them. It made sense to her.

'I came to give you this back,' Gary said, reaching into the duffel bag he was carrying and bringing out a battered, yellowed paperback.

She reached for it and looked at the title. '*Bonecrack*. Thanks, but I don't like Dick Francis.'

'You must have done once. You bought it.'

'Huh?'

'Look inside.'

Hillary, bemused, opened the cracked cover and read the inscription.

'Oh. It was your dad's,' she said flatly, and listened, frowning and sipping her coffee as Gary told her about the call from the sergeant at Bicester nick.

'If I was you, I'd forget all about that,' she advised wisely. Which reminded her. 'Have you seen the Yorkie Bars yet?'

'Yeah. A preliminary interview when they first got here. They reckon, as far as I can make out, that I was too young to be Dad's accomplice before joining the force, then too lowly afterwards. I suppose they must have heard that Dad never rated me much, and agree with him.'

'My, my, you are in an upbeat mood today,' Hillary said, grinning. 'If I were you, I'd thank your lucky stars that your dad finally did you a favour.'

Gary fought against a smile, then had to grin. He rubbed his face, which, thankfully, mirrored his mother's more than Ronnie's, and sighed. 'Well, I'm on nights, so I'd better get some kip myself.'

Hillary nodded. 'You can doss down here if you like. Save driving back to Witney.'

Gary looked around the cramped room and imagined the narrow bed and claustrophobic walls that must compose her bedroom.

'No, thanks,' he said quickly.

Hillary grinned wryly. Good choice, she thought.

She watched him gulp his coffee down, then glanced back at the book in her hand.

Odd, she couldn't remember ever giving Ronnie a book. The bastard wasn't interested in the written word, unless it came in *The Sun* and was accompanied by a picture of a top-less model.

She tossed it down on to what passed for a bookshelf, and went back to bed.

The mobile woke her, barely three hours later. For a mo-ment, she had an uncanny sense of déjà vu. The last time she'd laid in bed and been woken by a mobile, it was a sum-mons to Dashwood Lock and the unlovely body of Dave Pitman.

'Yeah, DI Greene,' she mumbled, sitting up, running a hand across her head and wishing, from its grainy texture, that she'd washed her hair before climbing back into bed. But a shower was out of the question until she'd filled the water tank.

She hated living on a boat.

'Boss, it's me,' Janine said. 'We've found out where *Time Out* was moored before Gascoigne, Makepeace and Pitman took it out. A siding down in the smoke. Mel wants us to check it out.'

Hillary yawned widely. Oh, did he? Well, thanks a lot, Mel. Obviously he was still pissed off with her.

But if she was in London, she couldn't be in the office where the Yorkie Bars wanted her. Come to think of it, she might be doing Mel down in assuming he was still giving her scut work as a slapped wrist for yesterday's shenanigans.

'Right. Tell you what, you come here and park up and we'll take my car down. I don't suppose you feel like driving much.'

Janine didn't. Usually it was an unspoken rule that the ju-nior officer always drove, especially if they were heading into alien territory. She supposed she should feel grateful to have a DI as thoughtful as Hillary.

'Right, boss,' she said heavily.

The siding was in the north of the city, surrounded by the usual graffiti-covered red-brick warehouse walls, illegally parked cars and litter. Even so, the community of barges looked bright and cheerful, their colours covering the spectrum of the rainbow, their side panels painted with the traditional flowers, castles and nature scenes.

One boat, *Halcyon Daze*, was festooned with kingfishers. As Hillary approached it, amused at the dry wit who'd named it, she reckoned the nearest they ever came to seeing a kingfisher around this urban hell-hole was when someone threw an orange and blue chocolate wrapper off the bridge.

'We're to see one George Harding. On *Willow Wand*. Should be up here, boss,' Janine said, pointing.

Hillary nodded. 'You're sure Mel cleared it with the locals?'

'Yes, boss,' Janine said, but like Hillary, didn't really expect anyone from the local nick to turn up to give them a hand, or even to see what the Oxonians wanted. Nobody had staff to spare these days on anything but the essentials.

'Here it is,' Janine said, unnecessarily. The boat was a small, strictly one-user boat. It would have driven Hillary mad within a week. She thought her own home was tiny enough.

'Mr Harding?' Hillary called, having no intention whatsoever of getting on board. She reckoned it had three rooms at the most. A lounge-cum-kitchen, with a tiny cubicle loo and shower off, and one turn-around-and-you-knock-your-elbows bedroom.

A moment later a bald head appeared from the prow and then a little garden gnome of a man popped up and on to the towpath. He had rounded red cheeks, twinkling brown eyes, and really should have been dressed in blue trousers and a red jerkin with big brass buttons.

Beside her, Hillary could feel Janine struggling not to laugh.

Hillary held out her ID card. 'I'm Detective Inspector Greene, this is Sergeant Tyler. We're here about the boat *Time Out* that was moored here for some time earlier in the spring. I believe a colleague of mine has already been in touch?'

'That's right. I was expecting you. Can't say as I know what it's about. Mind you, it don't surprise me if that curly-haired lout is in trouble with the law. His sort always are.'

Hillary nodded. At least the witness was going to talk. In fact, they'd probably have trouble stopping him. Living on the boat, he probably didn't get much chance to talk to folks. Still, that was better than listening to him squeeze out every word, like a reluctant orange.

'You mean Jake Gascoigne?' she said, recognising the description.

'Never knew his name. Didn't want to.'

'Can you remember when the boat was first moored here, Mr Harding?'

Harding, who could have been any age from 40 to 70, scratched his bald head alarmingly. Janine looked hastily across the canal, her eyes fixing on the silver, bloated corpse of a fish.

Who would have thought they'd even have fish in a waterway like this?

'I reckon it were April. Or maybe late March. Anyway, the buds were coming out on the trees.'

Hillary blinked, then noticed a solitary tree—birch, was it?—on the opposite bank. More likely alder. It didn't look exactly magnificent, whatever it was. Still, if she lived here, amongst all this man-made mess, she supposed she'd notice the annual life cycle of the one and only thing of any natural beauty.

'I see. But the curly-haired lout wasn't on it, then, is that right?' she asked, with a winning smile.

Mr George Harding brightened perceptibly. 'No. The curly-haired lout wasn't,' he agreed. 'He came later. Along with the older one and the ugly git. The good, the bad and the ugly, I called 'em,' he added, chuckling.

Actually chuckling. Not laughing, or sniggering, or making a sound like a rusty Tesco trolley. Instead, he had a full, rich, chortling chuckle. Just the kind a garden gnome would have.

Janine bit her lip and focused harder on the dead fish.

'I see. So you got on all right with the older man?' Hillary said. 'I mean, he'd be the "good" one of the good, the bad and the ugly, right?'

'Yeah, right. He was OK. The ugly sod was a foul-mouthed so and so. Always effing and blinding. Alfie was always polite.'

'He told you his name?' Hillary asked, surprised.

'Nope. I heard the ugly one call him that once. They didn't seem to like the curly-haired one much, neither of them. Showed good taste, if you ask me.'

'Can you describe the man who actually moored the boat up here?'

'Nope, didn't see him. Just woke up one morning, and there was a new boat. Happens all the time. Boats come and go. Nobody stays here long. Not unless, like me, they got a job nearby.'

Hillary nodded, recognising it was an invitation to ask him what he did, but knowing they'd be here all day if she did.

'Did you ever see anyone else visit the boat? With bags, or boxes, or anything like that?' she asked instead.

'Nope.'

It figured, Hillary thought. Whoever had delivered the boat, delivered it already stuffed to the gills with dope.

'I wonder if you might be kind enough to look at a picture

for me,' Hillary said, nodding to Janine who withdrew one of the pictures of Dave Pitman's body from her briefcase. 'I'm afraid the man in the photograph is dead, but it's not really gruesome.'

The pink cheeks paled a little, but George Harding was a trooper and nodded willingly. He only had to look at the photo for a short while.

'Yeah, that's him. You can't mistake a face like that, can you?'

Indeed you couldn't, Hillary thought. She prodded and prompted a bit more, but there was nothing more useful to be gained from the witness.

Still, it put Dave Pitman firmly on the boat when it left in April.

Of course, proving he was still on the boat, let alone that he'd fallen off it—or been pushed off it—in early May in Dashwood Lock was something else entirely.

Frank Ross was not happy. His little canary of two days ago had gone missing. Probably owed too much money to the bookies. Either that, or the news of a blow to Luke Fletcher's fortunes had prompted the little weasel to head for the hills, just in case anybody had noticed him talking to a copper barely a day before.

Still, Frank knew where there were plenty more of his kind to be found, and was currently feeding one of them.

He watched, with a half-hearted disgust, as Cyril Jackson wolfed down the last piece of cod and started on the chips. Jackson was a sad sod, once a decent B&E man partnered with an old-time safe cracker. They'd specialised in offices, mainly solicitors, who'd likely have secrets they wanted kept, and could generally be relied upon to provide fodder for blackmail. When his partner had died of old age, he'd spent a lot of time in and out of nick, before falling in with Fletcher's gang, strictly as a gofer.

Frank reckoned he wouldn't be holding on to that job for long, either. He wasn't quite all there, as his granny would have said. His bats weren't roosting in the right belfries. He was two spuds shy of a hundredweight.

Which was probably why he didn't have the sense to tell DS Frank Ross to shove his free fish and chips. No doubt word would get back to Fletcher that Jackson had been seen talking to him, but that would be Jackson's problem.

'So, you were saying how hard the lads took Pitman's death,' he prompted.

Jackson, his grey hair greasier than the chips he was eating, nodded up and down, his laden fork moving in motion with his head. 'Oh, ah. Not because anybody liked him, of course.' Jackson suddenly laughed, startling the other patrons of the fish and chip shop, and making the owner scowl over at them. 'He wasn't called The Pits for nothing. But everyone knew Mr Fletcher would be angry about it. On account of the skimming, like.'

Jackson, impervious to the jolt he'd just given Ross, reached for the vinegar bottle and splashed it across the chips. He then added a huge amount of salt.

'Oh, the skimming,' Ross said casually, his heart racing. 'He thought the old geezer, Alfie, was up to no good, then?' he said craftily, making Jackson convulse in laughter again.

'Not him. Old Alfie's straight as a die. Everyone says so. No, it was Knifey they was keeping an eye on.'

'Knifey? You mean Jake Gascoigne?'

But Jackson, who only knew what he knew from keeping his ears open and his mouth shut while simultaneously being thought of as having a screw loose, didn't know Knifey's real name.

But Frank reckoned it didn't matter.

It was the best couple of quid he'd ever spent on fish and chips in his life.

As he left and drove back to the Big House, it never once occurred to him to care that he had almost certainly cost the harmless and hapless Jackson a severe beating. Maybe even his life.

Hillary was at her desk when Frank came in, looking like the bee's knees. The Yorkie Bars, so Mel had told her, had been and gone on being informed that she'd been urgently required down in London. For some reason, he'd said with a bland smile, they'd gone away with the impression that she was going to be there all day.

It was nearly two, and she wasn't officially due to start work until three. So much for time off. She was reading the autopsy report in more detail. Regis, who'd been closeted with Mel most of the morning, wandered over.

'Anything?'

Hillary looked up, realising for the first time that his eyes were really dark green. She didn't know many green-eyed people.

'No. Well, maybe. It's puzzling. Read this.' She put her thumb on the relevant passage, and Regis read it quickly.

'Hmmm, not very helpful, is it? Death due to a combination of massive shock, loss of blood, inhalation of water and trauma. The pathologist seems to think practically everything killed him.'

'That's not what I meant,' she said. 'Did you notice the injuries all seem to centre on the pelvic area?'

Regis hadn't. He read again. 'Well, I suppose if you went overboard in a narrow lock, it would be the pelvic area that would take the most gyp, wouldn't it?'

Hillary wasn't so sure. If you were in the water, struggling for your life, wouldn't your head, neck and shoulders be likely to take the most punishment? Unless the lock was empty at the time, and Dave Pitman was standing on his feet, not free-swimming at all. In which case…

'Sir, I've just heard something interesting.' Frank Ross's voice, rich with self-congratulation, made both of them take notice.

'In which case, we'd better have DCI Mallow here,' Regis said, but Mel had already seen the little gathering at Hillary's desk and was making his way over.

Tommy Lynch and Janine Tyler also began to sidle closer.

'What's up?' Mel asked, his eyes carefully avoiding Janine's and ricocheting instead off Frank's gloating orbs.

'Sir, one of my snouts has just come up with something juicy. Apparently, Fletcher suspected Gascogine of skimming.'

Even Frank was satisfied by the reaction this got. Regis especially perked up.

With relish, and care, he recited how he'd got Jackson to talk, skipping over Jackson's mental defects and perhaps slightly emphasising his 'in' with the Fletcher outfit.

'So that's why Alfie Makepeace asked especially for Pitman,' Mel said, making Hillary do a double take. Had he? Obviously it was something Frank had reported directly to Mel, who hadn't seen fit to tell her. If she'd known that yesterday she might have had the wedge she needed to crack Makepeace open a little.

'Because if Gascoigne was skimming,' Regis followed his line of thought out loud, 'and Fletcher had put Alfie, his regular eyes and ears, on to the task of getting proof one way or the other, Makepeace would need some back-up. Someone with muscles and a rep.'

'And The Pits had a reputation for being a hard bastard,' Mel chimed in.

Regis glanced at Hillary, and saw her frowning.

'DI Greene?' he said softly, but it had the effect of turning all eyes on her. 'You don't agree?'

Hillary shook her head helplessly. The moment they'd

started to talk, her mind had turned back to the interview yesterday. Gascoigne had started to run the moment he realised Makepeace had company. OK, that was to be expected. It was a villain's natural instinct. But he'd come back. OK, perhaps that might be explained by the simple fact that he'd had time to realise that there was nothing to be scared of. The drugs had already been offloaded, after all.

During the interview he'd been bolshie and sneering, which, no doubt, were mere manifestations of his usual charming personality. But it had been *Makepeace* who'd overruled him about letting the police do an unofficial search of the boat. It had been *Makepeace* who'd done all the talking. Without doubt, it had been the older man who was in charge.

In short, Gascoigne hadn't responded like a man with guts enough to skim from Luke Fletcher.

'I don't know,' she said quietly. 'Gascoigne didn't strike me as a worried man.'

Frank Ross snorted sneeringly. ''Course it was Gascoigne. The nark called him "Knifey". And we all know Gascoigne has a rep with the knife.'

Hillary paid him no attention at all. Mel merely scowled at him. Regis was still staring at Hillary thoughtfully.

'He didn't strike you that way?' Regis said eventually. 'Interesting. If Gascoigne *had* been skimming—and that was almost suicidal, anyway—he would surely have been suspicious of Alfie Makepeace asking for Dave Pitman to come along for the ride. If this earlier nark of Ross's had heard that Makepeace had asked specifically for Pitman, then surely Gascoigne would know about it too?'

'Oh, come on, it all fits,' Ross said, not liking the way the Vice man was making eyes at Hillary Greene. 'Gascoigne was skimming, Fletcher suspected, and sent Alfie Makepeace, his regular little watchdog, to find out. He sends Pitman to be

Alfie's muscle, in case things go pear-shaped. And Pitman gets clobbered. It's obvious, innit?'

Mel tended to agree.

The fact that Hillary wasn't so sure, and Regis seemed inclined to agree with her, didn't much matter.

'Right, we'll take this as our working hypothesis,' Mel said, rubbing his hands with glee. 'Well done, Frank,' he added, flatly.

Watching Frank Ross gloat was a salutary experience for everyone.

12

THINGS had been happening while Hillary had been in London, a fact that was rammed home to her when she got to the office the next day.

Janine smiled a hello, then frowned as Mel came out of his office, Regis and his near-silent sergeant hot on his heels.

'Hillary, how did it go?' he asked, but it was perfunctory at best, and he hardly seemed to listen to her report. It didn't do much for their investigation, save, perhaps, to give a little extra weight to press down on Gascoigne and Makepeace. In their bid to get them to admit that they even knew Dave Pitman, let alone that he was their boat-mate for most of the journey from London to Oxford, it might pay a few dividends, but nothing more.

'We're just off to see Marcus,' Mel said, when she'd finished. 'We're going to ask to bring in Makepeace and Gascoigne for formal questioning. With what you got from London yesterday, and Frank's snout coming across with the info that Makepeace asked for Pitman specifically, it's worth sweating *him*, especially.'

Hillary nodded, but didn't look enthusiastic. She saw Mel give Janine a searching look, realised it had more in it than mere concern about an injured colleague's wellbeing, and bit back a surge of annoyance.

If there was one thing Janine didn't need now, it was a confidence-sapping bout in Mellow Mallow's bed. She was almost certain it would lead to nothing more than her boss cutting yet another notch in his belt, whilst Janine became the butt of office innuendo and gossip.

She'd have to hint that he should keep it buttoned in his trousers—never a task guaranteed to win friends and influence people.

If he even bothered to listen to her.

She looked up from shedding her jacket, only to find Regis giving her a long, knowing look, which made her want to grin and scowl at the same time.

'You don't think it would do much good?' he said, and it took her a moment to realise that he hadn't been reading her mind, but was talking about the proposed plan to sweat Makepeace and Gascoigne.

She snorted. 'Not really. I think Gascoigne, if he has been up to no good, will have at least enough sense to go hedgehog. And as for Makepeace—let's face it, he's as old a pro as you can get. He wouldn't be one of Fletcher's pets if he wasn't.' She glanced at Mel, who was trying not to look down Janine's cleavage. 'So, when are we bringing him in?' she asked.

Mel opened his mouth to tell her there was no 'we' about it, then didn't have to. His expression iced over instead by several degrees. With a sinking heart Hillary looked over her shoulder at the approaching Yorkie Bars.

'Oh, marvellous,' she said softly.

Mel went off quite happily to set about bringing in and interviewing their main suspects, with Regis, to his credit, looking less sanguine.

Hillary thought there was something comforting about the way he shot her an amused smile as she set off with the internal investigation officers, and she found herself thinking about him when she should have been thinking about Paul Danvers and Curtis Smith.

DS Smith looked slightly hungover, and she wondered, idly, what he'd been celebrating the night before. She doubted he was married with kids, so probably not an anniversary or one of the sprogs getting into uni.

She took a seat in the small interview room, not unaware of the irony of being an interview*er* forced into interview*ee* mode. She wondered, even more idly, how cops went about interviewing other cops, knowing that the person they were trying to wrangle information out of knew just as many tricks of the trade as they did.

Paul Danvers was looking as smooth as his partner looked rough. His blond hair was newly washed, and fell across his forehead in a way that many women would have found very attractive indeed. He was wearing a good-quality dark blue suit that complemented his eyes.

Eyes that were watching her closely.

Belatedly, the hairs on the back of her neck stood up.

Mel's good luck in having got rid of Hillary without being the bad guy was the last bit of fortune he was going to have that day.

He knew it when he heard that Gascoigne, who was supposed to be tucked up cosily on board *Time Out*, was in fact nothing of the sort.

'I thought we had a watch on him,' he said sharply to a miserable PC, who shifted uncomfortably in size elevens. 'We did, sir. But there were only the two of us, and it was dark. There's not a street light in sight out there.'

'There's only two ways to go on a towpath, son.' Mel gritted his teeth, wishing he hadn't asked Janine out yesterday. Or wishing that she'd said yes instead of no.

'There's up, and there's down,' he carried on, in a rare sarcastic mood.

The PC flushed. 'Sir. But there's plenty of gaps in the hedges and miles of open fields. There wasn't even a moon.'

'All right, all right,' Mel said irritably. 'I take it the old man is still on board?'

'Yes, sir. He had his bedroom light on all night, and I could see in. He didn't stir from the time he went to bed at about ten, until seven-forty this morning.'

'Fine. Think you can radio to your replacements and get them to bring him in?'

The PC flushed again. 'Yes, sir.'

'Ever heard of a Captain Ryan MacMurray?' Detective Sergeant Curtis Smith said, glancing across at his (technically at least) superior officer.

Hillary hadn't. 'No,' she said flatly.

'Doesn't ring any bell at all, huh?' Curtis smiled amiably.

Hillary, knowing he was trying to rile her, smiled pleasantly back. ''Fraid not. Is he a naval captain, pilot of a BA jumbo, or captain of the local rugby team? A hint might be helpful.'

Paul Danvers bit back a grin. Hillary was looking particularly good today, he thought. A plain white blouse pulled enticingly tight across ample breasts, and her nut-brown hair had a sheen to it.

He wasn't to know that Hillary would have been aghast to know her blouses were getting too tight for her, and her hair shone simply because she'd run out of shampoo (and shower water) and had heard that beer was a good substitute. So she'd used a bottle from the fridge, then had to spend an hour filling the water tank because she'd forgotten how much beer stank.

'He's the captain of a fishing vessel up in Ayr. Ever been to

Ayr? A nice port. Very picturesque,' Curtis said, leaning back, mentally acknowledging the fact that she was too savvy to lose her temper, and switching tactics.

'I've never been to haggis land full stop,' Hillary said, deliberately dumbing down. What her old English professor back at Ruskin would have said about 'haggis land' made her shudder to think.

'Oh. Strange, that. Because Captain MacMurray seems to know you,' Curtis lied smoothly.

It was just a pity that his superior officer shot him a surprised look. And it was even more of a pity (from their point of view) that Hillary caught it.

She felt, suddenly, extremely tired. Why the hell was she here playing silly buggers with the Yorkie Bars when she had work to do?

'The man must have good eyesight then, to be able to see me all the way down here,' she said flatly.

'He knows your husband very well,' Paul said, deciding he'd let Curtis rule the show for long enough. 'In fact, Captain MacMurray has been very talkative.'

'Why? Catch him out doing something naughty?' Hillary said dryly.

Paul smiled. 'Bingo. Captain MacMurray was caught with some very illegal goods on his boat the evening before last. Caviar, would you believe. Claims he bought it legitimately off a mate of his on a Russian trawler. He's a fisherman too, by the way. You'd be surprised what good ol' Cap'n MacMurray brings in with his catch of the day. Everything from silk to illegal used aeroplane parts.'

Hillary grimaced. Great. Ronnie used a skell who'd even sell duff aeroplane parts. She wondered, with a shiver of real loathing, just how many people had died in plane crashes because of MacMurray and the people who bought from him.

'I take it Ronnie used him as part of his animal-parts smuggling operation?' she said, getting straight to the point, 'or why else would you be talking to me about it?'

Paul inclined his head. 'It seems the not-so-good fisherman and your ex did a lot of business together, yes.'

'Yeah? Well, like I said, I've never been north of the border, so why don't you go fish elsewhere? Now, if that's all…'

She placed her hands firmly on the table and hoisted herself up.

'So you won't mind if we show your photograph around the harbour, then?' Curtis said, eyeing her with a tight smile.

Hillary laughed. 'Knock yourself out,' she said pleasantly, wishing that they really would.

Knock themselves out, that is.

Hillary learned about Gascoigne doing a runner from Tommy, who'd just come in for his shift, and had been gossiping with one of the PCs who'd pulled the now infamous night duty in question. Not surprisingly, he was feeling a little woebegone and hard done by, and Tommy Lynch, for all his size, was known to be a bit of a soft touch.

'I'll bet that's pleased Mel,' Hillary said after Tommy, with some amusement, had reported the fiasco to his boss. 'Have they brought in Makepeace at least?'

Tommy nodded. 'Interview room twelve. You gonna take a look, guv?'

Hillary shrugged. She wanted to tell him no. She wanted to tell him that they were still supposed to be looking into other, non-drugs-related reasons why someone might want to off The Pits.

But curiosity won out over piqued professionalism. 'Sure. Why not. Wanna come?'

Was the Pope Catholic?

★ ★ ★

Mel and Regis were up, Mel playing good guy to Regis's more believable bad guy. But from the moment she walked into the viewing room, she could tell that both men's acting prowess was utterly wasted on Alfie Makepeace.

He was wearing a blue and red checked shirt, unbuttoned at the top, and a pair of dark brown slacks, shiny at the knees. He was looking as comfortable as any cat on a mat in front of a fire in the interview room's ergonomically designed chair. His eyelids were half-closed. He looked like he could sit there for twelve hours straight, not that current interviewing procedures would ever permit that he should sit there that long. Then there were the meals he was entitled to, the refreshments, the presence of his lawyer,, and anything else he might need to make his stay at Thames Valley Police Headquarters a pleasant little interlude.

'Come on, Makepeace, why don't you admit Dave Pitman was on board, at least up until the night of the eighth? We know he was. We have a signed witness statement from someone in London who saw all three of you aboard the boat when it left its moorings.' This was Mel, sounding reasonable.

'What was it? Did you think you were invisible, perhaps?' This was Regis, sneering and spoiling for a fight. 'Or did you just think we couldn't back-track you that far?'

Makepeace said nothing.

With a sigh, Mel ostentatiously pulled a folder towards him and made a great show of reading it.

'Alfred Daniel Makepeace. Born seventeen, eight, thirty. Educated at St Helen's Primary, then a stint at the local comprehensive till you were fourteen. Left to work in a shoe factory. Then moved on and up to a boat-building yard, followed by a stint in the merchant navy.'

Regis snorted. 'Is that why Fletcher put you in charge, Alfie? Did you like being captain of HMS *Cokehead*? What was he in the navy, Mel? I'll bet he was a stoker. One of those grease-monkeys that never see the light of day.'

Makepeace said nothing.

Tommy stirred restlessly beside her. Although nowhere near as experienced as Hillary, he was obviously getting the picture that the two DIs were wasting their time in there.

Makepeace looked about as worried and intimidated as yesterday's leftover canteen rice pudding.

'We've had the dogs out at the boat, guv,' Tommy said. 'Nothing. The handler reckons they've gone over the whole boat with disinfectant.'

Hillary nodded, not at all surprised.

'So why did you ask for The Pits, then, Alfie?' Regis said, trying to catch Makepeace off guard. If Makepeace lifting his eyes from the table to give him a slow, thoughtful stare could be said to have worked, then it worked.

'Oh, yes, we know all about that,' Regis laughed, a very nasty laugh that sent definite trickles down Hillary's back. Very nice trickles. Of course, if she'd been a perp they wouldn't have been so nice, but she was a policewoman, and, moreover, a policewoman who'd been celibate for far too long. And Regis, though hardly the Hollywood tall, dark and handsome standard issue, nevertheless had that *something* that set a girl detective's toes a-tingling.

Now, wouldn't Detective Inspector Paul Danvers of the North Yorkshire Riding Constabulary be disappointed to know that?

Hillary barely stopped herself from snorting aloud.

'We know a lot about Luke Fletcher and his little problems lately,' Regis carried on, curling his upper lip like a Doberman spotting a stray cat.

'Not so little now, though, are they?' Mel slipped in mildly. 'His problems, I mean. After our raid in Oxford, I imagine he must be feeling the pinch.'

Makepeace said nothing.

Tommy sighed heavily beside her. 'He's not going to crack, is he, guv?' he said quietly.

'Not in a month of Sundays,' she agreed gloomily.

Just then the door to the interview room opened and Frank Ross stuck his fat head through the door.

'Guv, a word,' he said, ignoring the miffed look Mel sent him.

Regis shot him a look, and Mel got up. 'I'll have to leave you alone with DI Regis for a short while, Mr Makepeace,' he said, hoping for any sign, however minute, of unease in the suspect at this less than happy news.

Makepeace didn't so much as look up from the table top, which he seemed to find utterly fascinating.

'Frank looks fit to bust a gut,' Tommy said, transferring Hillary's attention to her nemesis.

Tommy was right. Frank looked fizzing.

'Come on,' she said quickly, slipping out the door. Normally Mel would have given her a rollicking for looking in on his interview, but he was too busy listening to Frank to care.

His face looked incredulous, then tight, then furious, then thoughtful.

Hillary felt her heart leap.

She moved up, just as Ross finished speaking. '…in that lay-by, not far from Sturdy's Castle, heading north.'

Mel looked beyond Ross's shoulder, saw Hillary, and nodded curtly.

'We've found Gascoigne,' he said simply. And, before she could ask why that should be such a cause for celebration, he added curtly, 'Dead.'

13

JANINE and Tommy glanced up as Hillary's ancient Volkswagen pulled in on to the side of the road. Luckily, since the building of the nearby motorway, this Banbury to Oxford A-road was nowhere near as busy as it used to be, and even at 5:30 on a weekday, traffic wasn't *too* bad. It was an added bonus that the body had been found in a lay-by, as it meant that the police tape cordoning wasn't disrupting traffic. Nevertheless, what with police cars and assorted paraphernalia parked up on the side of the road, plus the usual drive-by gawkers slowing down to get a thrill, there would inevitably be a bottleneck sooner or later.

To make matters worse, the coroner's pick-up men were already there, plus the exhibits officer, the man in charge of overseeing the removal of the victim's clothes and personal belongings, ready to bag them for forensics. It was unusual for him to be already in situ.

The public tended not to realise how many police officers had specific and crucial duties at any crime scene. Most knew, from TV detective series, about SOCO officers, and forensic pathologists, and psychological profilers. Less was known about people like exhibits officers, pick-up crews and all the other less-than-glamorous personnel that could be found at any normal crime scene.

Tommy, however, knew it was never usually *this* crowded. But he also knew why this was different. Because of the magic name, of course. Luke Fletcher. Everybody wanted in on this case.

He saw Hillary climb out of her car, looking good as usual, but with no Mel in tow. He'd probably had to stay behind to report to Superintendent Donleavy, he supposed. He imagined Mike Regis, the Vice man, would be pretty busy too. Perhaps it was just as well the two senior men weren't on the scene yet. Things weren't looking good.

'Janine, Tommy, what have we got?' Hillary asked crisply. She didn't need to ask what they were doing there ahead of her. She was not the SIO any more.

'Boss,' Janine said. 'One Peter Cornis, an estate agent from Banbury, pulled in to get some fish and chips roughly forty-five minutes ago. It's a bit early, but he said he had an evening showing out in Chipping Norton, and missed lunch due to a no-show in Summertown. He bought the standard cod and chips from Fred Cummings's mobile van.'

Hillary paused to look at the van in question. It was the usual specimen. White-painted, with a big service hatch in the centre side panel. Cummings Fish & Chips was painted, rather unimaginatively, on the side, with a rather lacklustre, laughing cod painted beneath it.

'Cummings is a regular here, he says. The pub up the road doesn't like it, and think it's a bit cheeky, but even with the motorway and all, Cummings still seems to make a bit on this stretch. Enough to make it worthwhile, at any rate.'

Hillary nodded. Others, she knew, would probably chivvy Janine to get on with it, but she'd found that getting the background was always useful.

'Anyway, after Peter Cornis bought his dinner, he wandered up and down to eat it. Said he'd been sitting in an office all afternoon, and fancied some exercise.'

Hillary frowned, and Janine grinned. 'Yeah, I know. My guess is he didn't want to get fish-and-chip smells in his motor.' She pointed with her pen.

Hillary glanced over to a new Alfa Romeo and rolled her eyes. Oh, men and their cars.

'Right,' she said dryly.

Janine grinned, while Tommy continued to stare at the car longingly.

'Anyway, he was walking past a gap in the hedge.' Janine pointed to where SOCO were already hard at work. 'He noticed what he thought was a tramp, sleeping it off in the ditch.'

Hillary nodded. The usual. It was at this point she usually began to feel sorry for the witness. Although most cops tended, automatically, to regard any finder-of-the-body with deep suspicion, nine times out of ten the witness was innocent. And it was hard to see why an estate agent from Banbury should kill Jake Gascoigne, then buy fish and chips the next day, right by his body, and be on the scene when the cops were called in.

'Right. Go on,' Hillary said.

Janine read from her shorthand with ease. 'He says he called out, but the tramp didn't stir. Something about him seemed "off". His words, not mine. Anyway, it was enough to make him step off the tarmac, push aside the bushes and bend down to give the "tramp" a poke.'

Hillary nodded. She'd come across this phenomenon many times before from witnesses. 'Something didn't seem right.' 'I had this funny feeling.' 'Something made me look closer.'

It was a common thing. In nearly all cases the explanation was simple. In this case, for instance, she was sure that the hapless Peter Cornis's subconscious had realised that the tramp's clothes were too good to actually belong to a tramp. Maybe he had noticed Jake Gascoigne's dark hair. Most members of the public associated tramps with old men. Winos. Perhaps, who knew, the busy Peter Cornis's subconscious had failed to pick up the scent of booze or meths. Whatever. It had all gone back into the fabulous computer called the human brain, and sent back the message to Peter Cornis that 'something was off'.

'When the body didn't move he looked closer,' Janine was continuing briskly, 'and subsequently lost what fish and chips he'd already eaten.'

Hillary groaned. 'Tell me, not all over the crime scene?'

Janine wrinkled her nose. 'No. He managed to stumble away and upchuck in some dock.'

Charming.

Hillary sighed. 'Go on.'

'After he'd got over it, he says he went back to his car and used the mobile to call us. In the meantime, two lorries had pulled in and their drivers were champing down oblivious. Thought Cornis was either just a regular sick bloke, or maybe a drunk trying to throw up some excess booze. Whatever, it never occurred to them that Fred's fish and chips might be tainted. They'd all but finished their last chip when the first of the squad cars showed up. They're not happy at being detained. One said he's hauling perishables—lettuces, I think—and has to meet a deadline.'

Hillary groaned. 'Right. Better get on to interviewing him first. The usual. Tommy, take the other lorry driver. I'll take Cornis. He's in his car?'

Janine nodded.

Another late night, working long past shift. With no overtime, natch. Her back hurt. She wanted to be home. Instead, she trudged towards the big navy blue lorry, and the driver whose eyes visibly lit up at her approach.

Janine groaned inwardly.

As Hillary approached the Alfa Romeo, she saw two more cars arrive. With Mike Regis in one.

She dragged her mind firmly back from thoughts of the Vice man and tapped on the window of the Alfa. It wound down with an electronic ease that made her instantly hostile to the man inside. Her own Volkswagen had windows that wound down with elbow power—and then only if they felt like it. The passenger window wouldn't even wind down if she had the upper body power of Arnold What's-his-face.

'Mr Cornis. I'm Detective Inspector Greene. Would you like to step out, or would it be easier if I sat in?'

Peter Cornis shrugged. He was a twenty-something, with the regulation 'in' haircut, the 'good' suit, the fake watch and the latest car toy hung from the mirror. The only thing that didn't scream 'man on the way up' was the look in his eyes. Without waiting for an answer, and feeling a lot less anti, Hillary moved around to the passenger seat and slipped inside.

It smelt of leather and wood. And a car freshener. Hillary, who didn't even bother to buy air freshener for the boat, sighed softly.

'Mr Cornis. I'm sorry about this, but I need to ask you some more questions…'

When she left the car a while later, Peter Cornis was fighting back tears. Reaction, of course—one of the things the TV detective shows didn't go into much. People finding bodies tended to cry about it. And have nightmares afterwards. And feel all sorts of things from fear to anger and resentment to depression.

Even estate agents.

She saw at a glance that Mel had arrived and was taking over. By his side, Frank looked particularly gleeful. Hillary felt even more depressed.

'Looks like we got sod all,' he said to Hillary, without preamble, when she walked up to him. 'The doc's here. He reckons the body's been there all night, of course.'

Hillary snorted. She hadn't really expected anything else. In fact, she'd been unconsciously working on the supposition that Gascoigne *had* been murdered sometime in the dark hours of the night. Why else had he slipped off the boat and done a runner? He had nothing to fear from the police.

'Think Fletcher gave him a buzz and arranged a meet?' she asked, rhetorically.

'Not in person,' Mel responded, just as offhandedly. 'No doubt another of his gofers did the actual dirty.'

'Perhaps Frank can check into that,' Hillary slipped in, with a nice warm feeling inside.

Frank looked furious. It was a scut job, and he knew it. 'Like hell,' he growled. 'As if any snout is going to be talking now. Everyone will have headed for the hills long since. I can think of better ways to waste my time than—'

'Well, I can't,' Mel snapped, butting in. 'You're always boasting about being an old-fashioned copper, a real hard man who knows where all the bodies are buried. Well, now's your chance to show what you can do.'

Frank shot Mel a killer look and stomped off.

Mel sighed heavily. 'Every day I pray I'll get into the office and find Frank Ross has applied for a transfer.'

Hillary laughed. It was a genuine, lovely sound, and had not only Tommy Lynch's head swivelling in her direction. Mike Regis, talking to the doc, also looked over at Mel and Hillary, and wondered how much fall-out she was still carrying from her ex.

If he should chance his arm.

'It would have been well dark, probably in the wee small hours when the body was dumped,' Hillary speculated out loud.

'The road wouldn't have been busy,' Mel put in.

'And the lay-by bends away from the road, with plenty of bushes between it and the main road,' she concluded glumly.

'Let's face it, our chances of a wit are practically nil,' Mel said.

For a moment, the two of them were silent. Then Hillary sighed. 'Who's with Makepeace?' she asked.

'Regis's man.'

'He talks, then?'

Mel smiled. 'On occasion. Not that he'll get anything out of Makepeace.'

Hillary contemplated the silent Makepeace, and the equally taciturn Vice sergeant. What a pair they must be making back at the Big House.

'It's going to be a long night,' Mel said, glancing over at the hedge and its group of interested people. Hillary wondered when hawthorn, squitch-grass, dock and dandelions ever got such intense scrutiny from humans.

'Was that a hint to go home and take it easy, sir?' she asked cockily.

Mel smiled tiredly. 'Why not? No reason for us both to be here.'

Hillary winced. Ouch. Still, Mel was right—he was the SIO here. He could do without her.

Without a word she turned and left.

Mike Regis and Tommy Lynch were the only ones who seemed to notice.

Back on the boat, she poured herself a glass of white wine. It was Riesling and had been left opened, in the fridge, since last Sunday when she'd opened it to go with her chicken dinner.

She sat down, felt the boat move ever so slightly beneath her, and leaned her head back against the wall. It was fast coming on to twilight, and through the half-open window she could hear a blackbird singing, beautifully, in one of the willows on the opposite bank.

The pub down the way was beginning to murmur, as pubs

did, but here on the boat the sound was muted, as was that of the cars passing by on the road beyond. A fish rose and plopped outside, sending circles of ever increasing circumference across the surface of the dirty water.

She sipped her wine and tried to unwind.

So Fletcher had had Gascoigne bumped off. Because he was skimming? Probably. Makepeace had been given the task of proving him dirty. Had he failed or succeeded? She frowned. And did the answer to *that* have anything to do with Dave Pitman winding up dead in Dashwood Lock?

Somehow she couldn't seem to make it fit.

If Gascoigne had been skimming, Luke Fletcher had suspected and Makepeace had found him out, why was it Pitman who had died first?

Had the two men had a fight? Gascoigne was known to use the knife, almost exclusively, but the ME's report on The Pits had found no knife injury at all.

Accident, then. Accidents happened to people all the time—including bad guys. Coincidences, too. In real life, coincidences abounded. It was only in detective novels where you couldn't get away with them. Because readers didn't like it, or so she assumed. But in real life, coincidences didn't give a sod whether you wanted to believe in them or not.

Even so, she didn't like it. She couldn't shake the feeling that she was missing something.

Her eyes fell to the book on the shelf beside her, and she lifted it, frowning. Dick Francis's *Bonecrack*. She wasn't much of a reader, not nowadays, and certainly not for this kind of thing. When she *did* read, she liked something decent. One of the Brontës. Austen. Eliot, maybe. Give her a classic anyday.

She opened the book and read the inscription more closely. 'To Stud. It takes one to know one. Hillary.'

Stud.

She snorted. When the hell had she ever called Ronnie 'Stud'? Never, that's when. Oh, she caught the pun, of course. Weren't Dick Francis's books always about race horses and stud farms? And wasn't the hero always some macho man who could stand any amount of pain? Just the sort of book Ronnie *would* go for.

She frowned. The writing looked vaguely like hers. But…

The phone rang. Quickly she tossed the book back on to the shelf and reached for it. 'DI Greene,' she said sharply, only now realising how tense she still was.

'It's me, guv,' Tommy Lynch said. 'Just thought you'd like to know. Doc's preliminary says Gascoigne was killed somewhere between eleven and four last night. Cause of death, subject to full post-mortem, natch, is multiple blows to the head and neck with our old friend, a blunt instrument.'

Hillary sighed. It figured. A typical 'lesson' murder. Anybody else skimming from Fletcher was going to think twice about it now.

'Right,' she said wearily. 'See you tomorrow.'

'Right, guv,' Tommy said warmly, and hung up.

Back in the lay-by, Tommy thrust the mobile into his trouser pocket and wondered what she was doing now. Probably drinking a glass of wine, maybe watching telly. No, reading, probably. He knew she'd gone to Ruskin. What had she read? English? History? Sociology?

He wished he was there with her, drinking wine and being able to talk to her about…whatever. Instead he got in his car and drove back home to his mother, Mercy. As soon as he reached the house, he knew that Jean was there. And that his mother had probably invited her.

He was smiling manfully when he walked through the door.

★ ★ ★

A load of reports waited for Hillary the next morning, sitting ominously on her desk like a paper mountain about to topple. Hillary looked at them with a jaundiced eye and sighed. Already her day was mapped out. Paperwork. Break for coffee. More paperwork. Break for lunch. More paperwork.

'Hill, can I have a minute?' Mel said, popping his head out of the door, looking like a man who'd been working all night.

Hillary, who'd finished off the bottle of wine last night, ran a tongue that felt like it could line a snooker table over dry lips and followed him inside.

'How's the background work on Dave Pitman coming along?' he surprised her by asking.

'Fine,' she said. 'I ran down the previous rape cases. No joy. I'm due to see his mother today.' She paused, thought about the paperwork, and amended, 'No, tomorrow, maybe.'

Mel nodded. 'Well, push on. Regis is overseeing Frank Ross and the Fletcher end of things,' he said, trying to sound casual, but if she'd been in a cartoon, a light bulb would have abruptly appeared over her head.

Ah. So that was it. Mike Regis was in charge of the drugs aspect, leaving poor old Mellow Mallow out in the cold.

'Right,' she said.

Spotting Janine and Tommy walking through the door, she decided to spread the sunshine even further.

'Janine, Tommy, just the job. I want you to re-interview Deirdre Warrender and her daughter Sylvia. Actually, Sylvia will be a first interview. She wasn't there when I talked to her mother.'

Janine looked at her blankly. Tommy, who had a better memory, nodded. 'Pitman's last rape victim?' he said quietly.

'*Alleged* rape victim, if you please,' Hillary corrected. 'He wasn't brought to trial for it, remember?'

Janine felt like swearing. More scut work. The action was

back at the lay-by, or following up the witness statements. Hell, she'd rather be with Frank Ross than chasing off after years-old red herrings. At least *he* stood more chance of coming up with something useful.

'Right, boss,' she said flatly.

Hillary, reading her far more easily than she would a Dick Francis novel, could have told her that things could easily get worse. Much worse. But as a senior(ish) police officer, part of her job was to drum up new recruits for the force, not chase off already broken in detective sergeants.

'Her poor titties,' Deirdre Warrender said, stirring her cup of tea and shaking her brassy red curls.

Janine wondered, vaguely, what sort of hair dye she used.

Tommy wondered if he'd misheard her.

'That's what I remember most about it, you know,' she said, looking up at the big handsome black policeman. 'The state of her poor titties. Black and blue, and scarred. Poor girl can't take her top off on any beach now, I can tell you.'

Tommy took a hasty swallow of his tea.

They were in Deirdre's kitchen, waiting for her daughter to come home. Apparently she had just got a new job nearby and returned home for lunch. Janine wondered if that was because the trauma of the rape was still with her, making her 'run home to mother' on a regular basis, or whether it was just cheaper to eat at home.

From the looks of the place, the Warrenders didn't exactly have money to burn.

They'd taken it in turns to read DI Greene's report of her first interview on the way over, swapping driving duties halfway out.

Now she nodded sympathetically. 'Yes, Dave Pitman had a bit of an MO for that,' she said.

Which was true. All three rape victims had come in for se-

vere battering about the breast and genital area. Stitches. Scars.
At least flesh healed, eventually. But at nearly 30 here was
Sylvia Warrender still living at home with her mother, com-
ing back for lunch like a little girl needing to be looked after.

As if responding to some telepathic call, the kitchen door
opened. Janine noticed Deirdre Warrender glance anxiously
at the door. She was obviously wishing Janine and Tommy
were a million miles away. Still, that meant nothing. They were
cops, and that alone made them the enemy to people like the
Warrenders. And to make matters worse they were there to
question her daughter about something they must both want
to forget.

The girl who walked in looked thin. Pale and thin. They
were the two things that immediately struck Janine. She looked
washed out, faded, drooping. Like a wild flower after a long
drought-ridden summer. The pale eyes—impossible to tell
what colour—zeroed in on them and became, if possible, even
more dull.

Tommy didn't dare move. She looked ready to bolt.

'Cops, love,' Deirdre said at once. 'Remember, I told you
I had a visit from one of them the other day? These two work
for her. Come on in and I'll get you some toast. Beans? Egg?'

Sylvia Warrender slipped, eel-like into a chair. She was
wearing a plain black pair of trousers and a white, satin-look
blouse. She was wearing make-up, but it didn't seem to work,
somehow. The only thing that immediately stood out on her,
to Tommy's mind anyway, was her necklace.

His girlfriend Jean was, on the whole, what people would
describe as a down-to-earth girl. Not the kind to lavish her
money on expensive holidays. The kind who had a building
society account, steadily growing. The sort who bought next
year's Christmas presents in the January sales. The sort his
mother loved. But she had one extravagance—jewellery. Not

that she bought a lot, or that she was silly over it. It was just that what she bought was always good, always gold, and always expensive.

And the necklace Sylvia Warrender was wearing would be something that Jean would definitely salivate over.

Except that she was not a Gemini.

The necklace was gold, with a plain but very nice box-cut chain. It was the pendant, however, dropping neatly in the milk-coloured *V* underneath Sylvia's almost non-existent chin, that immediately caught the attention. For a start, Tommy could have sworn it was not mass produced. He'd been dragged to enough craft fairs by Jean to know. This pendant, two back-to-back outlines of pretty young girls, the Gemini twins, had the smack of hand-made, one-off individuality. Cameos in gold wire. Very fine.

And surely very expensive?

If she had a boyfriend, he obviously rated her highly. Or was it a present from her mother? Like Janine, he knew some rape victims never recovered. Never dated, but instead retreated into a safe world, peopled only with close relations like parents, or not peopled at all.

Tommy glanced at Deirdre while Janine gently questioned Sylvia about Dave Pitman.

Could she have afforded to buy such a gift for her daughter? He wouldn't have thought so. Perhaps she hooked, now and then, purely as an amateur. Even so, she didn't look the sort who'd go for hand-crafted jewellery. A bottle of Chanel would probably be Deirdre Warrender's definition of class.

He sighed, listening as Janine, with genuine finesse, went through the paces.

Both Sylvia and Deirdre Warrender had an alibi for the night Dave Pitman was killed. So that was another dead end.

As Hillary had already ascertained, the father was a shadowy figure at best, and Sylvia seemed to know next to nothing about him.

Another dead end.

They were wasting their time.

When they got back outside, some twenty minutes later, Janine sighed heavily, and put her notebook away. Then said, shortly, 'I'm glad Pitman is dead.'

Tommy, for a second, felt a little frisson of shock, then nodded in understanding when it passed.

Sylvia Warrender was probably just as dead as Pitman. Only the fact that she breathed differentiated them. She'd been terrified of even looking at Tommy, and had answered all of Janine's questions, even the more knuckle-biting ones about the rape itself, in a kind of monotone that would have had any psychiatrist looking anxious.

He could almost imagine her life. Get up, force down some breakfast, go to work, come home for lunch, go back to work, come home, eat her mother's cooking, then spend the night in front of the telly. No men. No friends. No social life. All those things were dangerous. All those things must have led to her meeting Pitman in the first place. Led to her being in the wrong place at the wrong time.

Yeah, he could understand why Janine, or any other woman, would be glad Pitman was dead. Hell, he only had to think of Jean or his mother or Hillary and Dave Pitman in the same mental breath, and *he* was glad Pitman was dead.

Back in the car, the radio was squawking.

Janine reached for it eagerly. Obviously something was happening back at the Big House.

14

'WHAT'S UP, boss?' Janine asked, the moment she walked into the office. There was a definite buzz but one she couldn't quite pin down.

Hillary glanced up from the path report she was re-reading on Dave Pitman. Something about it was still bothering her.

'Huh? Oh.' Her eyes focused, and she leaned back in her chair, running a hand through her lush, still faintly beer-scented brown hair.

Tommy watched carefully. Careful not to be seen watching, that is.

'Oh, an appeal went out on the lunchtime news for anyone driving by Sturdy's Castle late last night to get in touch. We got the usual, but one's come up trumps. A woman driver, returning from a visit up at the Radcliffe. Sister, apparently, in a bad way. She'd been hanging around, waiting to see if the worst was gonna happen. Apparently, around one, quarter past, in the morning they told her it was safe to go home. According to the wit, a hairdresser at a salon in Deddington, she was driving past the lay-by going on one-forty, one-fifty time and saw a car parked up.'

Tommy sat down in his chair, using his feet to wheel it from his desk back to Hillary. Janine took off her lightweight coat and tossed it towards her desk chair ignoring it as it hit the floor.

From his office, Mel saw her, and into his mind, like a determined waft of lust, flitted the image of her doing a striptease. Taking off the blouse next, then the skirt, she'd be wearing stockings, of course, and…

He cursed, and answered the phone.

Oblivious to her superior's discomfort, Hillary continued to bring her team up to speed. 'She saw a single male, white, between thirty and thirty-five, well built, probably dark haired, lugging something from the boot of the car.

'As you know, the streetlamps over there aren't brilliant, but she recognised the make of car because her husband used to own one. A Vauxhall Carlton, dark in colour, black, dark blue, maybe dark grey. At the time, she assumed it was just somebody doing a spot of illegal dumping. When asked to describe the object, she stalls a bit, saying it was dark, she was going by at fifty miles an hour plus, but it was big and bulky, sort of like a rolled-up carpet. That's what she thought he was dumping. Old carpet.'

'Yeah, well, it's usually that, or old mattresses, ain't it?' Janine said laconically. But she knew what everyone was thinking. A dead body, rolled up in something, looked a lot like a rolled-up carpet.

'Regis is still talking to her now, going over it a second time. Mel took the original interview. So, tell me about the Warrenders,' she finished.

Janine went over her notes. Then Tommy told her about the necklace.

'Thing is, guv,' he ended, 'it looked like good-quality gear to me.'

Hillary frowned thoughtfully. She could understand why Tommy had noticed it. From her own memory of Deirdre

Warrender and the household, it wasn't the kind of place you expected to find gold. Literal gold, that is.

'Right. Well, let's leave it for now.' She couldn't really justify Tommy's time checking it out because she couldn't see any connection between a gold necklace and Dave Pitman's death.

And no matter how much she wanted to turn over every stone, just to show Mellow Mallow and Donleavy that she could still function like a good police officer, even when being shafted and given the shitty end of the stick, she wasn't about to go overboard on it.

'OK. I'll be going to interview the mother tomorrow. Janine, see if Mel wants you for anything.'

She didn't notice her sergeant go white then flush. 'Right, boss.'

'Tommy, you'd better start trying to trace any stolen Carltons, dark in colour. Go back two days. If nothing, go back a week.'

Tommy groaned inwardly. 'Right, guv.'

Mel glanced up as Janine walked in the door. Feeling wrong-footed by the mental striptease image, he tried to smile like a benign uncle.

'Sergeant,' he said, foregoing her name.

Janine scowled and wondered what was biting him. 'Sir,' she said crisply. 'DI Greene wants to know if you have an assignment for me.'

Mel didn't. 'Look, about the other night. The cinema. And…everything. I wanted to say I'm sorry it didn't work out.'

Janine shifted uneasily from foot to foot. He was looking good today. All the late nights and tension had given him a bit of a rough edge. He wasn't quite so polished and smooth. She liked it.

'Yeah, well, it just felt a bit awkward, sir, didn't it?' she said miserably.

Mel nodded. Then looked up. 'Want to try again?'

Janine smiled instantly. 'Sure. Why not?'

It wasn't until gone five, when Hillary and all but the next shift were thinking of going home, that the call came in.

A car, just off the Woodeaton turn, which was part of the local rat-run to Headington, had been found burnt out. It had been run off the road, through a hedge and into a field beyond a dip, so it was invisible from the road. It wasn't until the farmer came across it that it was discovered. Thoroughly pissed off, he'd only just reported it.

Tommy caught the call just as he was putting on his jacket, then relayed it to Hillary, who rolled her eyes but nodded. 'Better tell Mel,' she said, because after the rollicking he'd given her about the second boat, she was punishing him by reporting every little move she made.

Mel merely waved her off with his blessing, and Janine, catching sight of them getting into Tommy's car in the car park, jogged over.

'No need for you to come, if you'd rather get off,' Hillary said through the wound-down window, mindful of her sergeant's still stiff and aching back. 'We've found a possible burned-out that matches the description of our Sturdy's Castle lay-by wit. Might be nothing.'

Janine, thinking about going home, soaking in the tub before changing into something sexy, then waiting for Mel to show up with a bottle of wine and a packet of condoms, shrugged.

Sod that.

She wasn't that sad that she had to have nearly four hours to get ready and wait for a man. She'd be back in plenty of time.

'I'll follow you down, boss,' she said. 'Where is it?'

Hillary told her then nodded to Tommy, who drove out and headed up the main road to the roundabout.

He wanted to say something to her, but couldn't think what. Hillary, for her part, simply sat in the passenger seat, her elbow on top of the wound-down window, saying nothing. The fierce breeze felt good on her face. Her eyes felt gritty, as they always did when she wasn't getting enough sleep, but the thought of going back to the cramped, empty boat depressed her.

She wondered what sort of place Mike Regis had. A conventional semi? A smart bungalow? How about a flat, one of those nice Victorian conversions in north Oxford? Up near Keble College maybe, by the park.

Then her mind supplied a wife and a couple of kids, and she grimaced. She was blowed if she was going to ask around about his marital status—in six seconds flat it would be doing the rounds of the canteen. And she was still wincing about the unfounded rumours that she and Mel were doing (or had in the past done) the old horizontal tango. Taking a trip on the same bloody carousel didn't appeal at all.

Tommy heard her heave a huge sigh, and felt his hands tighten on the wheel.

He negotiated the usual traffic hazards at Islip, and a few minutes later was indicating to turn off to the small, historic village of Woodeaton. Didn't people from all over the globe come to the church here because it had something rare in it? A tapestry—or a goblet or manuscript or something. He couldn't remember what it was. His mum could probably have told him, though.

'Here it is, guv,' he said unnecessarily, since a marked police car and an unhappy man in a tractor were parked off the road.

Janine pulled in behind them, and together they walked to the glum-looking man in the tractor. The uniforms on the scene began to look vaguely interested now that some 'brass' had shown up.

Hillary eyed the grass, the hedge and the dip beyond and heaved yet another sigh. Great. Join the police force and get your clothes and hair messed up with hawthorn, your legs stung by nettles, and your shoes ruined by cowshit and dirty ditch water.

Some uncomfortable and curse-laden moments later, they were all clustered around the burnt-out car. By now the light was starting to go, and the setting sun was generously casting a pleasant golden light on the field, already green with barley. Except for a blackened area surrounding the car where the fire had fizzled out.

'It's a Vauxhall Carlton, all right,' Tommy said and, being a gentleman, got on his hands and knees and peered underneath it in search of unsinged paint. 'And it used to be a dark grey,' he added, standing up and wiping mud and grass and ashes off his hands and the knees of his trousers.

Hillary nodded. 'OK. Let's work on the assumption that it's too much of a coincidence that our wit sees a man dumping an old carpet at Sturdy's last night and us finding the same sort of car burnt out today. Tommy, take the village, see if anybody noticed anything. Since it was the middle of the night, don't hold your breath.'

Tommy grinned. As if he would. He set off uncomplainingly, whilst Janine, staring morosely at the car, wished she'd gone home and taken the bath. She had some nice gardenia-scented salts left over from a birthday present.

Girl power was all very good when it didn't cost you anything to practise it.

'Janine, have a talk with Farmer Jones up yonder,' Hillary said, again in the dead, flat tone most coppers used when they knew something was a pure waste of time, but had to be done anyway.

Janine sighed and trotted off, back up across the ditch, and through the hedge.

'Gives a whole new meaning to the phrase "been dragged through a hedge backwards",' she muttered to herself as she approached the tractor.

But it was Janine who made the breakthrough, some half an hour later. Not through talking to the farmer, who, as expected, only complained about the amount of joyriders who wrecked cars in this part of the county, but through walking along the side of the road and casting about for 'clues', those things so beloved of mystery readers, which were so scarce in reality.

True, what she found wasn't a cigarette end of a rare and wonderful quality that could only be ordered through the internet from Panama, nor was it a footprint or even a dropped hankie/key/piece of paper or any other variety of Christie-like mystery. It wasn't even on the same side of the road as the car, but just opposite. This side of the road didn't have a ditch, but it did have a hawthorn hedge with a slight dip, and, more importantly, lots of tall, trampled-down grass. Below the line of sight of the road, out of the wind and well-sheltered, it was as perfect an example of a tramp's hotel as you'd find.

Hillary, when called over by her sergeant to take a look, nodded knowingly.

'Well spotted,' she said, which, much to Janine's chagrin, made her feel good. 'If our pal was curled up there last night, he'd have had a perfect view of the fun and games,' she mused, looking across to the gap in the hedge where the car had gone through.

Janine nodded. 'And tramps are curious, aren't they? If he'd seen a car either being carefully driven, or maybe pushed, into a hedge, he'd want to take a dekko. Maybe even warm himself by the fire afterwards?'

Hillary pursed her lips. 'Possibly.' But tramps tended to come in two varieties. The mentally retarded, too uneducated not to poke their noses in where they weren't wanted, and the very canny, who knew enough about survival to keep their heads well and truly down.

Tommy, disillusioned and almost invisible in the near-dark, came back up alongside them. The tramp's nest was virtually indistinguishable in this light.

'What you looking at?' he asked, not even bothering to report to Hillary that the village had been a bust.

Janine told him.

'Now you get the fun of trying to find our sleeping beauty,' Hillary added.

Janine groaned. 'Not me, guv. I've got a date.'

'Right, get off, then.' Hillary thought, then grinned evilly. She reached for her mobile and dialled the Big House. As she thought, Frank had come on for his later shift.

She gave him the good news.

Frank, furious, hung up, rumbling under his breath. No way was he going to check out the sewers and dives of scum-life Oxford looking for a tramp who liked to kip out at Woodeaton.

Senior officer or not, screw her.

If only he knew where that cunning bastard Ronnie Greene had stashed all his dough, he'd use it just to make his old lady's life a living misery.

Janine put the plates in the sink, wondering if she should wash up or leave them.

Mel had arrived with a Thai take-out, introducing her to culinary delights she already knew about but pretended not to. Her last boyfriend but one had been a backpacker, and had introduced her not only to Thai but to Creole cooking as well.

Still, Mel liked to play the big sophisticate, so why not let him?

They'd drunk the wine, called each other by their first names right from the start, discussed the latest in the case, listened to some Norah Jones, and now looked ready to get down to the nitty gritty.

Hence the wash-up-now-or-later conundrum.

When she went back into the 'lounge', Mel was leaning back in the armchair, eyes closed. Her room was the biggest bedroom in the house she rented with her mates, but in exchange for having it, she had to use it as a living area too, leaving the real lounge downstairs free for one or the other of her mates to entertain in.

She didn't normally mind, but now she was acutely aware of her underwear lurking in the chest of drawers to the right, along with her sanitary towels. He opened his eyes suddenly and looked at her.

Then there was the bed—not a double bed, but a three-quarters effort.

'Do you want to?' Mel said simply, not even looking the bed's way.

Janine thought of her back, which still hurt. Thought of the nudge-nudge, wink-wink jokes that were bound to start the moment people realised they were an item. Did she really need this hassle?

'Why not?' she said.

Tommy, for a man who was checking out shop doorways late on a chilly night, was a happy man. Probably because, on the other side of the deserted road, Hillary was doing the same.

Hillary knew it was madness, a DI doing scut work like this late at night. Most people under the rank of sergeant thought any DI belonged behind a desk doing paperwork.

So be it. She'd simply rather be here than back at the boat. Sad, sad, sad.

It was Tommy who found him.

He wasn't old, but he wasn't young either. He was, how-ever, very drunk. Perhaps that was why he actually answered when Tommy asked him where he usually slept. If sober, no doubt he'd have lied about it.

'Guv,' Tommy called softly, bending down to get a better look at his prize, ignoring the smell of cheap booze, urine, and—curiously—strong soap. 'This here chap usually kips out Woodeaton way,' he said casually as Hillary joined him.

The area they were in was not quite into the suburb of Botley, but it had plenty of carpet warehouses, car plants and dark alleys where a chap could rest out of the hustle and bustle of the city.

It wasn't a place Hillary would choose to be alone in at night.

'Nice and warm,' the tramp slurred in confirmation. He was wearing a dirty, padded parka. 'Mission, up yonder.' He suddenly burped out the unasked-for information, which probably accounted for the smell of soap. 'Full,' the tramp said, nodding wisely, in that one word explaining why he was on the doorstep. But the real question was, of course, why was he here and not back at Woodeaton?

With a sigh, Hillary nodded to Tommy to bring him in. Once he'd slept it off, had a good meal and sobered up, he might be worth his weight in gold.

He threw up as Tommy hauled him to his feet, a thin, greenish, chemical spume that made her gag.

Then again, maybe not.

When Hillary got in the next morning, she was furious to find that Mel was already interviewing the tramp. His name, ac-cording to the blackboard outside the interview room, was Michael Ryan. No relation, hopefully, to the man in Hungerford who'd gone crazy and killed so many people in that shocking rampage nearly twenty years ago now.

Knowing that she couldn't just burst in on the interview, even though it had been her and Tommy who'd done the dirty work, Hillary stomped up to the office, in a foul mood, only to find Janine already in and looking good.

Not that she wasn't glad to see her looking better, but there was something about her that raised all of Hillary's instinctive hackles. I'm just in a really shitty mood, she thought to herself, slinging her bag down on her desk and smothering a yawn.

'The Yorkie Bars were in looking for you, boss,' Janine said.

Hillary swore long and graphically, making several heads, not just her sergeant's, turn to her in surprise. Although she could curse with the best of them, Hillary wasn't known as such a spectacular sewer-mouth.

Well, sod that. Batting her eyelashes at the infatuated Paul Danvers wasn't going to improve the quality of her day at all. She grabbed her bag again. 'When Mel comes up, tell him I'm interviewing Dave Pitman's mother. Oh, and tell Tommy hard luck. He'll know what I mean.'

The big black constable would have been looking forward to reaping the rewards of his efforts last night, Hillary knew, and would also be gutted to find Mel in there well before him.

After all, Michael Ryan hadn't spewed up all down Mel's label-bearing shirt and shiny new Oxfords.

Mrs Pitman was one of those women who looked much older than you knew they must be. The Pits had been 32 when he died, but even if his mother had had him later in life, she still shouldn't have looked like a near octogenarian. Hillary could see the pinkness of her scalp showing through her sparse white hair as she led her into a painfully clean sitting room. She was wearing a flowered apron and comfortable slippers.

Hillary sat where the obviously nervous woman indicated,

and from the pale, near translucent tone of her skin, wondered if she ever ventured out of the house at all.

'It's about your son, Mrs Pitman,' she said (as if it could be about anything else), and turned down an offer of tea. Usually she always said yes, because hospitality broke the barriers, but Muriel Pitman didn't look as if she had enough energy left to even fill the kettle.

She remembered back to the constable's report who'd first interviewed her, and his comment that he thought she must have gone in mortal fear of her son. She found herself agreeing with him. Pitman was an only child. Probably her husband, either long gone or long dead, had been the bullying kind as well, teaching The Pits that a woman's place was to be battered, beaten and kept indoors.

'You found out who did it yet?' she asked, but in the watery brown eyes Hillary could see no real question. There was no emotion in her voice either, neither anger nor curiosity. Perhaps, when it finally sank in that her son was gone, that she was free and clear, she might take off the apron, put on some shoes and go outside and find herself a life.

It was hopeless, of course. Hillary asked all the usual questions, but there was no way The Pits would have told this poor old soul about what he really did for a living, let alone who he did it for.

On the shelf were a few token photographs, one of a man who looked like a mean Wurzel Gummidge character, taken on what was obviously the local allotment, and who could only be Mr Pitman senior, and one of the The Pits himself, posing by a chrome monster of a bike. In the background lurked what appeared to be old barn buildings, sheds, and something tin and ugly, the kind of thing you came upon unexpectedly when driving through the countryside. It was usually annexed to a nice period farmhouse. Or a manure heap.

She knew the locals were still trying to find Pitman's lock-up, and even though she asked, Hillary knew that his mother would have no idea where her son kept his pride and joy. And what did it matter if they found his bloody motorbike anyway? Was it going to explain how it was him, and not Jake Gascoigne, who'd gone off the back of that boat in Dashwood Lock?

She left a short while later, her day irretrievably ruined. First of all Mel nabs her hard-won wit, then the Yorkie Bars were on the prowl, and now this.

As the door closed respectfully behind her, she imagined Muriel Pitman's shoulders slumping in relief as she shuffled back to the kitchen, probably the warmest room in the house.

She hoped she had a cat. The thought of Muriel Pitman living in that insanely clean house with not even a cat for company made her want to just get in her car and howl.

Shit, she hated days like this. Days when everything conspired to depress her. She walked towards the car, then noticed the neighbour. No doubt he'd been coiled, waiting to strike. Had probably seen her car arrive, and knew what that meant. No doubt Dave Pitman was the local celebrity now, and would be for some time to come.

'Found out who killed him, then, have you?' the man asked bluntly. He was mid-50s, balding, rounded and avid-eyed. 'Ask me, the poor soul's better off without him. Used to come here, Sunday's like, for his dinner. Never paid her nothing, I can tell you. Sometimes he'd use her garden for a mechanic's shop. Remember once, she'd just put out marigolds. Lots of 'em, French ones and them gold ones, lovely it looked. And up he comes, with that dirty scrambling bike of his, and just dismantles it on her lawn. Oil and bits of metal everywhere. But she never said nothing. Daredn't.' He nodded wisely. 'He'd have given her some of this, see, if she had,' he said, holding up his hand, palm inward, in the classic gesture of someone about to give you a good slapping.

Hillary nodded, letting him ramble on, half listening to the usual tirade against a no-good thug and what his poor saint of a mother had to put up with.

In the back of her mind, though, something tickled. Eventually she realised what it was. 'He had a scrambling bike, then?' she said, thinking back to the photo. Not that gleaming chrome monster, that was for sure. So he must have had more than one bike. She thought back to the picture on the mantelpiece. Farm outhouses. Was it possible that he didn't have a lock-up at all? Not a garage as such, because a collection of bikes wouldn't fit, but some disused barns or something might just be the ticket. Farmers, nowadays, had to scrape a living as best they could. No doubt Dave Pitman, with his passion for bikes, would have paid good money to keep his babies safe in a nice waterproof barn somewhere.

'Oh, aye. Used to do a bit of illegal scrambling out by Woodstock way. Farmers were all up in arms about it, but they couldn't catch him at it, see. I reckon the Duke of Marlborough will be as glad to see the bugger dead as anyone. I wouldn't have put it past him to go haring across the fields out near Blenheim. He'd have considered that a right laugh. And a dare. You know, to cock a snook at the Duke.'

Hillary did know.

She thanked the man, who was still reminiscing about big bad Dave Pitman even when she got in the car and firmly shut the door on him.

Reaching for her mobile, she called up the Big House and got hold of Tommy.

'Hey, Tommy,' she said. 'Fancy coming out to Woodstock? Meet me at the Duke's Head. We'll have a bite to eat. There's something I need you to help me with. Oh, and don't tell Mel, eh?'

15

PAUL DANVERS pushed open the door to the open-plan office and saw at a glance that DI Hillary Greene wasn't at her desk. Surprise, surprise. Any lesser man might be beginning to suspect that people were deliberately avoiding him.

By his side, Curtis Smith smiled obliquely. 'Well, look who's not here. Again.'

Paul shrugged. For some reason, it made him angry that his sergeant should be thinking the same thing, and so he was careful to keep his voice even. 'I daresay she's busy. She *has* got a case on. And an important one at that.'

'Yeah. And whose fault is that?' Curtis asked aggressively.

Paul glanced across at Mel Mallow's cubicle. The door was firmly shut.

Curtis, spying Frank Ross staring at them openly, nudged Paul's arm. 'You ask me, if we want to run DI Greene to earth, we'd be better off asking the poison cherub over there.'

Paul sighed. 'You seem hot to confront her all at once.'

'We've got new evidence.'

Paul snorted. 'Remember who you're talking to, OK? Our new evidence isn't worth the paper it was written on.'

Curtis smiled softly. 'So? DI Greene won't know that.' So

saying, he began to amble over towards DS Ross, who put on a sneer especially for them.

'DS Ross, just the man we were looking for,' Curtis said, glad to see the sergeant go slightly pale at this rather ominous beginning.

'We were wondering if you could tell us where DI Greene is,' Paul put in flatly, for some reason in no mood to play bait-the-poor-sucker.

Frank Ross fought briefly with the war that said you never but *never* talked to filth like this and the delicious sensation that came whenever he managed to shaft Hillary Greene.

Delicious sensation won.

Now there *was* a surprise.

Tommy was happy. He'd arrived at the pub, half expecting the call to have been one of those mirages (albeit an auditory version) that some poor sap got when crawling through the desert, only to find that Hillary actually and truly was waiting for him. At a table in a big bay window, to be precise. They ordered chicken, leek and ham pie, with a side salad, and talked about the case.

Tommy would have preferred to talk about anything else. Literature, music, telly, hell, even childhood memories or their favourite colours.

Yes, he was that desperate.

But the case it was. And if Hillary wanted to find The Pits's lock-up, barn, bikes, what the hell ever, he would search through hell and high water for them. Well, at least around the environs of Woodstock.

The meal passed all too quickly, and soon they were driving past an outlying village, the name of which escaped him.

'I'll drop you off here, search the next village on, then

come back for you. We'll keep it up, on a clockwise sweep around the town.' Hillary paused, then added wryly, 'You never know your luck.'

They hadn't pulled out of the pub car park more than two minutes before the Yorkie Bars pulled in behind them.

The barman was no help, but the member of staff who'd served their pies and pints recalled them discussing tactics for searching barn outhouses in the immediate area. Paul wanted to give up there and then, a mixture of reasons making him reluctant to carry on. One was sheer laziness—the thought of driving through cow-shit-covered lanes in search of one car made him depressed to the marrow of his bones, and he longed for Leeds, his home town, where villains stayed near cafés, pubs and decently paved streets with buildings on either side. The chances of finding Hillary out in the sticks was remote, and painstaking tasks always made him shudder. He was beginning to feel like one of those characters in the American films of the thirties and forties, where brutal prison guards with blood-hounds tracked some poor hapless bastard through the swamps.

But Curtis had other ideas. For some reason, he was deter-mined to confront her, and Paul was willing to bet that he wouldn't have minded slipping the cuffs on Humphrey Bogart or George Raft in a Mississippi swamp, given the chance. Curtis would even buy the bloodhound a chump steak for its pains.

Hillary couldn't believe her luck. The first farm she'd tried and she'd struck gold. Now what were the chances of that? As if to make up for the really crappy start to her day, she was sud-denly given a pat on the head and a *there, there* like this.

The farmer's wife didn't look like a farmer's wife in that she wasn't rounded, rosy cheeked and cheerful. She was blonde, nearly as pretty as Janine, wore pricey jeans and looked to be on her way out, probably to do some shopping in Harvey Nichols or to buy expensive wallpaper for the dining room.

The farmhouse was huge and square, and no doubt under this lady's auspices had been decorated inside to within an inch of its life, but it was surrounded by the usual accompaniment of barns, sheds and outhouses, and that's all that mattered.

Particularly when one of them had been rented by David Pitman.

'Yeah, Mr Pitman rented the old pig house from us,' she said, on answering the door. 'That one, over there.' A red-painted nail pointed out a large, rectangular building with a corrugated iron roof and stone walls that looked at least a foot thick.

'Mind if I take a look?' Hillary said. 'You may have heard that Mr Pitman met with a fatal accident some time ago.'

'Really?' Big blue eyes widened innocently. 'I didn't know that.'

Hillary smiled. Yeah. Right. Then again, she looked the type who probably only read *Home and Country*.

Or *Horse and Hound*.

'So, I'm sure, under the circumstances, you have no objection to me looking around?' she tried again.

'Oh, no. He only kept his bikes in there anyway. Oh, you might like the key to the padlock.'

Before Hillary could reply, she popped back into the house, leaving the DI speculating furiously. Why would The Pits, a bike fanatic, leave a spare key with the farmer's wife? Perhaps her husband had insisted. Or perhaps they'd had a spare key cut, on the sly? Or maybe The Pits had been only too pleased to give her a second key. No. Surely not. Surely they hadn't been doing the horizontal tango together. Not someone that pug-ugly, and the wannabe sloane ranger?

'Here it is,' the farmer's wife said, dangling a key helpfully. Hillary took it, grunted out a reluctant thanks and set off briskly across the courtyard.

In olden days, she thought wistfully, there'd have been free-range hens clucking contentedly around a trough, scrounging for corn and grass seeds. A sheepdog would lie panting a welcome in the shade. Perhaps the odd goose or two would honk at her in passing.

But this was the new millennium, and the only thing that gave away the forecourt as belonging to a farm was a tractor, pulled to bits and awaiting reassembly, parked up against a far wall.

That and oil and drying cow-shit everywhere.

Paul Danvers spotted the car first and pulled on to the side.

'See, told you it wouldn't be so bad,' Curtis had the cheek to say. In truth, he'd never thought they'd find her either, but it beat sitting around back at the Big House, trying to prise out facts about Ronnie Greene that no-one wanted to set free.

Paul climbed out and looked around. A vague odour of manure hung around on the air, helped by an overnight rain that was quickly being steam-dried by a fast-warming sun.

The corn was green, and in the hedge a corn bunting sang jubilantly from the highest branch. The country lane was traffic free, and it was hard to imagine that a city existed anywhere.

'Hell, what a depressing dump,' Curtis said flatly. 'Come on.'

In the old pig house, Hillary stared at a row of bikes. They gleamed. In fact, they seemed to ooze the smugness that she usually associated with extremely well-looked-after cars. Without doubt, they had that pride-and-joy air about them. Except for one bike that was in pieces by the wall. What was it with men and machinery, Hillary wondered vaguely. Why did they always want to pull stuff apart?

The pig house was utterly bare. There wasn't an old cupboard, a tatty stuffed chair, a wooden bench or even a cardboard box anywhere. Just the bikes, a toolbox, a tarpaulin covering the ground around the dismantled bike, and a few old-time farm implements hanging, neglected, from the rafter beams.

Great. All this time and energy to find *this*. She sighed and went towards the gleaming bike. The scrambling bikes looked less impressive but not a scrap of mud trespassed on any of them.

She moved over to the bike that lay strewn on the tarpaulin and squatted down disconsolately beside it. What the hell was she doing checking out barns and bikes when Mel and Mike Regis were back at the Big House, questioning her witnesses and taking the juiciest bites out of her case?

She prodded the exhaust, which fell over with a clang and bounced off the empty fuel tank, making it roll over ponderously on to its side.

Inside it, something thudded.

Hillary frowned. The fuel tank was painted a bright scarlet and had a painted finger of flame down each side. A silver petrol cap rested on top. She moved and rolled it back, and this time felt, as well as heard, something thud inside. Not slosh. Not like old petrol or water would slosh. It was something firm and solid. Like a brick. Except it didn't clang against the metal. Something padded?

Hillary, her pulse rate quickening, got on to her knees and pulled the petrol tank around further into the light coming through the open doorway.

And saw it.

A faint line, all around the middle of the petrol tank. In the dim light, it had been impossible to see. Now she could tell that at some point the petrol tank had been cut apart. And soldered together? No. There was no tell-tale thickening along the line.

Pulling on one side, keeping the other firmly anchored be-

tween her knees, Hillary grunted and strained and swore.
When the two parts suddenly separated, she nearly punched
herself on the chin with her knuckled hand.

Something solid and white wrapped fell out on to the tarpaulin.

She stared at it hard. Another drugs find? She reached for
it, noticing it was wrapped in that stiff white paper you found
between stacks of sugar in supermarkets.

She should take it back for forensics. Let it be opened by a
lab officer. At the very least, inform Mel.

Yeah, right. And have *this* taken off her as well.

Slipping on a pair of tissue-thin latex gloves that she kept
permanently in her pocket, she slipped her finger under one
end and carefully, patiently, disturbing it as little as possible,
began to open the package.

At last she unwrapped it enough to look inside.

And blinked.

Money.

Lots and lots of money, all in fifties by the look of the colour. A solid cube of it. There must be…what? A hundred
thousand? More.

'Well, well, looks like you finally struck hubby's gold,' a
voice drawled from the doorway.

Hillary, slack-jawed, looked up and saw Curtis Smith smiling at her like a wolf spotting deer spoor. Behind his shoulder, Paul Danvers looked worried.

And disappointed.

Hillary stared at the pile of cash in her lap, then up at the
Yorkie Bars.

And suddenly remembered that old saying about Murphy's
law. She really should have known that a day that started as full
of crap as this one had could only get even crappier.

★ ★ ★

Hillary couldn't believe she was being driven into the parking lot of the Big House in the back of the Yorkie Bars' car, practically under arrest. She wondered if Tommy would be able to get a lift back to Kidlington OK, then realised that the abandoned PC was the least of her worries.

Paul opened the back door for her, but it had nothing to do with courtesy. For shit's sake, what did they think she was going to do? Try and do a runner right here, right now, with half the force looking on? Hell, she wasn't even wearing flats.

She shot him a fulminating scowl, then watched as Curtis Smith pulled the bag of money, now safely ensconced in an evidence bag, from the back seat.

Great. Right in full view. She wondered how many eyes were now peering down from the windows. She sighed heavily and resisted the impulse to applaud Smith. Danvers might have the look, but Smith sure as hell had all the theatrical talent.

They walked into the station, past the bulging eyes of the desk sergeant and on up the steps. Some sort of telepathic osmosis seemed to occur as together the three silent officers continued up the stairs. Everyone they met fell silent and watched as they passed.

Hillary fumed and for the first time felt scared. Oh, not about her ability to prove that the damned money wasn't Ronnie's now famous 'stash', but by her realisation of what it felt like to have everyone assume you to be guilty. As a police officer, being given a lesson on how it felt to be a prime suspect was really something she could have done without.

Mel looked up, his jaw dropping as he saw Hillary being escorted by the two Yorkie Bars across the office to his door.

Over by his desk, Frank's face was so gleeful it looked as if it was about to pop loose from his skin. A grin so wide it split his face almost in two was even more sickening to watch.

As his office door opened, Mel's eyes fell to the transparent evidence bag and the money showing clearly through it. He looked up into Hillary's furious eyes, then, his own expression hardening, looked at Paul Danvers.

'What the hell's going on?' Mel said, immediately wishing he could come up with something more original, but feeling too sick to think it up. 'Hillary?'

She glowered at him. 'Sir,' she said smartly, but hardly helpfully.

'We found DI Greene in possession of this money, in a barn outhouse just outside Woodstock,' Paul Danvers said heavily. 'So far, DI Greene has refused to discuss it. I suggest you get her the office eagle.'

Meaning, Hillary knew, the solicitor and legal expert whose job it was to protect the rights of police officers accused, or about to be accused and/or charged, with a criminal offence.

'I didn't discuss it because it's part of an ongoing case that's no damned business of yours,' Hillary snapped. And because, if she was honest, she felt too stubborn. From the looks on their faces it was evident what they thought, and she was damned if she was going to gabble out the truth like some piss-scared good little girl.

No, far better to let them think they had her and then pull the rug out from under their interfering feet.

'But by all means, call in the eagle,' she continued sweetly. 'He might just be able to think of something I can charge *you two* with. Like false arrest. Impeding an officer in charge of her duty. Oh, stuff like that.'

'You're not under arrest,' Paul said automatically, then could have kicked himself in the balls as she shot him a jeering smile.

Damn it, what was it with her? They catch her red-handed with mucho dinero, and still she was trying to put them in the wrong. You had to hand it to the lady. She had guts. And style.

'Not yet,' Curtis corrected him smoothly.

Hillary turned thoughtful eyes on him, then smiled slowly. Oh boy, she was going to enjoy this.

'Sir, if we can discuss this alone,' she began, but already both Paul and Curtis were shaking their heads, as she'd known they would.

'Hillary,' Mel snarled. 'Just spit it out.'

So Hillary did. Starting with her interview with The Pits's mother, the photograph, co-opting Tommy to help and the search of the barn.

'I think you'll find Dave Pitman's fingerprints all over the bag and the money, sir,' she finished, shooting the Yorkie Bars a triumphant smile. 'Besides, if it had been Ronnie's dough,' she added, 'it would have been a hell of a lot more than that.'

And with that nice little parting shot, she leaned casually against the wall and studied her nails. Curtis Smith wasn't the only one with theatrical talent. She'd done a stint in the college drama group way back when. OK, a non-speaking part, but the critics had raved. Well, mentioned her name in the list of characters, anyway.

Mel leaned back in his chair, trying not to laugh, and wishing he could haul her out. She had no business opening that package before he and forensics had had a look at it, but he didn't have the heart to say so in front of the Yorkie Bars. Not after that wonderful piece of entertainment. Smith in particular looked ready to spit tin-tacks.

Besides, it had been damned good police work on her part.

'I think we'd better get that down to forensics right away,' Mel said, pointing at the evidence bag, but Curtis Smith's fingers closed on it protectively.

'I'll take it over personally,' he said, with distinct disrespect. 'We wouldn't want anything to happen to it, would we, sir?'

'Sergeant.' It was Paul Danvers who reprimanded him. It

wasn't like Smith to let things get to him. True, they'd just been made to look right prats, but even so. Mel was a CDI.

Curtis took a deep breath, then looked from Mel, who looked fit to bust a gasket, to Hillary who looked, suddenly, bored. 'We want you to be available for a line-up,' he said flatly. 'Our wit from Scotland now tells us that he once saw a second person in your husband's car, during one of his operations.'

'Fine,' Hillary snapped back. 'Just let me know when and where.'

The air was thick with tension and mutual dislike. Paul tried to catch her eye when he left, but she wasn't having it.

The moment the door shut, Hillary slumped down into the chair opposite Mel and began to laugh.

He watched her for a while, knowing she needed the release, and wishing he kept a bottle of the hard stuff in his drawer.

He didn't, of course. Too incorrect.

When her chuckles had finally subsided, he leaned forward and asked her, icy-voiced, just what the hell she'd been thinking of, opening the packet *in situ*. But they both knew what she'd been thinking, and with some justification. She'd been working her arse off on this investigation, even though she'd been shafted well and truly, and every lead she got was taken away from her.

She apologised. Mel felt guilty enough to be magnanimous. Then they began to think.

'What was Pitman doing with that much dough?' Mel said as an opening gambit, wondering just how long he could put off telling Mike Regis about this latest development. After all, it wasn't, necessarily, drugs related, right? Not strictly Vice's business.

'He's obviously the one who's been skimming,' Hillary said,

snapping his mind back from thoughts of staking out his territory and bringing it back sharply to the real matter in hand.

'Not necessarily,' he said cautiously. 'Pits could have been doing some petty dealing on the side.'

'Right,' Hillary snorted disbelievingly. 'As if Fletcher would stand for that.'

'Could be proceeds of robbery.'

'What, a bit of private enterprise?' Hillary said. 'If you were working for Fletcher, would you be up for doing a bit of pilfering? Come on, we know *somebody* had been skimming from Fletcher, right? It wasn't much of a secret if even Frank's stoolies knew about it. We'd assumed it was Gascoigne, but what if it was Pitman all along?'

Mel leaned forward on the desk, his shirt sleeves rolled up to reveal a light matting of dark hair and a plain, expensive-looking watch. Hillary wondered if it was deliberate, or if Mel was just like one of those women who seemed to 'do' elegant as easily as they breathed?

'So Pitman being killed never was a mystery. Or an accident. He was meant to be bumped off all along?' Mel offered tentatively.

Hillary frowned. 'Yeah,' she said, but equally dubiously. 'But in that case, why was Gascoigne killed later?'

Mel scowled at her, as if all this uncertainty was her fault. 'Perhaps they were both in on it,' he said at last.

'Oh, come on,' Hillary scoffed. 'You're not going to tell me that Fletcher had two bad apples? But supposing, just for a moment, that he did, and that he knew they were both skimming. Why get one to wipe out the other?'

'Why not? There's no honour among thieves. Perhaps Gascoigne jumped at the chance of offing his partner. More for him then.'

But Mel's heart wasn't really in it. It sounded way too far-fetched. But with Hillary he always felt on the defensive, al-most compelled to fight his corner, no matter how much of a shmuck it made him feel.

'But why take the chance?' Hillary shot back. 'Fletcher, I mean? What if Gascoigne tells Pitman he's been hired to bump him off, or vice versa. What's to stop them getting together, decide things are getting too hot and, what the hell, just make one final big score and leg it?'

'Too risky.'

'Yeah, but if they're skimming, they're not the brightest bulb in the light factory anyway, right? But the real question is why would Fletcher take that sort of risk, when all he had to do was farm out the contract to an independent and off them both. No pain, no comeback, and no risk.'

Mel sighed heavily. 'You're right. It's just not fitting to-gether. So, let's back-track. Pitman was definitely the one skimming, yeah? The dosh proves that.'

Hillary nodded. 'Sounds reasonable.'

'Fletcher knows that it's one of his mules. But suspects Gascoigne?' he offered tentatively.

Hillary nodded cautiously. 'OK. Let's go with that.'

'So he tells Makepeace, his eyes and ears, to watch Gascoigne, catch him out maybe, and sends The Pits along to act as his muscle just in case things get rough.'

'That's what the word on the street says,' she agreed, thinking of Frank Ross and his nose for dirt. 'And, so far, fits all the facts.'

'OK. But something goes wrong,' Mel continued, warm-ing to his theme now. 'Perhaps Gascoigne finds Makepeace searching through his things, or doing something off. And Pitman, coming to the rescue, gets offed by Gascoigne. Perhaps, who the hell knows, accidental-like.'

Hillary thought back to the autopsy reports, and about Gascoigne's reaction to Makepeace during their time on the boat.

She shook her head. 'Still doesn't feel right.'

Mel sighed. 'OK. So perhaps Fletcher knew all along that it was Pitman who was skimming, and it was Gascoigne's job to off him. Which he does, making it look like a boating accident.'

'Yeah. But then why is Gascoigne dead? You're not trying to say that hit didn't have Fletcher written all over it.'

Mel sighed. 'Perhaps Gascoigne botched it. Perhaps Fletcher wanted to know where The Pits kept his stash. Perhaps he wanted to know if he had help. Perhaps Gascoigne didn't follow orders, resulting in The Pits dying before he could talk.'

'That's a bloody lot of *if*s. If I may say so.'

'Can you think of anything better?'

But Hillary couldn't. That was the problem.

When she left Mel's office a half hour later, Tommy was back, and looking worried. Of course, word had spread about her run-in with the Yorkies, and half the station seemed to expect her to be led down to the cells in cuffs.

Frank Ross beamed at her, looking happy, happy, happy. It had set him up for the next month, seeing her being escorted into Mel's office like she had. He only hoped the shit, when it hit the fan, stuck to her like Superglue.

Hillary, ignoring him, asked Tommy to drive her back to Woodstock to pick up her car. She was still too deep in thought about this latest development and where it left them to bother wiping the smirk off Ross's face.

She wished she could talk to Mike Regis about it. She was forming the distinct impression that she and the Vice man had minds that worked very much alike.

As they pulled out of the car park, Curtis Smith and Paul Danvers watched them from an upper storey window.

'She didn't seem too scared about standing up in an identity parade,' Paul said, wanting to rub Curtis's nose in it.

He felt like a right prat, and blamed his sergeant for it.

'That only means she never went to Ayr,' Curtis said stubbornly. 'Not that she wasn't in on it.'

Paul sighed heavily. 'You think this suspect's fingerprints of hers are going to be on the money?'

Curtis nodded gloomily. Yeah, he thought so. She'd been too damned smug for it to be a bluff. Besides, she was right. Her hubby must have made on or around a million with his dirty animal trading scam. And, if he'd stopped to think about it, he'd have known Ronnie Greene wasn't the cash-hidden-in-an-old-barn kind of guy.

No. Once word got around about this fiasco, they were going to be the laughing stock of the Big House.

Which only made him more determined than ever to nail her.

16

'WE HAVE to let Makepeace go,' Mel said, just as Hillary was getting ready to go home.

'Perfect,' she said sourly. Really. The perfect end to the perfect day.

Mel smiled sympathetically. 'Time's a-wasting, his brief is screaming blue bloody murder, and we've got no evidence to hold him. So far we've not even been able to prove that David Pitman was even on that boat when it went through the lock. With Gascoigne dead, Makepeace can say whatever he likes, and we've got nobody to say any different. Besides, as his brief was at such pains to point out, though Makepeace has form, none of it is for violence. Even his age is working against us. Can't you just see the press—Thames Valley's finest picking on an OAP?'

Hillary shrugged. Mel didn't need to convince her. She was as aware as anyone that their case was going down the toilet. The euphoria of the earlier huge drugs bust was starting to wear off, and how.

'Fletcher's fuming.' Frank Ross's voice oiled across the office as he walked towards them. Gloomy, he looked even worse than when he was smirking—and that took some doing. He nodded back to his desk, and the phone he'd been on all afternoon. 'Nobody's talking, he's got everything buttoned down so tight his people aren't even wearing shoes that squeak. We've about as much chance of finding the take-out artist who offed Gascoigne as England has of winning back the Ashes.'

Mel, who quite liked cricket, winced. 'Go home, people,' Mel said wearily (because he'd always wanted to say things like that), and Hillary, for one, didn't need telling twice.

Hillary awoke the next day, convinced that things could only get better. When she arrived at work, the desk sergeant gave her such a cheerful welcome she actually wondered if something had broken during the night.

'Hear the Yorkie Bars are trying to find a nice deep hole to crawl in,' he said, and Hillary grinned, albeit a little hollowly. Oh. So that was it. Her humiliation yesterday had turned into triumph. No doubt the whole damned Big House was having a quiet party.

'I take it forensics came through on the dabs,' she said, knowing that the desk sergeant was usually the one person in the station who knew everything about everybody on every case. Forget the omnipotence of the chief constable. If you really wanted to be in the know, ask the man on the desk.

'Sure did. The Pits, The Pits, and nothing but The Pits,' the desk sergeant reassured her with a wink.

Hillary was still grinning when she walked into the office, but the sight of Curtis Smith and Paul Danvers seated at her desk, the blond bombshell comfortably reading the morning paper, his sergeant nosing through her drawers, wiped the grin right back off.

'Gentlemen,' she said dryly as she approached them, slinging her bag under the desk, and manually, with a hidden grunt of effort, swinging her office chair, Curtis Smith and all, around to face her. 'Off,' she said simply.

The sergeant got off, looking rather more amiable than he had yesterday, and pulled up another chair to bring him into line beside his boss.

'We've come to tell you the line-up is off,' Paul said. He *was* senior, after all, so when it came to doing the dirty he did it, even if he blamed Curtis for yesterday's cock-up. *He* hadn't wanted to go chasing after Hillary Greene in the first place. But here he was, eating humble pie.

'Yeah. A hundred and sixty-two grand ain't nothing like the sum we figure your ex has squirreled away somewhere,' Curtis put in, watching her closely.

He'd had all night to get over his fury of yesterday's debacle, and was once again thinking clearly. He still wanted to nail her, but was beginning to think it wouldn't be easy. Hell, in fact, he was beginning to come around to Paul's way of thinking. If Hillary Greene was dirty, he certainly wasn't getting the right vibes about it. He liked to think he was fair, and persecuting *innocent* coppers was as abhorrent to him as the next bloke.

OK, she'd pulled a fast one yesterday. She could easily have said what she'd been doing in that outhouse with all that money and cleared it up within moments, but he could understand why she hadn't. If she was innocent, she had a right to be pissed off at being treated like dirt, and getting her own back was only fair dos.

Still. She might still be dirty.

Hillary smiled. 'Is that so. Your wit not quite so hot, hmm?'

'We're getting evidence coming in that your husband planned on retiring soon. No doubt to spend, spend, spend on the Costa Brava somewhere,' Curtis carried on, ignoring the snickering that was going on behind him. He knew damned well that all the ears in the office were flapping, just waiting for them to make another stinker, but he was damned if that was going to stop him doing his job. 'So what was the plan? Stay on here a few more years yourself, maybe even see the divorce through as a nice little smokescreen, then meet up with him later?'

Hillary leaned back. 'Oh, please. The Costa Brava? Give us some credit. We had figured on the Seychelles at the very least.'

Paul Danvers grinned. He couldn't help it. He glanced at Curtis, who was also, he knew from experience, trying to keep from smiling. The lady had style.

'We'll be in touch, DI Greene,' Curtis said mildly.

'Oh, be still my beating heart,' Hillary drawled, and Paul found himself wishing that she wasn't being sarcastic. He still thought it would be awfully nice to make DI Greene's heart really race.

Hillary watched them go, wondering if that last line of the sergeant's really meant that it was all over, and that they were finally giving up, or if he was just yanking her chain.

Mel watched the two Yorkie Bars retreat. Was it just wishful thinking, or was there something final in the way they slouched off? He walked over to Hillary, nodding at their departing backs. 'Everything OK?'

'Fine,' she said crisply. 'I think they're giving up.'

She felt drained all of a sudden. A feeling of lethargy, something that had never before attacked her in the middle of a case, washed over her.

It scared her.

She'd always had moments in between major cases when she got bored and tired, that old familiar is-this-all-worth-it feeling nibbling at her toes, but when it came this hard and fast when she was nowhere near to finding a solution to her case, what did that mean?

Perhaps it was time to quit.

From his chair, Tommy felt his stomach lurch at the sudden bleakness in Hillary's eyes. He swallowed hard. Surely it would go soon? Yes, it had. Her shoulders were coming back, she was forcing a smile, just as he'd always known she would. She was tough. It would take more than the Yorkie Bars to keep her down.

But what about the rest? The looming, hulking great shadow that was that bastard of a husband of hers was still making her life miserable now that he was dead and buried. Then there was Mel and Mike Regis constantly taking her work over, as if she were some damned green PC who needed constant supervision. And everyone knew she hated living on the boat. Until her solicitors got her husband's finances sorted and the Yorkie Bars put in their final report, she was being held in limbo. She couldn't even move back into her house.

Put together, wouldn't anybody buckle under all that pressure?

He thought about what life would be like if she quit, and the thought of Frank Ross's glee, Janine's quiet but well-hidden relief, and the dull acceptance of all the others that yet another cop had succumbed to burn-out only made his own expression as bleak as midwinter.

He turned back to his desk and buried his head in the computer.

'Janine, a word,' Mel said, when the sergeant walked through the door an hour later. Her shift started a little later than his own, and he'd been casting quick glances at the door all morning.

Janine slung her bag on her desk but made no move to join him halfway across the room.

'Yes, sir?' she said formally, as he approached.

Mel glanced around nervously. This was not what he had planned. 'I was wondering if you felt like dinner tonight. I thought that place up in Summertown. You know, that fancy French place. I've been longing for an excuse to try it out.'

He spoke almost in a whisper, and it put her hackles up. Hell, if he was so anxious for people not to know about them, why take her out at all? A quickie in the back of his car probably had more appeal.

Tommy, who could hear them clearly, didn't falter in his typing. So that was on the agenda, was it? He knew Mel had something of a reputation with women, but he was surprised that Janine had fallen for it. He'd have thought her too ambitious. Or did she think he'd be helpful? He kept typing steadily, writing up his report for the Yorkie Bars' records, confirming yesterday's events in Woodstock.

Would Janine sleeping with the boss actually help her? Tommy had no feelings one way or the other about Janine. He hadn't been promoted for long and so hadn't been working with her for much above three months. He wasn't the sort of man who had a problem with women as bosses, and was perfectly willing to accept that Janine had earned her sergeant's stripes because of sheer hard work and drive. But surely her and Mel sleeping together could backfire on her? And him, if it came down to it. Tommy was never sure of station house politics. What was the current thinking on legovers with juniors?

'Sorry, sir, I don't think so.' Janine, lower and softer-voiced, wasn't so easy to hear.

'Why? What's wrong?' That was Mel, sounding just a little too eager, and perhaps a shade petulant. Had he got it wrong? Was it the boss doing all the pushing? Since his latest divorce, Tommy supposed he'd been keeping his head down, so to speak. Perhaps he was ready to play away again.

But if he was taking advantage of being boss, should he do something about it? Hell, no. Even he wasn't that green! And besides, if anyone could look after herself, it was Janine.

'Nothing's wrong, sir. I just don't think it's a good idea.'

Behind him, Mel opened his mouth to argue, then shut it

again. 'All right,' he said quietly, and took himself back to his office.

Janine watched him go, wondering if she'd done the right thing. On the one hand, it turned their night together into a tacky one-night stand. Cheapened it, maybe. But then, what the hell, she was a big girl. She and the rest of her sisters were supposed to take things like that in their stride nowadays. And besides, he hadn't put up much of a fight, had he? Hadn't tried to talk her 'round. OK, the office wasn't the time or the place, but he could have looked just a little bit sorry.

She sighed angrily and pulled out her chair, realising that it didn't even hurt her shoulders to do so any more. Come to think of it, last night she hadn't dreamt she was being beaten up, either. She was beginning to feel more like her old self. So screw Mellow bloody Mallow.

Or rather *not screw* him.

She grinned and pulled a stack of paperwork towards her.

Mike Regis wasn't happy to hear Makepeace had been re-leased, but like Hillary, he was philosophical.

The questioning of the tramp had proved worthless. He'd flat out refused to admit that he'd been anywhere near Woodeaton when the car had been dumped. Whether he was too drunk to actually remember or just too canny when sober to talk was neither here nor there. In his gut, he knew, Gascoigne's killing was going to be left open. He suspected Mel knew it as well. They'd given Fletcher one hell of a whack when they'd intercepted his drugs shipment, and now he sure as hell wouldn't be using the barges again. It would take him a while to recover, but he would. And it wasn't as if Makepeace was ever going to grass up his boss. Pitman and Gascoigne were dead. Whoever had done the hit on the latter was long gone. And even Frank Ross admitted nobody was talking, even in their sleep. Unless they could bring Pitman's death to Fletcher's doorstep, the bastard was going to walk.

He pushed open the door, spotted Hillary and detoured from Mel's office to her desk.

Frank Ross, he was glad to see, was absent. He didn't know how Mel and Hillary could bear to work with the slob.

'Hello. How are things?'

Hillary looked up. The Vice man was looking rumpled, tired and downhearted.

She knew how he felt.

'About as bad as they can get,' she said sourly. 'In fact, I was thinking not half an hour ago of quitting.'

Tommy Lynch stopped typing.

'I've got a degree, I could always retrain. Do some teaching maybe. Adult learning. The pay's better, the office hours easier, and I might even get to live in a proper house with four solid walls and everything.'

Mike nodded. Who was she kidding?

'Are you anywhere on Pitman? What are you reading?'

'No. And the autopsy reports,' she said, answering him in strict order. 'I keep coming back to them,' she admitted.

'Start from the beginning,' Mike advised, then shut up, realising he was in danger of teaching his grandma how to suck eggs.

Hillary shot a warning glance at him, saw it wasn't necessary, and smiled.

Tommy, who was watching her, didn't like the smile, but at least she'd stopped talking about quitting.

'I hear you gave the Yorkie Bars a bloody nose yesterday,' Mike said, running a hand over his face.

It was a long, bony hand, Hillary noticed. Sensitive-looking.

'It wasn't hard,' she said dryly.

Mike guffawed, loud enough to make Mel notice. He looked up and beckoned him through the glass.

Mike sighed and got up. 'My boss is signing us off, for the moment,' he said. 'We've got the drugs shipment, busted up the distribution, and now we're concentrating on Fletcher. Surveillance. Trying to figure out his next move. He's got to start buying or selling and re-organising soon.'

Hillary nodded. He was right. 'Good luck,' she said, her voice heartfelt.

Mike smiled at her, his eyes softening. 'We'll still be keeping in touch,' he promised.

Hillary's eyes flickered. 'Sure,' she said carefully.

Things were looking up.

Tommy watched the Vice man go, his jealousy simmering with surprising strength. He hadn't thought the green-eyed monster was one of the things he had to watch out for.

He wheeled his chair to Hillary's desk. 'Guv,' he said by way of greeting.

Hillary sighed. 'Tommy. Anything?'

'No, guv. Nothing new.'

Was there ever?

OK. Go over everything again. 'I'm not in the mood for hanging around here,' she said, suddenly anxious to be gone. The office, so familiar, so much a part of her day-to-day life, seemed stifling. 'We must have some leads to check down. Anything?' she asked, not even trying to hide her desperation.

Tommy, sensing her need for escape, wracked his brains. She needed him. That one sweet fact was enough. Trouble was, there weren't any leads.

Except...

'Well, we still don't know about the locket,' he said. 'Sylvia Warrender's locket.'

Hillary groaned. 'Is that all we've got?'

'Well, it's possible the rape allegation wasn't kosher. I mean,

The Pits might have had a regular girlfriend, and that might have been Sylvia Warrender. Perhaps they argued and she brought the allegation to get back at him. And after kissing and making up, we know he had money enough to buy gold jewellery.'

Hillary shook her head. Never in a month of Sundays. Still, what the hell else did she have to do?

'Tell me about it again,' she said flatly.

Tommy brightened. At least he had a chance to shine a bit now. 'Thing is, guv, I asked my...girlfriend...about it,' he said, then added quickly, as she shot him a hard look, 'Not that I let on it was part of a case or anything.' He hadn't wanted to mention having a girlfriend at all, really, but he could hardly explain how he came by this new knowledge without doing so. 'She's something of a jewellery buff, you see? All I said was, I saw this necklace the other day, one I thought she might like. I described it, making out it was one of the WPCs here who was wearing one. She had no idea it was related to a case.'

Hillary nodded. 'OK, Tommy. No need to bust a gut. You were discreet. Go on.'

But she wasn't really interested. She was fed up. More and more she wanted out. Both out of this office, here and now, but more generally out. But there was nowhere for her to go.

'So, anyway, I described it—gold box-chain, hand-made looking design, zodiac, all the rest. And she recognised it.'

Hillary's somewhat glazed look sharpened on him momentarily.

'What? You mean she knows Sylvia Warrender?'

Why that should engender surprise, she couldn't say—she didn't know Tommy's girlfriend from Adam. It was a sure sign of how desperate she was to get a life of her own when even a titbit from a detective constable's private life made her mildly curious.

'No, guv. She recognised the amulet. Said you could only get them from this little workshop-jewellery shack in the covered market. Apparently some Romanian or Hungarian or someone makes them. A woman. She's getting quite a rep, apparently. You know, designing for bigger and bigger names. Local celebs. That sort of thing. Jean thinks it won't be long before she heads for London.'

And she'd hinted, quite strongly, that she was a Capricorn herself. So Tommy would probably have to buy one, perhaps for Christmas, or he'd never hear the end of it.

'Nobody else makes them?' Hillary said. Well, whoop-dee-doo. Give the man a peanut.

'No, guv. Thing is, they're pricey. Right pricey. And I still don't see how somebody like Sylvia gets to be wearing one.' It would take a good chunk out of his savings to get one for Jean, that was for sure.

'Well, come on then,' she said, grabbing her bag. 'Let's check it out.'

The covered market stretched from Cornmarket Street to the High Street, taking up a good acreage of prime real estate. It had several entrances and exits, so they parked illegally and walked down the pedestrianised street.

No matter how famous the city, or beautiful its buildings, shopping precincts always looked the same. Hillary walked past a Burger King, trying to ignore the scent of hamburgers and fries, and those delicious ice-cream milkshakes.

The moment they stepped into the Covered Market, her appetite fled. The smell of fish, meat, fruit and vegetables turned her stomach, doing her an unknowing favour. Hillary never had liked markets.

Scattered amongst these stalls of comestibles, however, was more esoteric fare. This was Oxford, after all. A second-hand bookshop, tiny, cramped and dark, was literally packed from floor to ceiling with everything from tomes of John Donne and Trollope to the latest Jilly Cooper.

A shop called Next to Nothing (because it was next door to a shop called Nothing) sold knick-knacks and assorted fripperies. There was an old-fashioned ironmonger's a few yards on, and then braces of pheasants (this was Oxford, after all) hung up in front of a row of hares and partridges. A stall selling fine Belgium lace nestled cheek by jowl with a shop selling fragrant real leather belts and handbags.

'Here it is, guv,' Tommy said, pointing to a well-lit but rather ramshackle jewellery store. The costume jewellery, of course, was laid out at the front. Bizarre things in beads, pierced and tooled leather bracelets and chokers that looked like they belonged on dogs (and Staffordshire Bull Terriers at that) were heaped in baskets for passing tourists and shoppers to manhandle and ooh and ahh over.

Inside, a woman wearing protective goggles was bent over something, busily at work with a soldering iron, and it was here that the real stuff was kept. Gold, silver, copper, bronze, platinum. A real Aladdin's cave.

And there behind glass, were the zodiac necklaces. Although each symbol was clearly what it represented, no two were the same. The scales of the Libra set, for example, were different, one set of scales being overlaid with mother-of-pearl, another being silver set against gold.

'Hello, can I help?' The soldering iron had been turned off, the goggles removed.

The woman looked to be in her 50s, and her hair, tied back under a bandanna, was silver where it escaped. She had big eyes and high cheekbones and her voice did indeed have Eastern European overtones.

Hillary could see why Tommy's girlfriend thought Oxford

would soon lose her to the richer pickings to be found in the capital.

'Yes. Police,' Hillary said, showing her identity card. Tommy did the same.

The woman slowly slid off her stool, her eyes wary now.

'We were wondering if you could help us. We're trying to trace a necklace. We know it's one of yours. A zodiac pendant. Gemini. Tommy, you saw it best.'

Tommy described it. He hadn't finished when the woman began nodding her head.

'Yes, I remember. Twisted gold wire. I was trying to achieve a cameo-like effect. Didn't really think I'd succeeded, but I put it on display anyway. It sold almost at once.' Her wide, generous mouth twisted into a smile. There was, obviously, no accounting for taste.

'Do you remember who bought it? Do you keep records?'

'No, not records. But I remember the man who bought it clearly. He paid cash. Not many customers do that any more. I remember him bringing out a wallet and peeling off the money.' The jeweller smiled, obviously remembering the incident with pleasure. 'As a child we were very poor, you see? Nowadays,' she said, shrugging graphically, 'I don't have to scrimp and scrape, so much. But still…something like that sticks in the memory. There's something about the look and feel of money still that makes me warm all over. So much more beautiful than ugly plastic credit cards.'

Hillary nodded, not really interested in her life history. 'This man, can you describe him?'

'Oh, yes. He was old, easily in his sixties. Tallish, gangling, with a big nose.' She stopped as both Hillary and Tommy gaped at her. 'Did I say something wrong?'

Hillary quickly shook her head. Did she have a photo on her? Damn, she didn't.

But Tommy did. She saw him hand over a mugshot of Alfie Makepeace.

'Is this him?' he asked, holding his breath.

The jeweller beamed and nodded enthusiastically. 'Yes, that's him,' she said simply.

17

JUST like that, sometimes it happened, just like that. Hillary managed to thank the jeweller then walked out of the shop, negotiating the crowd in the smelly covered market with the careful control of someone almost drunk.

'Guv, they've had to let Makepeace go,' Tommy said, himself in a nice little euphoria of shock. His first big case, and he was there when it was cracked. Surely it would go well on his CV when he took his sergeant's exams?

'Shit,' Hillary said. Then she set off fast, weaving through Cornmarket Street, almost running. Of course, with his long legs Tommy easily—and annoyingly easily at that—kept up with her. To make matters worse, she was beginning to pant.

'Back to the boat,' she said, careful not to gasp. 'Last I heard it was still moored up just past Banbury, right?'

'Yes, guv.'

'You drive,' Hillary said, not trusting herself to keep to the speed limit, or, for that matter, from getting themselves killed with reckless overtaking.

She wanted this so bad it almost hurt.

Mike Regis was probably still at the Big House, wrapping up the liaison with Mel, and she desperately wanted to present them with the solution of the case. In her mind's eye she even could see it. She'd waltz in, sit without waiting, smile and tell them they had the killer and a full confession waiting for them downstairs in the cells.

It would be beautiful.

When they got to the canal, the boat was gone. Hillary felt so frustrated she could have wept. Beside her, she heard Tommy swearing graphically under his breath.

For a second she felt like bursting into tears.

Think, dammit, think.

'OK, we know he's on the boat,' she said grimly. 'Because if one of Fletcher's men had been sent to move it, it would have set off all kinds of alarm bells with the Vice people watching him. And he'd know that. Fletcher's a smart bastard. So odds on it's Makepeace who took off in it. And he can't have got far.' Hillary smiled, for once glad of a narrowboat's limitations. 'Hell, four miles an hour, and he wasn't released more than…what, two hours ago?'

Tommy's face split into a wide, white grin. He glanced up one side of the canal then the other.

'But which way, guv?' He hoped she wasn't going to tell him they should split up. He didn't want her having to face Makepeace alone. He was probably a killer. 'Perhaps we should call for back-up,' he said, hating to say it, knowing why she was so determined to crack the case without Mel or Regis breathing down their necks. She deserved it, but not if it meant putting her life at risk.

Hillary was grinning. 'Constable, the one thing about a narrowboat is it's long. Very long. And can only be turned at special custom-made places along the canal.'

Tommy, confused, looked at the opposite bank, not more than six or so feet the other side of him, then realised what she meant. Makepeace couldn't have turned it around here.

But which way had it been pointing? He screwed up his

eyes, trying to remember which way the pointed bit had faced when last he'd seen it.

He couldn't.

'Come on,' Hillary said, already power-walking away to the north. Tommy fell into step beside her. He trusted her memory implicitly. That was probably why she was a DI and he only a humble DC.

They found the boat moored up beside a lock. Of course, Makepeace was alone now, Hillary thought, and negotiating a lock single-handedly wasn't something to be recommended.

She walked straight on to the prow, pushed open the door without knocking and went inside. Tommy, scared by her recklessness, whilst at the same time admiring it unconditionally, rushed up fast behind her, ready to throw her to the ground and cover her should Makepeace appear holding an uzi.

Alfie Makepeace was sitting in the armchair drinking a cup of tea and reading the paper.

'Hello, Mr Makepeace,' Hillary said, moving forward and leaning against one wall. The ceiling, barely a few inches above her head, gave her the usual feeling of claustrophobia.

'DI Greene, isn't it?' Alfie Makepeace said, ostentatiously folding away the newspaper. He was wearing a knitted beige cardigan, the same kind that her father had favoured. His thinning hair was combed neatly back. He smelt, vaguely, of Old Spice. No doubt he'd showered first thing after getting back from the nick. Most people did.

A less likely-looking murder suspect was hard to imagine.

'Your lot have just let me go,' he told her. He glanced down at the paper he'd been reading—three days old, she noticed vaguely—then tossed it aside.

Tommy tensed at the sudden movement.

'Yes, I know,' she said. 'But that was then, this is now. I'd like you to accompany us back to the station, sir.'

She'd have to read him his rights. Mel would be furious enough with her for jumping the gun without her handing any defence lawyer a golden opportunity to recite overlooked technicalities.

On the other hand, before she got him back to Kidlington she needed to shake him, to be sure he'd give it all up.

She thought she had it, but how best to play it?

'Aren't you frightened of your boss at all, Mr Makepeace?' she asked, raising one eyebrow, managing to make her tone sound mildly curious. 'I mean, if I'd conned Luke Fletcher into supplying me with one of his men, just so I could kill him, for personal and private reasons, it would make *my* palms sweat a little.'

Alfie's somewhat rheumy eyes squinted at her. Was it her imagination, or had he tensed up?

'Don't know what you're talking about,' he said softly. But his fingers were plucking at one of the buttons on his cardigan, the restless, subconscious gesture telling her volumes.

She had him on the run. Yes!

'Did you know that it was David Pitman, and not Gascoigne, who was raking off a cut for himself?' she asked, and saw him literally jerk in the chair. 'No, I didn't think so,' she said, oozing sympathy.

Tommy, content to watch, listen and learn, tingled pleasantly. Some day, he'd be the one doing the questioning. He'd be the one wearing the stripes and making the decisions.

'You're lying,' Alfie said flatly.

But Hillary was already shaking her head. ''Fraid not, Alfie,' she said sadly. 'I myself found his stash, not above a day ago, in that outhouse he keeps his bikes in. You know, out Woodstock way? It's even been fingerprinted. All that lovely money, *Luke Fletcher*'s money, with The Pits's fingerprints all over it. You know, if I was you, right about now, I'd be worrying what Fletcher will do when he realises that not only did he kill the wrong man, but that his trusted old mate Alfie Makepeace has been yanking his chain all this time.'

Alfie's fingers twisted the button almost off. Then he shrugged. Then smiled.

'No skin off my nose. Nobody's going to pin any murder on to Fletcher.'

'He's still not going to be pleased with you, though, is he?' she said quickly, trying to keep the edge of anxiety out of her voice, to keep on top of it. But she was losing him.

He was the toughest of the tough under that nice-old-man exterior.

Alfie shrugged again. 'So he'll be mad. Anyone can make a mistake. Even me. He won't hold that against me.'

'Right. Like Fletcher is known for his forgiving nature,' Hillary snorted.

But when his eyes looked back at her they were hard and old. And suddenly she got it. What did he have to lose? For a second, she thought she'd lost, and all her dreams of a glorious collar sailed out the window.

Then she realised she'd been on the wrong tack all along.

She moved forward and sat down carefully in the chair opposite him, leaning forward, her arms lying loosely atop her knees, hands dangling.

'Tell me about Sylvia, Alfie,' she said softly now, and saw his face tighten. Even his wrinkles seemed to iron out, so hard was his jaw clenched. She heard him take a ragged breath.

'You know,' she said softly, 'what with DNA and bloodtyping and stuff, it wouldn't take a lab nowadays much over a week to prove paternity. Of course, it would mean Sylvia being served with papers forcing her to take a blood test. Her mum,

Deirdre, will be upset about that, I daresay. Then, if you still refuse to co-operate, it'll all be brought out in court. The rape, all the nasty details. Pitman was a bit of an animal, wasn't he?'

Tommy shifted his eyes from the old man to the wall. Suddenly he was very glad he wasn't the one asking the questions. Would he be able to do it? Would he ever be able to do what his guv was doing now? He knew why she'd changed tactics, of course. They had to get Makepeace to confess. With sod all by way of witnesses, and pitiful forensics and hard evidence, a motive and a confession was all they could hope for.

So she had to go for the jugular. His weak spot. But as he thought back to the Warrenders, the pitiful, listless Sylvia, and her defiant but frightened and blowsy mum, he felt himself wavering.

'Leave 'em be,' Makepeace said gruffly.

Hillary shrugged. 'I'd be glad to. Personally. But my boss is Superintendent Marcus Donleavy, and he's looking for promotion. So's the man who'll probably replace *him*. You met him. DCI Mallow. They'll both be hot to get a conviction in a high-profile murder and drugs case. They won't think twice about ferreting out every bit of information and dirt they can. About you. And about your family. Well, I call them that, but I don't suppose many people will count them as quite that. After all, what did it amount to? A bit of a fling with the local bike, then buggering off to sea when you learned she was up the duff. Hardly the story of your average loving family setup, is it? Jury won't be sympathetic at all.'

'It weren't like that,' Alfie said, but without any bite. His voice was tired now, old, and without hope.

Hillary took a long, steady breath. 'So what was it like, Alfie?'

The old man shrugged. 'I had form. Nothing heavy, mind, but Dee was one of the few who didn't hold it against me. We were together nearly three months. Then I got offered this job on this Norwegian oil tanker. Nothing skilled, useless pay, long hours. But it was work. And, truth to tell, I fancied the thought of seeing the world. Mid-life crisis or what?' He laughed. Then shook his head. 'Dee never told me she was preggers. Maybe she didn't know.'

He looked out of the window, seeing who-knew-what memories rolling out along the canal bank. 'I never really gave her another thought. Not till I ran into her last year. And she told me about Sylvia.'

'And about the rape,' Hillary said flatly.

Makepeace's face hardened. 'Yeah. That too. I had a daughter. I never thought of stuff like that. You know. Normal stuff. Stuff that matters. To think I had a little girl. She used to go dancing, her mum told me. Was bright and pretty and funny. Now...now she didn't do nothing. Woke up at night screaming. Popped pills like her mother drank gin. And all because of that scum.' He spat out the last word with real venom.

Hillary nodded. 'And you knew him, didn't you? That's what made it so hard, I bet. Made you flip. The fact that you'd worked with him. What, had a drink with him? And all that time, when you didn't know it, he'd raped your little girl. I bet he even used to brag about his way with the ladies. The rapes he'd got away with. Yeah?'

Reluctantly, Makepeace nodded.

Hillary sighed. 'No wonder you wanted to kill the bastard.'

'And did,' Makepeace finally said, with so much satisfaction it made Tommy fold his arms protectively across his chest.

But he'd not yet confessed back at the Big House, Hillary was thinking, far more concerned with practical matters than matters of conscience. He hadn't said a word with a tape recorder playing, after being read his rights.

She bit her lip. Careful now.

'So what happened that night? You threw him off the back of the boat?'

Makepeace shrugged. 'Not threw. Just pushed. We were in the lock. I jiggled the starter motor, made out something was jammed. I said maybe the propeller was fouled, and he leaned over to look. A quick shove in the back, and he was in.'

'Where was Gascoigne during all this?'

Makepeace grunted, the laugh full of contempt. 'Him? Drunk, on his bunk. What else? I told Pitman I was gonna have to wake him up to close the lock and flood it. But I never went near him.'

'So Pitman was in the water. And you just…what? Reversed over him?'

Makepeace shrugged. 'Weren't that hard. Locks are narrow. There was nowhere for him to go, was there? No way he could avoid being crushed. I waited until he was trying to climb up the back, and then, when his precious dick was just where I wanted it, deliberately crushed him against the lock gate or wall. I wanted to castrate the bastard, you see. Dee told me what he did to Sylvie. Her…breasts…you know. So I thought, Right, you bastard, see how you like it.'

Over in his corner, Hillary heard Tommy gulp.

'Yes,' she said simply. So that was why she'd kept going back to the autopsy reports. Her subconscious had been trying to point out to her that the wounds, all being centred around the genitals, meant something far more than she'd been seeing. Far more than mere coincidence.

'So all this time, while we were faffing about, convinced it was drugs, it had been a plain and simple murder all along. A classic family revenge thing.' She shook her head. Wouldn't they be sick back at the Big House when they heard this? Especially Mel, who'd given her the 'personal' angle to begin with, but only because he'd been convinced there'd been nothing personal about it.

Just how wrong could you get?

'I've been very dim,' Hillary said softly. Makepeace looked at her, not particularly interested, then shrugged. 'So what did you tell Gascoigne when he sobered up?' she prodded.

Makepeace shrugged. 'Just that there'd been an accident. Pitman had fooled around while the boat was in the lock and went overboard. It wasn't hard. Jake wasn't particularly bright.'

'And now he's dead. Because Fletcher believed you when you told him he'd been skimming,' Hillary said, her voice hard again. 'But then, why should you care about that?'

Makepeace leaned back in his chair, his old bones creaking. 'Exactly. Do you know how many people Gascoigne cut up on Fletcher's orders? Not that I'll be repeating that on tape,' he added quickly.

Hillary nodded. No, of course he wouldn't. Any more than he'd admit that he had known Gascoigne wasn't skimming. But Fletcher was Mel's and Mike Regis's problem. She'd solved *her* case.

'But you will admit to offing Pitman? For their sake. Deirdre must have guessed it was you who'd done it, the moment she heard Pitman was dead. I always felt as if she was hiding something. Tell me, does Sylvie know you're her dad?'

'Yeah. Dee told her. On her birthday. I bought her a birthday present. For the first time, I had someone to buy a present for.'

He sounded so happy, Hillary simply didn't have the heart to tell him it had been the gift that had nailed him.

Instead, she repeated her question. 'So you'll cop to it? All nice and legal, a signed confession. Save Sylvie and Dee the pain of going through all that again? No courts or cross-examinations for them, huh?' she cajoled softly.

Makepeace nodded silently. And Tommy tried not to notice the tears rolling down the old man's face.

Perhaps he shouldn't be in the police force? If he felt this guilty when nicking a cold-blooded murderer, how would he feel the next time?

It wasn't often you had a dream come true so when Hillary walked into the office later, with Makepeace's taped confession from the interview room still ringing in her ears, she was determined to make the most of it.

Frank Ross was at his desk and scowled at her when she walked in. She beamed and flipped him the finger.

A nice little bonus, that.

Then she pushed on to Mel's office, and again couldn't believe her luck. Donleavy was there.

He smiled at her. 'Hillary, so glad you're here. I was just telling Mel, the York…shire policemen sent to investigate Ronnie's…er…activities, have just told me they no longer consider it likely that you had any involvement with his scam. As of now, they've signed off on you.'

Hillary smiled. Yeah, that was nice, too.

'Sir,' she said by way of acknowledgement, then looked at Mel. 'I've got David Pitman's killer in the interview room. I've read him his rights, he's waived his right to his solicitor and given a full taped confession. I've left him writing up the same confession in longhand. He'll be signing it about now.'

Mel blinked.

Marcus Donleavy slowly scratched his eyebrow.

Sometimes she loved this job.

The Boat was crowded. Not that the Thrupp village pub was usually this hot on a weekday, but tonight it was filled with celebrating coppers.

Mel and Janine were in one corner, drinking camparis and looking tense. Hillary, just slightly the worse for vodka, wondered what plans they were hatching.

Frank Ross, playing darts with a local, was trying to look as if he wasn't churning with impotent rage.

Even Superintendent Donleavy had put in a brief appearance and made a little congratulating speech, which had been wildly cheered by Tommy, Janine and the rest of the office regulars. It mightn't have been, strictly speaking, their case, but they'd followed it and were pleased for her.

Seeing the back of the Yorkie Bars only added to the general air of hilarity and triumph.

Hillary, another vodka in hand, wandered rather haphazardly over to Tommy's table, accepting back-pats and jokes as she went. She guessed the older black woman was his mother, and the pretty girl beside him his jewellery-loving girlfriend.

'Tommy. Mrs Lynch.' She glanced at the younger girl, who smiled and held out her hand.

'Jean.'

'Jean. Nice to meet you.' The two women solemnly shook hands.

Tommy didn't like the way his mother sniffed and glanced suspiciously from him to Hillary. He looked away. What was it with mothers?

But before Mercy could say anything, Hillary quickly looked up, then smiled. 'Hey, Gary, over here.' And to Tommy's mother, said simply, 'My stepson. Excuse me a minute, please.'

Mercy Lynch looked, much to her son's vast relief, slightly mollified. In her eyes, his boss was now a happily married woman with a family. Tommy, for one, was not about to let on that the situation was any different.

A ragged cheer went up as Mike Regis and his taciturn sergeant walked in. Tommy watched, gloomily, as Hillary introduced her stepson to them, and the foursome went to the bar.

Jean reached out and squeezed his hand.

Hillary was slightly drunk. She knew she was when she waved off Gary and nearly lost her balance and fell over. It made her walk very carefully along the towpath.

The landlady had chucked them out bang on closing time, and who could blame her? Frank Ross for one would undoubtedly have reported her for licence violation. Now that the last of the celebrants was on his way home, no doubt hoping that someone had warned Traffic to look the other way, there was no getting away from the waiting *Mollern*.

She was almost tempted to walk into Kidlington and seek out a B&B. At least it wouldn't be floating about on water.

She made it to the boat without mishap and leaned against it for a while, savouring the night. Summer was coming and it was warm. Somewhere a bat swooped and squeaked. Who said they made sounds beyond human hearing?

She fumbled with the lock, got the door opened, and staggered down the stairs.

Coffee.

She made it strong and black, then wavered and added some milk and a big spoonful of sugar. Next, she collapsed into her chair, sloshing some of the drink on her skirt, but was in no mood to care.

Mike Regis had been really pleased for her, she could tell. And Frank would be at home by now, eating his heart out.

All was right with the world.

She was too high to go to bed but there'd be nothing on the box. She reached for the book in the wastepaper basket, wondering what the hell it was doing there, then realised it was Ronnie's bloody Dick Francis.

She stared at it. Perhaps because she was slightly drunk and feeling so good, or perhaps because she was at that stage where her brain synapses were being nicely illogical, a thought popped into her head so bizarre it made her laugh out loud.

This was it. This was what the Yorkie Bars had been looking for for so long. Ronnie's secret hoard. Numbers for his legendary offshore account.

She put down the coffee and looked at the first page. All the numbers were on the bottom. She leaned forward, positioning the book well into the light of the lamp. And holding it carefully, from the back, slowly let the pages whiffle past, her eyes glued to the numbers on the bottom of the page.

Not one of them was ringed or marked.

She laughed. So much for Mrs Sherlock bloody Holmes.

Then she yelped. Something blue. She turned back the pages, slowly, and there it was.

Not a number underlined, but a word.

Sex.

She snorted. Yeah, right. Just the word Ronnie *would* underline.

But, come on, Hills, her drunker inner voice suddenly whined, not even Ronnie was such a pathetic loser that he went around underlining dirty words in books.

Frowning now, she started at the beginning, turning the pages over quickly but carefully.

There! Another word underlined. The word *for.*

For? *Four?*

Another ten pages over and the word *one* was marked. Then, later, the word *there.*

There? An anagram of three?

The words *too, heaven* and *mine* were added. Seven and Nine?

Feeling a little sick now, she reached for a pen and paper and wrote the numbers out in order.

What had Gary said? His father had told him he had an account…where the hell was it? The Caymans? And it wasn't under his name, just numbers.

But surely any bank would need some kind of password as well?

She looked at the book cover, then the inscription.

Stud.

Of course. Stud. She giggled. What the hell else? Oh, Ronnie, Ronnie, you stupid prat.

She leaned back in her chair but the book suddenly felt as if it weighed tons, making her drop it to the floor.

How many banks were there in the Caymans? How long would it take her, armed with a possible code word and the all-important numbers, to find it?

She had some holiday time due. She could fly to the Caymans. The Yorkie Bars had given up on her. Or so they said. She could actually pull it off.

She stared at the wall in front of her—so close, so cramping.

She could get off this bloody boat. Give up the bloody job. No more Frank. No more Mel and Donleavy giving her shit jobs. No more shift work, no more dead bodies, no more rapists and their victims.

Just beaches and sand and palm trees, and tropical drinks with bits of fruit floating in them.

Hillary closed her eyes. She was drunk, right?

Yeah.

But seriously tempted.

'Oh, shit,' she said softly.

OLD INSTINCTS DIE HARD FOR EX-COP JOSEPH SOYINKA

Joseph made many enemies fighting corruption but refused to be intimidated – until his wife was killed. Now he lives with his young son in the anonymous safety of New York City. By day he drives a yellow cab. By night, he tries to forget about the past.

But when his friend Cyrus is framed for a brutal murder, Joseph knows the only way to find the real killer is to take Cyrus's place in a deadly game.

OUT NOW

www.blackstarcrime.co.uk

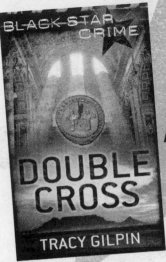

A POWERFUL SECRET ORGANISATION.

AN INTELLIGENCE AGENCY DETERMINED TO DESTROY IT.

When Dunai Marks finds her boss and mentor Siobhan Craig murdered in their office, she's convinced it's not just 'a burglary gone wrong'.

Only it seems Siobhan had many secrets that will change Dunai's life forever, drawing her into a terrifying new world. A world Siobhan would have sacrificed life itself to protect.

www.blackstarcrime.co.uk

1108/BSC/BOOKS

If you enjoyed this book, then make sure you also read other titles in the Black Star Crime™ series. Order direct and we'll deliver them straight to your door. Our complete titles list is available online.

www.blackstarcrime.co.uk

Book Title/Author	ISBN & Price	Quantity
Runaway Minister Nick Curtis	978 1 848 45000 4 £3.99	
Streetwise Chris Freeman	978 1 848 45001 1 £3.99	
A Narrow Escape Faith Martin	978 1 848 45002 8 £3.99	
Murder Plot Lance Elliot	978 1 848 45003 5 £3.99	
A Perfect Evil Alex Kava	978 1 848 45004 2 £3.99	
Double Cross Tracy Gilpin	978 1 848 45005 9 £3.99	
Tuscan Termination Margaret Moore	978 1 848 45006 6 £3.99	
Homicide in the Hills Steve Garcia	978 1 848 45007 3 £3.99	
Lost and Found Vivian Roberts	978 1 848 45008 0 £3.99	
Split Second Alex Kava	978 1 848 45009 7 £3.99	

Please add 99p postage & packing per book
DELIVERY TO UK ONLY

Post to: End Page Offer, PO Box 1780, Croydon, CR9 3UH

Please ensure that you include full postal address details. Please pay by cheque or postal order (payable to Reader Service) unless ordering online. Prices and availability subject to change without notice.

Order online at: www.blackstarcrime.co.uk

Allow 28 days for delivery.